THERE CAME
TWO ANGELS

THERE CAME TWO ANGELS

A LOY LOMBARD MYSTERY
BY JULIA LIEBER

alyson books
los angeles

THIS TRADE PAPERBACK ORIGINAL IS PUBLISHED BY ALYSON PUBLICATIONS,
P.O. BOX 4371, LOS ANGELES, CALIFORNIA 90078-4371.
DISTRIBUTION IN THE UNITED KINGDOM BY TURNAROUND PUBLISHER SERVICES LTD.,
UNIT 3, OLYMPIA TRADING ESTATE, COBURG ROAD, WOOD GREEN,
LONDON N22 6TZ ENGLAND.

FIRST EDITION: MAY 2004

04 05 06 07 08 a 10 9 8 7 6 5 4 3 2 1

ISBN 1-55583-797-2

LIBRARY OF CONGRESS CATALOGING-IN-PUBLICATION DATA
   LIEBER, JULIA.
      THERE CAME TWO ANGELS : A LOY LOMBARD MYSTERY / BY JULIA LIEBER.—1ST ED.
      ISBN 1-55583-797-2
         1. WOMEN PRIVATE INVESTIGATORS—NORTH CAROLINA—ASHEVILLE—
   FICTION. 2. MALE PROSTITUTES—CRIMES AGAINST—FICTION.
   3. GAY MEN—CRIMES AGAINST—FICTION. 4. EX-POLICE OFFICERS—
   FICTION. 5. ASHEVILLE (N.C.)—FICTION. I. TITLE.
   PS3612.I33T47 2004
   813'—DC22   2004040993

CREDITS
COVER PHOTOGRAPHY BY JOEL ROGERS/GETTY IMAGES.
COVER DESIGN BY LOUIS MANDRAPILIAS.

1

JASPER SLADE WAS A FORMER UNITED STATES SENATOR, having left office to establish his right-wing foundation, the American Family Freedom Campaign. He had made his fortune in tobacco and his reputation in Republican politics. Now in his early fifties, he was at the peak of a long and dedicated career in the cause of restoring traditional values in American citizens and top-heavy wealth to American corporations. He was the peerless emissary of Southern conservatism, the self-appointed champion of decency and morality. Presently, he was naked but for a towel draped across his trembling lap, blood streaked and spattered all over his body. On the bed beside the chair in which he was hunkered lay the mutilated corpse of a young, nude man, his throat slit through to the spine.

Lt. Mike Church of the Asheville Police Department had just arrived in the room, a third-floor suite at the Rosemond Inn Bed and Breakfast on Watauga Lane. Two other policemen were in the room along with men from the crime lab taking photographs of the dead body. Church glanced at the body, at the pale, somnolent features, calm in contrast to the blood-soaked sheets and coverlets that half-concealed his smooth, slender hips and legs. "Who's the dead guy?" Church asked.

"Name of Jay Hughes, according to the register downstairs," said one of the cops.

Church glanced at the thin, hunched shoulders of the bewildered-looking man in the chair. He was staring into space, pulling at his lower lip with his left hand. "Is he the suspect or a witness?" Church asked, pointing at the man.

"Both," said the cop. "He was in the room when we busted the door in."

"Has he said anything?"

"Nope. He was screaming earlier, according to the lady that runs the place. She called 911. We sure as shit didn't expect to find this mess."

Church nudged one of the forensics officers collecting blood and semen samples around the bed. "Weapon?"

"Combed the room for it," the forensics officer said irritably, "but there's not a one to be found. The bathroom window's open, though. He must have thrown it outside. We've got men down there searching the perimeter of the house." The officer added, "You took your time getting here, Mike."

"It's 2 A.M.," Mike Church said. "I got here as fast as I could in that fog." He looked out the window, where, three floors below, fog hugged the earth and the ghostly glow of police flashlights flickered in and out of the haze. "They'll never find anything down there tonight." Church turned around and pointed at the man in the chair. "So who is he?"

"Jasper Slade," said the cop with the camera, playfully pointing it at Church. "Okay, Lieutenant. Smile and say *queer*."

———

For a quiet mountain town of some 70,000 people, Asheville, North Carolina, was unusual in the South. It was the kind of town that attracted arty people, the young and gay, the self-appointed hip, the vegan-pagan-yoga lot. Still, there were gentle reminders of the down-home place it used to be. Next door to mountain craft stores now stood shops selling Tibetan gongs and African tribal masks. Barbecue-and-rib joints now competed with vegetarian cafés and fancy coffeehouses where young people with tattooed necks and pierced navels gathered to listen to poetry and folk music. Jazz and blues clubs outnumbered bluegrass venues. Asheville was an oddity of the South, its cheerful, languid streets laid out like welcome mats for diversity.

Loy Lombard's bungalow sat a few miles south of all that, a mile or so down a county route that veered off of Hendersonville Road and better than a hundred yards from where her mailbox peeked through a bushy tangle of forsythia along the lane. There were no neighboring houses in sight; the few acres of land surrounding her house were trimmed in the distance by forested foothills of the Blue Ridge Mountains. Ross McKenna arrived at the narrow gravel driveway without warning. He hadn't called ahead, and it was early. He was used to getting people's attention, though, and had found that with enough money and a little intimidation, he could be more than persuasive.

He rapped at the door for more than a minute before hearing the door unlatch. A woman peered out from the dark interior of the house.

"Are you Miss Lombard?" he asked.

She looked tired and suspicious. Quietly, she said, "Who's asking?"

"I'm Ross McKenna, from Raleigh."

"I don't talk to missionaries, not even on Sunday."

McKenna smiled. "Ma'am, I'm not a missionary. I'm interested in your professional services, Secure Services, your business."

She glanced over his shoulder—he thought in the direction of the Mercedes he had rented for his stay in Asheville—and after what seemed like a few grudging seconds of deliberation, invited him inside.

McKenna followed her inside and sat in the armchair she pointed to. She asked him if he wanted coffee. "Please," he said, and watched her move slowly toward the kitchen. Her short, thick black hair was disheveled, and she was wearing a flannel robe, sweatpants, and flip-flops. It occurred to him he had rousted her out of bed.

"I'm sorry if I awakened you," he said in a loud voice.

There was no response from the kitchen. He heard a cabinet slam shut, and the clap of ceramic on Formica. After a few silent seconds, she appeared holding two steaming coffee mugs. "I'm not used to home visits from bidders," she said lazily. She handed him his mug.

She was an attractive, imposing woman—nearly six feet tall—with a large build, though not at all fat. Her eyes were dark, deep-set, and narrow, with slight folds that gave her a rather Asiatic look. Her wide brow, long nose, and full mouth made McKenna guess she was of Mediterranean stock. McKenna had always prided himself for his ability to spot racial distinctions. "Lombard," he said, almost to himself. "Is that a French name?"

"Italian," she said, easing onto the sofa. "Used to be Lombardo, back in the old country." She set her mug on the coffee table and leaned back into the armrest, shifting so that one leg reclined along the length of the sofa cushions, and rested her other foot on the floor. She closed her eyes and rubbed her temples with her fingertips.

"Maltese, then," said McKenna suddenly, and Lombard gave a start. "I'd bet anything some of your people came from Malta."

"I don't know," she said. "These days they're mainly in Independence, Louisiana."

McKenna moved on. "I've come to discuss an urgent matter." He stopped when he noticed her pained expression. "Are you all right?"

"I will be after a few cups of coffee." She raised her mug to her lips. "What kind of urgent matter brings you here on a Sunday? You need guards for a church?"

"Guards? No. I understand you operate a private investigation firm."

"Where did you hear that?"

McKenna frowned. "Sigmund Mashburn told me. He says your firm provides private investigative services."

She arched an eyebrow. "Sig Mashburn. The lawyer?"

"Yes. He told me you're an investigator."

"Was. I *was* an investigator. I thought you dropped in to see about a guard."

"I beg your pardon?"

"Guards. My business contracts out bodyguards and security guards. I have about sixty men working all over the western region."

"So you don't do private investigation? That's strange. Mashburn said you were the best in your field."

"I've never met Mr. Mashburn. He must have heard about my days as a cop in Charlotte. A lot of people have, I'm sorry to say." She put down her coffee mug. "I got a private investigator's license when I started my business, and I've been offered jobs, but the guards have kept me in good stead, and I haven't got any offers from PI clients worth bothering with. I have no interest in sneaking around cheating spouses or tracking down runaways. I worked homicide cases for the Charlotte police, but there's not much demand for a homicide PI around here."

"I'm afraid the matter I've come to discuss is right up your alley, Miss Lombard."

She looked surprised. "You got a murder case for me?"

"Yes."

"And Sig Mashburn recommended me?"

"He did."

"And he's your lawyer, I take it," she said.

McKenna nodded. "I retained his services yesterday, on behalf of a friend."

"Then what do you need me for? Doesn't a big-time lawyer like Sig Mashburn have his own investigator?"

"I told him I want our lawyer and investigator to work separately."

"Why?"

"Because I say so," he said flatly. He straightened his shoulders and crossed his legs. "I told Sig Mashburn I needed a private eye who can stay behind the scenes, uncover every stone, find every clue, and keep his mouth shut. And I told him what I'm going to tell you, Miss Lombard. I control this case. I call the shots."

Lombard shrugged. "How much you call 'em for?"

"I'll make you very happy with the advance." He looked around the plainly furnished room, made homey with potted plants and hanging baskets and brightly colored prints. Still, he marked her lack of real success. "I gather you could use the business."

"I suppose so, but like I said, I've turned cases down. So what have you got?"

"It's high-profile. Very demanding, because I demand the best, and Mashburn said you were the best in your day."

"He's right."

"I would say, based on your record, that I agree. Of course, you did leave Charlotte in disgrace, according to my research."

She frowned. "Who are you? I mean, who do you work for?"

"I'm the executive director of the American Family Freedom Campaign, headquartered in Raleigh. And I know all about you." He pulled a manila envelope from his briefcase. "This is your Internal Affairs file from the Charlotte Police Department. I hope you don't mind."

She pitched him a dark glare. "How did you get that?"

"A friendly source gave it to me, yesterday, after Sig Mashburn's reference. We have a nice little network of info-getters," he said, not the least bit perturbed by her cold look. "So. Here's what I've got. Correct me if I'm wrong. You were born in New Orleans in 1962. Your few relatives still live there. Cousins, mainly. You're an orphan. Went into the Navy. After your discharge you came to Charlotte, North Carolina, where you joined the police force. Decorated cop, rose up quickly through the ranks, by age thirty-five got to be a top-dog detective, and then, *boom!*" He dropped the file folder on his lap. "It all came crashing down. You tucked tail and headed for the hills of western North Carolina."

Lombard said, "Mr. McKenna, I've no time for this bullshit. What do you want?"

"I was merely reviewing what happened to you in Charlotte. It's shameful, but there's something about it all that I like. Your partner was indicted for graft, and you were investigated by the FBI for your connection to a sleazy drug dealer. That part I don't like. You know what I do like, though?"

"At this point, I don't give a damn," she said. "Show yourself the door, Mr. McKenna. It's too early on a Sunday for games. Get out."

He ignored her and went on. "You could have saved your career if only you had testified against your partner. They had nothing on you. Only tried to bully you into thinking they did, and you called their bluff. You had information they wanted, only you took the Fifth and wouldn't give it to them. You wouldn't have incriminated yourself because you hadn't done anything wrong. You knew it, and they knew it. Yet you used the Fifth Amendment privilege as an excuse to avoid giving any testimony that might hurt Sam McLean. That was brave, and it was loyal." He flipped a page over and shrugged. "I noticed some police psychologist's reports. You once shot a suspect, and he died. Bothered your conscience, according to what you told the shrink." He looked up from the folder and studied her saturnine features for a few seconds. "But you wouldn't talk to the shrink about allegations against your partner, Sam McLean. You can keep your mouth shut. And in fifteen years on the force, nine of them as a detective, you never left a case cold. Not one."

McKenna closed the folder and slipped it into his briefcase. "That's the kind of dedication I need for this case, Miss Lombard." He looked at her. "For my friend accused wrongly of murder, the former senator Jasper Slade."

Lombard's lips parted, and she more or less exhaled, "I'll be damned."

"I take it you read the papers yesterday."

"All about it. He's accused of murdering a young hustler."

"He's been convicted by the media," McKenna said.

"Where is Mr. Slade right now? The TV news said he posted bail."

"We bailed him out yesterday morning. He's at a safe house with friends of our organization, out of the glare of the media."

"Good idea."

"Meanwhile, the TV news you refer to skewers him as a murderer, and worse."

"Worse?" Lombard asked quietly. "What's worse than murder?"

"He's been portrayed as a homosexual."

"Oh, of course. Indeed he has," Lombard muttered. She slowly rubbed her jaw. "Do you know anything about his—um—friendship with that young fellow who died?"

"He didn't know him. At least, he didn't know him very well at all. Only as long as it took to frame him."

"Frame him," Lombard echoed softly. "Hmm. Who framed him?"

"That is what you are going to find out." McKenna raised his coffee mug primly to his lips and stared at Lombard. "You look awfully disturbed all of a sudden, Miss Lombard. Have I said something to upset you?"

"I'm a little confused. Why do you think Mr. Slade got framed? Do you have—you know, what lawyers like Sig Mashburn call it— a rational basis for believing something like that?"

For the next several minutes McKenna described the ongoing battle between conservatives and left-wing groups, particularly gay rights lobbies and the liberal media. He explained how Jasper Slade had for years led the fight to restore decency in America and how his very name had become a rallying cry against moral degeneracy. McKenna told Lombard that her work would include investigating various gay rights organizations that had publicly threatened to destroy Slade. "You will see. These people had a motive for framing Jasper Slade, to make him out as a homosexual and as a murderer," McKenna explained. "They want to ruin his mission in this country. It sounds outrageous, but the idea that Senator Slade could consort with men and then kill one of them is much more outrageous. They sought his destruction, and they killed one of their own to carry out their scheme." He glanced at his wristwatch. "Now let's talk about the money. I have to get going soon. You'll meet me in Raleigh this week for more details. Your investigation will start there."

Lombard scratched her head and drew a long breath. "Whew!" she chuckled. "This one is round-the-clock. I'm gonna need a lot in the way of an advance." As if on a sudden thought, she asked, "Who did you say you work for?"

"The American Family Freedom Campaign, the AFFC."

She stared at him blankly.

"Mr. Slade's conservative foundation."

Lombard 's eyes widened. "Oh! Right. You're one of Slade's boys."

"I'd prefer if you didn't put it quite like that."

She closed her eyes again and resumed rubbing her forehead. "I should have picked up on that, but I have a hell of a headache. Go on. I'm listening."

"So you are familiar with our organization?"

She swung her leg off the sofa and sat up with great effort. Her hangover showed. "Yeah. I've heard of it. You're right-wingers."

McKenna raised his chin up and said, "Yes, we are. You'll take the case?"

She gave a bright smile. "I need the money. Of course, I'd just about sink my teeth in the Jasper Slade case for nothing if I could afford to. If what you want is help finding a way to dig him out of this mess, then you've come to just the right woman. If there is anything or anybody on this planet that can stop him from going to prison or the chair, I'll find it, him, her—I'll run them down from here to kingdom come." She leaned back into her sofa. "Now, Jasper Slade is in a lot of trouble, and I need the facts. Not your theories, but your *facts*. I want every detail you've got. Then we'll talk about the money."

Sam McLean was pacing back and forth in the kitchen of the brick rancher, situated on a cul-de-sac in a trimmed and tree-lined Asheville subdivision, that he shared with his wife and three young daughters. Ordinarily on a Monday morning he would have been at his desk at Secure Services Inc. by the crack of dawn. He worked long hours to provide for his family, but also out of loyalty to his friend Loy Lombard, who had offered him the job when he was at the lowest point of his life.

"How long will you be in Raleigh?" Selena McLean asked her husband. She was standing at the counter making sandwiches for their daughters' lunch boxes while the little girls alternately quarreled and giggled at the kitchen table.

"A couple of days," McLean replied, peering out the kitchen window to the driveway. "Loy's late."

"So what's this big case about?" Selena asked.

"I don't know yet." McLean winked at Selena. He looked younger than his thirty-eight years, a lean, nice-looking fellow with wavy dusty-blond hair and kind gray eyes.

"Don't know? You were out in her car for an hour last night." He glanced at the kitchen clock. "You know Loy won't talk case work over the phone. She never did. It's a big case, honey, worth a $20,000 advance."

"Who's going to mind the office? Did Loy tell you that much?"

"Retta's the office manager, honey, and a good one. It'll be fine."

"You'll call me when you check into your hotel room?"

"Of course I will. Ah, here she is. It's about time." Loy's car had just pulled into the driveway.

Selena frowned. "Isn't she going to come in?"

Then Loy laid on the horn.

"She's in a hurry," McLean said, grinning. "Now where's that thermos? You know Loy loves your coffee."

"She tolerates my coffee. She only drinks it to please you."

McLean took the thermos and embraced his wife, a petite, dark-complexioned woman with long black hair. He kissed her warmly. "You keep those doors latched, now. I'll call tonight before the girls' bedtime."

McLean rushed out to Lombard's Pathfinder and dropped his suitcase in the back. Lombard revved the engine, and he scuttled around the SUV and slid into the front seat, slamming his door as she shifted into reverse and skidded out into the cul-de-sac.

"Did you happen to remember the coffee?" she asked.

McLean showed her the thermos.

"And it's Selena's, right? Not that watered-down piss you brew at the office."

"It's the way you like it, Loy: Molten asphalt." McLean

unscrewed the thermos lid, and they peeled onto the freeway in good spirits. It was their first case together since Charlotte. It was The One, the case that could make them.

———

A few hours later, as they neared Raleigh, Lombard and McLean were in an argument. "We're a couple of whores," McLean said matter-of-factly, "is what we are."

"A little whoring never hurt anybody," Lombard said. "I'm doing this as much for the thrill of working the Slade case as I'm doing it for the money."

"It's an open-and-shut case. What are we gonna find out? That some 'liberal intelligentsia' framed him?" McLean said. He had a way of putting arguments in a frank, pointed manner that made him persuasive to a fault—except to Lombard, who always had thought he would have made a great lawyer. "We'll end up looking like fools, Loy."

"Sam, you're younger than me, yet you worry like an old woman, you know that?" Lombard smiled at him and punched him in the arm. "Snap out of it. We'll look just fine when it's all said and done, and we'll have worked a hell of a notorious case. This is good for business. People with money will come to us from now on."

"See, there you go again. It's all about money to you."

"You're damn right it is. We're scraping by the way things are right now. We need a shot in the arm."

McLean said, "I provide just fine for my family."

"Sure you do! And I provide just fine for my tomcats and the

roses out back and that's about it. What about your girls' college?"
She eyed him and looked back at the road. "What about if one
day you want to take Selena on a nice trip, someplace other than
the Outer Banks? We make ends meet just fine, and that's all we
do. Well, that's not good enough for me."

"So we're gonna chase after some queer conspiracy theory,"
McLean said with a caustic laugh.

"That's exactly right. And it will lead nowhere, but along the
way we'll work the case from our angle too, and we'll have a
respectable file built up by the time the case rolls around to trial,
or the plea bargain, more likely. So nobody's gonna look foolish.
We just have to humor the bank for a while with this frame-up
theory. Keep him happy."

"That's not real investigative work, Loy. I'm surprised at you."
He added reprovingly, "And for more reasons than one."

"Don't start that, Sam," she said wearily. "I never shrank from
busting a homosexual when I was a cop, or from investigating a
suspect who happened to be gay. This is no different."

"Sure it is. You're gonna be running around making a lot of
innocent gay people nervous, asking questions you know for a
fact make no sense. At least when you were a cop you followed
real instincts and the hunt was right. This isn't."

Lombard abruptly swerved onto the shoulder of the highway
and rolled to a stop. She took a deep breath. "You just infuriate
me sometimes, you know that? I'm trying to help business, so you
can just stop throwing the mirror up in my face. I may be a dyke,
but that has never and will never have a damn thing to do with
how I run my business or my cases. Now, if you're so high and
mighty you can't see how I'm trying to do right by us both and
our business, I'll turn around right now and take you back home
and work it by myself."

McLean shrugged. "I'm just telling you what I think, Loy."

"I know. You're too honest. I have to remind myself of that

every time I wonder why you didn't become a lawyer."

"And I'll say something else. I'll admit it. I don't like the case because of how sleazy it is. Conservative politician banging some gay hustler. It disgusts me. I hate to think what else we might dredge up."

"Now there's the homophobe I know and love," Lombard chuckled as she merged the car back into traffic. "I knew that line about 'innocent gay people' was bullshit, even though I bought it for the second it took me to get mad at you."

"I'm not a homophobe," McLean said. "I'm your friend, remember? I just think there's a time and a place for things, and the place for a conservative Republican senator is with his wife or his wife's memory, and not some gay pretty boy." He reflected for a moment and asked, "So is it a hate crime when a gay man murders another homosexual?"

"Murder is always about hate or money," Lombard said. "From the news reports, Slade's victim was a penniless hustler, so it's about hate, but a different kind of hate. It's self-hatred." She shook her head gently as she stared ahead. "I worked a case before you came on as a detective in Charlotte. Two men got together casually, a one-night stand. One of them was a closeted man with a wife and kids, and a bottomless well of self-hatred and shame stored up inside him. He was ashamed of his homosexuality, and he vented his shame by beating the living hell out of every stranger he had sex with. Nobody ever told on him because they were ashamed too." She shrugged. "Well, they didn't talk until he finally killed a man. He so hated who he was inside that he killed his victim for being attractive to him." She glanced at McLean. "That's a fact. So maybe Slade vented his self-hatred on that poor boy." Lombard paused for a moment. "On the other hand, maybe Hughes blackmailed him. Either way, it's not much of a defense."

"If it was blackmail, then it was about money, not hatred," said McLean.

"I've thought about that," Lombard said. "But listen to us. We're talking like cops speculating on a motive, when we've been hired to find a defense. We'd better start keeping our eyes on the prize."

———

They were from different backgrounds, but they were close. Sam McLean was from a small town in the piedmont and had grown up on Friday night football and Sunday dinner at Grandma's. He married his high school sweetheart and stayed married because he loved her. They lived quietly and went to church every Sunday. He became a cop because he thought it was an honorable job.

Loy Lombard came from a blue-collar family in New Orleans. She had gotten into drugs and petty crime as a teenager before an aunt took over and straightened her out. She joined the Navy, gave it four years, and got discharged out of Norfolk, Virginia. She drove down to North Carolina for a spot in a police academy because she didn't know what else to do. She moved up fast when she joined the force in Charlotte. By the time McLean had made detective and became her partner, Lombard was in her late thirties and was already a seasoned investigator.

Toward the end of his career in Charlotte, McLean was introduced by a detective friend of his named Lynn Stroop to a nightclub owner named Iman Casteel. McLean suddenly got a taste of a faster way of life. Iman Casteel and the men who hung out in his club wore the kinds of suits you couldn't find in North Carolina. They drove spectacular cars and owned vacation homes. McLean wasn't naive; he figured they had a crooked angle somewhere, but as long as he didn't know anything, it didn't bother him. He was having fun, smoking Cuban cigars, and drinking Hennessy with a crowd of real players. He laughed at their jokes and wondered privately what they might be hiding, but who cared? As long he didn't know for sure. All he had ever done was to get married and become a cop and have kids, and nothing was ever going to happen to him again. What was wrong with a little excitement with a slick buddy like Stroop and his highfalutin friend Iman Casteel?

Then it turned out Iman was a drug runner, and Stroop had been taking money from him for years. When the FBI descended on him, Iman Casteel gave them McLean's name as someone who sometimes accepted "gifts" from him. Then he gave them Lombard's name, because Iman had once met her too.

So the U.S. attorney came to Lombard for information, and he threatened her with an indictment if she failed to cooperate. He wanted to know about the gifts Iman Casteel talked about and how much time McLean spent with Casteel. The fact was that McLean had told Lombard about his association with Casteel. He had even talked her into meeting Casteel and Stroop for a drink one night. That night Casteel offered the three cops each a solid gold scarab as a token of friendship. Lombard had refused the gift, but McLean and Stroop had accepted the pieces.

Lombard never told anybody, though. Not the U.S. attorney, not the judge, not a soul. She didn't get indicted, but when the government indicted McLean and Stroop, she got subpoenaed and was forced to look like she was covering up a crime when she refused to testify, relying on the Fifth Amendment privilege against self-incrimination, though she had nothing to hide about herself. After the trial she was given the option of resigning or facing an Internal Affairs audit that most certainly would have resulted in a humiliating censure and dismissal, as had already happened to McLean. She resigned.

McLean never got over his feelings of guilt about the ruin of Lombard's career, and when she offered him the job in Asheville, he asked her why she wanted anything to do with him. She told him she respected and trusted him, and he accepted that as her reason. It never occurred to McLean that Lombard had felt sorry for him.

2

LOMBARD AND MCLEAN WERE AWAITING AN INTERVIEW with Ross McKenna at a tobacco plantation near Raleigh called Stonebridge Farm. Lombard studied a large oil portrait of a man and a woman posing in English riding habit in front of a fireplace identical to the one over which the painting was hung. "What did the housekeeper call this room?" Lombard asked. "A study?"

"The library," McLean replied. He sat down and glanced at his watch.

"She was kind of snotty, didn't you think?"

"She was just busy, I guess." McLean yawned and leaned back in his chair and closed his eyes. The room was gloomy despite the bright midday sunshine outside. Mahogany paneling and narrow casement windows stifled sunlight, so that even at one o'clock the glow of green banker's lamps was necessary to illuminate the titles of hundreds of books lining the shelves.

"Well, I thought she was snotty." Lombard pulled a pair of reading glasses from her jacket pocket and affixed them to her nose. She began inspecting the book titles. "Solzhenitsyn," she read aloud.

"Huh?" McLean grunted. "What'd you say?"

"Solzhenitsyn. They got everything he ever wrote."

"Who's that?"

"A Russian writer. Did time in the gulag for saying something smart about Stalin. Won the Nobel Prize."

"What about him?"

"Nothing. Just showing off how much I know."

"Yeah, you know a lot for a girl who barely graduated high school."

"I love to read books like these here," Lombard said, pulling out a volume. "Philosophy and religion and all that. This shelf looks like it's dedicated to anti-Communist writers. Here's Henry Kissinger. Good God, they've got Joseph McCarthy mixed up in there too. The lightweights with the heavyweights." She slid the book back in place and examined the other shelves. "There's a pattern to the way these books are arranged. This shelf is all economists. And over here, all these shelves have religious-sounding titles. They even got a book by the pope. Huh. Are the Drinnons Catholic?"

"I don't know. I thought you knew everything," McLean said, his eyes still shut.

"Smart-ass. Ooh. Looky here." She smiled mischievously and rapped her knuckles against the spines of a new-looking row of books. "All these are paperback. How cheap. But I guess the subject matter calls for cheap binding, in the eyes of our hosts."

"What is it?" McLean sighed.

"Homosexuality. Three whole shelves here. *The Sin of Sodom*," she said, pulling out one of the books. She opened it and scanned its preface. "Just as I thought. They never mention verses 30 and on."

McLean opened his eyes. "What are you talking about?"

"Fundamentalists. Every time they argue homosexuality is a sin, they point out the story of Sodom and Gomorrah—Genesis, chapter 19. It has thirty-eight chapters, but the God boys always stop at chapter 29, where Lot escapes the destruction of Sodom on account of how righteous he is in the eyes of the Lord. They must not know quite what to make of chapters 30 through 38."

"Go ahead," McLean said. "Tell me all about it."

"It's the story of how the sainted Lot knocked up his two innocent daughters."

"Good God. What are you talking about?"

"Aw, I'm surprised at you, Sam. I thought you Baptists kept a ready command of God's word."

"I'm Presbyterian."

Lombard said, "There's bound to be a Bible in here somewhere. Anyway, I know the story by heart. It follows Lot and his daughters into hiding, after Mrs. Lot gets turned into salt. According to the story, the three of them live in a cave and the girls start getting nervous about never having any babies. Not many eligible bucks up in the hill country above Zoar. So. They plot to get Daddy drunk and horny. 'Come, let us ply our father with wine and then lie with him, that we may have offspring by our father.' So poor old Lot was defenseless against the wiles of his nubile young girls. Just like every child-molesting scumbag I took off the streets in Charlotte, he was drunk and couldn't help his sorry self. Anyway, Lot's daughters got pregnant, and thus began the Moabite and Ammonite lines."

McLean said, "I never heard that story."

"Pretty scandalous, huh?"

"Scandalous!" a voice thundered. Lombard turned to the source of the voice, at the room's entrance, and saw a mannish-looking woman with long, slender legs and a thick middle. She looked well-bred, was not far past fifty, and had eyes the same color as the gray streaks in her dark hair. "What is scandalous?" The woman eyed the book Lombard was holding. "Of course. *The Sin of Sodom*. It's timely reading, in view of Jasper's situation. I'm Della Drinnon."

Lombard introduced herself and McLean. "You have a beautiful home, Mrs. Drinnon. I was just admiring that big painting up there over the fireplace."

"That is a portrait of my late husband and myself. I was younger and thinner," Mrs. Drinnon chuckled. A look of pride overcame her as she gazed at the portrait. "Alexander Clayton Drinnon was one of Jasper's best friends. Do you know how my husband died?" she asked dryly, as though they had three guesses.

Lombard remembered the name of A.C. Drinnon, a powerful tobacco mogul who, although he had been a native North Carolinian, had spent most of his life in New York. She knew he had committed suicide by shooting himself, but she said, "I'm afraid I don't."

"He committed suicide. Blew his brains out."

"Oh. I'm terribly sorry."

"I found his body half a minute after I heard the gun blast. He was slumped over that rolltop desk there in the corner," she said, pointing, "right here in this room."

Lombard tensed her brow in mock sympathy and glanced at McLean.

"Mrs. Drinnon," McLean said, glancing at his watch, "Mr. McKenna told us to be here at 1 o'clock sharp. Are you expecting him soon?"

"He's on his way." Mrs. Drinnon sat down on a sofa without crossing her legs. "Why don't you-all sit? Tell me about your work."

"There isn't much to tell yet," Lombard said, opting for a chair across the rug from where Mrs. Drinnon sat. "This is our first murder case in private practice."

"Yes, Ross told me all about that. So you're from Asheville? Like it there?"

"Nice town," McLean said amiably. "Good for raising a family."

"Hmm. Are you sure? I heard one of the councilwomen was a lesbian."

"Really?" Lombard asked. "Which one?"

McLean chuckled nervously. "It's a good old country town. My wife and three girls are very happy there. And safe too. Hardly any crime to speak of."

The phone rang. "Cora will pick that up," Mrs. Drinnon said. "Probably another reporter. They've been all over us. They're like rats, the media are."

"Amen to that," said Lombard.

"Mmm. Yes, I imagine you dislike reporters as much as we do, the way they went after you in Charlotte. It's abominable, the way they manipulate the public mind. It seems like they're bent on destroying anybody who dares to tell the truth about their grip on society. What they've done to Jasper is proof enough of that."

Lombard eyed the oil image of A.C. Drinnon, a strapping, robust man in his youth. He had died a hundred pounds over-weight. "I'll bet Mr. Drinnon had a thing or two to say about the media," she said, recalling his famous enthusiasm for conspiracy theories.

"A.C. was Jasper's inspiration," Mrs. Drinnon said solemnly. She got up and snatched a pamphlet off a bookcase. "Everything you need to know about the American media is in this booklet. It was printed shortly after Jasper started the AFFC four years ago, not long after A.C.'s death." She handed the pamphlet to Lombard. "See? The cover logo is a triangle, a symbol we have reclaimed from the militant homosexual anarchists who hold such powerful sway over the media. The sides of the triangle are red, white, and blue, each symbolizing God, family, and country, the trinity that binds our campaign. Red for the blood of Christ our guiding master, white for the purity of the family, and blue for the authority and majesty of our great nation."

McLean smiled. "I'd say that just about covers everything."

"The AFFC is gaining strength every day. Jasper Slade's downfall could be fatal to our cause, and the anti-Christian, anti-conservative media know that. Atheists and idolaters use morally corrupt forces to undermine the country by whatever means, to seduce the young and turn them against God and fam-ily. They fill young people's heads with ideas about sexual free-dom and single parenthood and homosexuals adopting babies. They're for abortions and adultery. They want to turn this great nation into Sodom, just like that book you were looking at!" Her voice swelled. "It's anarchy! God, family, country, everything Jasper Slade stands for, these anarchists despise. They'll do anything to ruin him."

Lombard asked, "I don't suppose you have one particular anarchist in mind, like as a suspect in the plot to frame the senator?"

"You'll have to ask Ross about that," Mrs. Drinnon said absently.

———

"I don't suppose you have one particular anarchist in mind, like as a suspect?" Lombard repeated an hour later. She fixed a hard stare on Ross McKenna, who had just finished his version of the sermon Mrs. Drinnon had delivered earlier.

McKenna smiled. "I like the way you get right to the point, Miss Lombard."

"A suspect for framing Senator Slade or for killing Hughes?" McLean asked. "Do you mean to tell us you think Hughes was killed as part of some conspiracy to set up Slade and bring down the AFFC?"

"That's what I've been saying all along," McKenna nodded. "I can understand your incredulity, but I'm prepared to show you evidence of this conspiracy."

They were sitting in an upstairs study, formerly that of the late A.C., and presently arranged like a shrine to his memory. He stared down at them from a more recent portrait made around the time of his death, dour and gray and bald and fat, glowering from over a barrister's bookcase lined with rare books. McKenna addressed Lombard. "You've been eyeing those rare books, Miss

Lombard. I noticed that bookcase in your living room yesterday. You read, don't you?"

Lombard shrugged. "I'm no scholar. I've never read anything like these here."

"Are you familiar with a quarterly newsletter published in Asheville called the *Carolina Vigilante*?"

"I've looked through it once or twice. Radical earth-mother rag they drop in coffeehouses and bookshops around town."

"Do you recall any articles about Jasper Slade?"

"No. I don't read that paper regularly. Bleeding-heart liberal. Turns me off."

"So you don't know the publisher, Wiley Faulks?"

"No." She turned to McLean. "Ever heard of him, Sam?"

"Nope."

"We don't know him. Fill us in."

"Well, Wiley Faulks is a flagrant homosexual," McKenna said. "He is the publisher *and* editor of the *Vigilante*. He once ran with Greenpeace, and he's a Naderite. He's a vocal opponent of the tobacco farmer, and he's made a career of attacking the AFFC. He ran a piece months ago suggesting that Jasper Slade is homosexual. We thought of suing then, but we let it go since few people outside the left-wing camp read the *Vigilante* anyway. Here's the issue I'm referring to."

Lombard took the paper from him and read aloud the highlighted caption. " 'Jasper Slade's Dark Pink Secret.' Hmm. Cute title."

"I don't think it's cute," McKenna said curtly, handing her another tract. "I want you to read the highlighted portion out loud. It will explain why I think Faulks knows something about this conspiracy, if he isn't behind it himself, which I certainly don't doubt."

Lombard began reading. " 'The *Vigilante* will not stop until Jasper Slade has been exposed as a dangerous pawn of the corporate powers that exploit and deplete the spirit of the working people of

North Carolina. We will not yield to his hypocrisy, his tyranny, or his threats. If it becomes necessary to destroy his organization in order to effect justice and liberty for our people, the *Vigilante* is prepared to endure combat.'"

McKenna said, "That issue came out a week ago Friday."

"A week before the murder," Lombard mused aloud. "Mr. McKenna, why would a person who wants to ruin Slade kill that innocent boy? Why not kill Slade? The killer surely had the chance to do them both in that night."

"You read it. He used the word *combat*. Combat, as in war. Revolutionaries are prepared to sacrifice innocents in their cause. It's what defines them. His motive wasn't to kill Jasper the man, but Jasper the power, and the AFFC as a whole. He's made it his mission, and he's backed by the gay intelligentsia."

"Who do you think did the actual murder?" asked Lombard.

"That's what I need help with."

"Okay. Go on. Tell me about the gay intelligentsia."

McKenna's voice took on the enthusiasm of a pastor who has won a convert. "You'll find its epicenter right here in Raleigh. The Piedmont Pride's offices are downtown. They run the whole gay network all over the state, and regularly contribute scathing material about the AFFC to Wiley Faulks's newsletter in Asheville. Here's another example, from the same issue," he said, this time handing the copy to McLean.

"'Slade Rides Again,'" McLean drawled in schoolboy cadence.

"A disgusting reference to a red leather motorcycle jacket Slade is alleged to have given his lover as a gift. You'll notice no byline, nobody taking credit for the report, only the editor's assurance that the information was 'confirmed' by sources in the Pride office here in Raleigh." He snatched the newsletter out of McLean's hands and held it up, shaking it. "They don't name the lover because there is no lover! That's journalism, huh? That's integrity. The deviants!" He threw the newsletter on his desk. "They made up the whole thing just to malign Jasper Slade. But it wasn't enough, because nobody reads their degenerate publications. They had to get to him so the public would notice. They had to contrive a scheme that would ruin him forever and destroy all that he has built."

After a few silent seconds, Lombard asked, "Is that everything you've got?"

"Yes."

"Where's Slade?"

"Upstairs."

"Upstairs? Good! Then let's talk to him."

"Not now."

"Not now?" Lombard repeated crossly. "Why not now?"

"He's sedated. He's been sleeping since he arrived on Saturday. He's in shock."

"Has he given a statement to anybody about what happened?"

"No. Like I said, he's been out of it all weekend."

"Well, he's said something, *anything*. Does he ever eat or go to the bathroom?"

"What difference does that make?"

"It matters who he talks to, McKenna. I want to be one of the first."

"I'll see that you are."

"I mean it," Lombard said emphatically. "When I was a cop the suspect was the first person I wanted to talk to about a crime. The trick was in getting to him before a lawyer did. Here I am in Raleigh, a few feet from the man accused, a man I'm working *for,* and you're telling me I can't talk to him!"

McKenna brought his hand to his forehead, as though he had a headache. "Please don't keep carping at me. I told you you'll see him as soon as he is able to talk."

"And why is he sedated if he's in shock?" Lombard demanded. "What's he on?"

McKenna sighed and looked down at his feet. "All right. I'm

going to tell you something the public doesn't know. Jasper has for many years suffered from a terribly painful nervous affliction that affects his muscles. He gets wound so tight he collapses in agony. A few years ago he began taking pain medication. He's needed it badly to get through this weekend."

"What pain medication?"

"It's a kind of…well, it's Demerol."

"Demerol? He shoots up?" Lombard shouted.

"He's injected with measured doses according to a physician's prescription. It soothes him."

"It damn well ought to!" Lombard and McLean traded surprised glances. She got up and said, "Well, when he comes out of La-La Land, let me know. In the meantime, Sam and I will check out these, um, 'gay intelligentsia' leads."

A few moments later Lombard drove silently past the gate and turned onto the county route that led back to the highway.

"What do you think?" McLean asked.

Lombard glanced at him and cracked. She laughed musically and loud. "He's a junkie! Senator Slade is a dope fiend with a yen for young men. Can you believe it?"

McLean arched his eyebrows and said matter-of-factly, "It staggers the mind. I hate to think what's next."

"What's next is the Piedmont Pride. I want you to find out where they're at in Raleigh. I have to stop by the motel and call Retta to check on things. You take the car and talk to whoever you run into at the Pride offices. Just so we have something to give that lunatic McKenna."

"How about you go talk to them?" McLean offered. "I can check in with Retta."

"Sam, don't be a baby."

"I'm being reasonable. I think you'd do better getting those people to talk, is all."

"*Those* people," Lombard repeated. "Sam, I want you talk to them because you can do as good an interview as I can and also because you need to get over your homo heebie-jeebies. Those activist types are the biggest squares on the planet. You haven't got a thing to worry about. You're more likely to be bored stiff than scandalized."

———

The Piedmont Pride office occupied a stucco cottage on a quiet tree-lined street of a residential neighborhood. A young man with prep-school looks and thinning brown hair came to the door, and McLean introduced himself as an investigator and showed the man his badge. The silver-plated badge was a fake, one of several Lombard had obtained through a mail-order catalog back when she and McLean had gotten their private investigator licenses. Lombard had explained at the time that people tend to spill their guts when they see a badge. When McLean flashed his badge at the Pride office, the young man introduced himself as Ben Hartley. He seemed nervous and distracted, his dark eyes glancing at any space not occupied by McLean, until McLean announced he was from Asheville. Hartley looked startled and asked, "Asheville? What brings you all the way here from Asheville?"

"A little story that appeared in the *Carolina Vigilante* about a week and a half ago."

Hartley sat down. "I'm all ears."

McLean leaned forward and handed Hartley the copy McKenna had given him. "See that highlighted part? Says, 'Slade Rides Again.'"

Hartley shrugged. "So? What's it about?"

"Oh, it's just some silly little article about how Jasper Slade gave a red leather jacket to a friend of his. Homosexual overtones, the like. Know anything about it?"

Hartley appeared to be searching his memory. "I can't say I do."

McLean arched his brow. "Huh, well that's interesting. How many people work here at the Pride office?"

"Just me and Jess. Jessamyn Frost, my boss. Well, there are volunteers."

"Any of them write articles for the *Vigilante*?"

Hartley gave his searching look. "I'm sure. Well, yes, we do, on occasion."

"I should think so," McLean said, unfolding the newsletter in question. "Because here in that very article, it says the information came from the Piedmont Pride office in Raleigh."

Hartley's brow tensed. "Well, that may be. If that's what it says. You know, come to think of it, I've heard rumors about that jacket too."

"What do you know about the identity of the so-called lover who got that jacket as a present?"

"Just rumors." Hartley gave a faint chuckle. "Nothing solid."

"I don't care. What have you heard?"

"Just hearsay."

McLean smiled. "I live on hearsay. I wonder if the rumor you heard jibes with the one I heard." He narrowed his eyes and lied smoothly. "Because I heard the lover who got that jacket was none other than Jay Hughes, or I should say the late Jay Hughes."

Hartley said thoughtfully, "That's the rumor I heard too."

"Where did you hear it?"

Hartley stared dumbly at McLean. "I don't know. I mean, I can't remember."

"I get the feeling you're holding back, Mr. Hartley," McLean said. "You wrote that article, didn't you?"

Hartley shook his head. "I don't know. I..."

"Well, hell, I'll settle this right now," McLean grumbled. "Go fetch your boss. What was her name?"

"Jessamyn Frost."

"She's here, isn't she?"

"She's out. And I don't want her involved."

McLean's complexion grew rosy. He said slowly, "Well, Mr. Hartley, I'm sorry you don't want her involved. But I'm out of options. I'll get to the bottom of this any way I have to. That includes getting it from Ms. Frost if I have to, today, tomorrow, the next day, or by a subpoena. Which is it gonna be, son?"

Hartley winced. "No. I don't want...just leave Jess out of it, okay?"

"That depends."

"Okay, just don't get mad. I'm just all mixed up. I heard about the murder. I know that's why you're here. I'm just really fucked up and scared, because I knew the victim. I knew Jay." Hartley was suddenly pale, his voice weary and trembling. "I liked Jay. He was a really good person, and um, I'm just so upset about what happened to him." Tears welled in Hartley's eyes. "I go to Asheville on Pride business, just every now and then. I go to this club called the Grotto. It's a gay men's club. Very private, very exclusive. A good-looking guy who looks like he has money can get in with no problem. Anyway, Jay hung out there. I noticed him because it was impossible not to notice him. He was so beautiful he glowed. I heard a rumor that he was dating a big-time closeted politician, and I thought that was interesting. So I approached Jay about it."

McLean scowled. "What happened?"

"Nothing at first. I just chatted with him the first couple of times I saw him at the Grotto. Then one night he showed up wearing this cool-as-shit red leather jacket. I mean, it was scarlet and soft as a lamb's ass."

"Soft as a what?"

"It's a figure of speech, sir. Please. Anyway, I complimented him on it and asked him where he got it. He said it was a gift. Being nosy, I asked from whom. He said his boyfriend gave it to him. So I could tell he was proud of whoever his boyfriend was, and I said something like, 'Your boyfriend must be in some bad business,' or words to that effect. You know, just joking around. Well, he was dying to brag about his sugar daddy, I could tell. I asked him, and he told me. Then he kind of freaked out, like he let the cat out of the bag. Begged me not to tell anybody."

"So he told you his sugar daddy was Jasper Slade."

"He didn't say sugar daddy, but yeah. It was Slade."

"And you told on him anyway."

"I didn't name Jay," Hartley said defensively. "There was no way the story could be traced back to him. Wiley left my name out of it. It was just a way to get at Slade that I couldn't pass up." Hartley averted his eyes. "I wish I hadn't written it. Otherwise, Jay might still be alive."

"What do you mean by that?"

"I don't know," Hartley said. "I just worry that the story got him in trouble, that maybe if I had left it alone, he wouldn't have got killed like that."

"Killed like what?"

"Butchered." Hartley leaned forward and buried his face in his hands. "Christ. I never thought something like that would happen. I never could have imagined it."

"What do you mean you didn't talk to her?" Lombard snapped. She and McLean were having a late supper at a Greek restaurant, and he had just summarized his interview of Ben Hartley and mentioned Jessamyn Frost as an afterthought.

McLean said, "She wasn't there. But McKenna will be real pleased that we got to the boogeyman that wrote that blurb about Slade ridin' again."

"Did you tell him you were a cop?"

"Of course not, but I let him think I was. He went on and on. So we've got one more lead, and that's Wiley Faulks."

"Two leads," Lombard said. "There's also the Grotto, and you're going."

"Why should I go? You're the homo!"

"It's a men's club, Sammy. Real nice one too. They wouldn't let me in."

"What makes you think they'll let me in?"

"You're a good-looking man! They'll be all over you." She laughed wickedly.

"You're interviewing Wiley Faulks, then."

"All right. But I'm talking to Jessamyn Frost before we leave here. I'll stop by tomorrow morning. While I'm there, you call that lunatic McKenna and tell him all about your chat with Ben Hartley, and about Wiley Faulks knowing Hartley, and the Grotto. One good thing about those leads: They're getting us back home, thank God."

———

The next morning Lombard packed her suitcase as she watched Court TV in her motel room. News of Jasper Slade filled the airwaves across the nation, but Court TV was Lombard's favorite channel, with its detailed investigative profiles and dramatic reenactments. In this morning's account of the Slade controversy emerged the allegation of what was billed as the "Whitehall Speech." Last year, the account held, Slade had visited Whitehall College, a conservative Christian school near Asheville, and delivered an unrecorded address to the graduating class in which he lambasted in scathing particularity the onslaught of homosexuality among the youth of America. He denounced proposed hate-crimes bills designed to protect gay victims, and suggested that conservative lawmakers draft what he called a Defense of Dignity Bill. The bill would create a defense for anyone accused of murdering a homosexual, if it could be established that the homicide was provoked by the homosexual's "unnatural advances" against the accused. The bill had never been introduced, and Slade later denied proposing it.

Lombard told McLean she would be back by checkout time and started off to the Piedmont Pride office. She was relieved to find Jessamyn Frost there, and willing to talk to her.

"Ben told me he talked to a man from your department yesterday," said Frost, a smartly dressed middle-aged woman with short, wavy hair and Betty Crocker looks.

"That was my partner, Sam McLean. He had someplace to get to and didn't have time to chat with you. So here I am."

Frost leaned against a desk. "So what do you want?"

"I want to know what exactly the Piedmont Pride does. What's it here for?"

"We lobby, mainly the state legislature. We're a resource center for people who want information about gay issues, like the state of the law, medicine, social and cultural concerns, as they relate to gay people. We connect gays to legal and health care professionals, to political, social, and religious institutions that aid gay people."

"So if you want to know what's gay about North Carolina, this is the place to be."

"We provide just about everything but a dating service, that's true." Frost smiled.

"The one thing *everybody* wants," Lombard chuckled, "you don't provide?"

Frost looked puzzled. "Do you have any more questions?"

"I sure do. Yesterday Ben Hartley told my partner Sam McLean that you-all have volunteers. Where are they?"

"Chapel Hill, Wilmington, Greensboro, Winston-Salem, Charlotte."

"College towns."

"Education centers are the best footholds for progress. Our volunteers are mostly young people, many of them students at universities."

"What about Asheville? Asheville is a college town too."

"UNC-Asheville, yes." Frost nodded. "It's very small, of course."

"And there's Appalachian State in Boone, up in the mountains," Lombard added.

"Boone and Asheville are both very small, regional places. Not very urban."

"Sounds like the Pride looks down on us western Carolina folks."

"That's not true. I love Asheville. It's a lovely town, and I go there with my partner for Bele Chere every summer."

"The arts festival. Crowds. Me, I keep my head low and stay home."

"UNCA is a good school, and very enlightened, I'm told."

"What do you know about Whitehall?" Lombard asked abruptly.

Frost pursed her lips. "It's a reactionary school not far from Asheville. Why?"

"Yesterday I sat in my motel room and watched Court TV. You ever watch Court TV? Got some good shows about crime and criminal investigation. Anyway, they're all over this Jasper Slade case.

Those cute little anchor girls' eyes are popping out their heads with each new rumor about Slade's secret homosexual past. Anyway, they played a tape of one of those wild speeches Slade gives—well, used to give—at colleges. This one they played was in Michigan."

Frost said distastefully, "I've seen it. It's a notorious gay hate speech."

Lombard leaned forward in her chair and raised her hands. She had a habit of gesticulating when she told a story, and she always clasped her hands together in front of her face when she began. She pointed both of her index fingers up on either side of her head, devil-style, and said, "Then this reporter—now, I think reporters, well, *most* reporters, are lying sons of bitches, so maybe there's no truth to it. But this reporter starts talking about a speech Slade gave at Whitehall College not too long ago. Now, it wasn't recorded, but if it was real, it made that Michigan speech sound like the Sermon on the Mount. He was talking about going easy on people that kill gays, just for the fact that the victim was making a pass at the killer."

Frost said solemnly, "I also have it on good authority that he has called for the Defense of Dignity Bill. Wiley Faulks heard him."

"Wiley Faulks? Who's that?" Loy asked casually.

"The editor of the *Carolina Vigilante,* the paper your partner discussed with Ben."

"An Asheville paper," Loy remarked.

"Do you read it?" Frost asked, as though surprised.

"I look through it every now and then. It agrees with my politics." Lombard's dark eyes crinkled at the corners as her smile broadened.

"You actually read the *Vigilante*? Now that is encouraging in a police officer. You don't sound like you're from North Carolina, though. I can't place the accent."

"I'm originally from New Orleans. I left when I got out of high school."

"How did you end up working for the Asheville police?"

Lombard's smile tensed. "Well, Ms. Frost, I'm not with the police. I used to be, back in Charlotte, but I'm in private practice in Asheville these days."

Frost's soft features darkened. "You're a private investigator? I don't get it. Who are you working for?"

"I'm working for Jasper Slade's defense team."

Frost stared at Loy for a few seconds and then shook her head. "I feel that you should have been up front about that from the beginning. I'm really troubled by this."

"I know. Sam should have been clearer about that, and I thought he was, really." She saw that Frost was unconvinced. She went on, "The thing is, Ms. Frost, my job is to find out the truth about what happened back in Asheville. The defense will use what I find out or not use it depending on how it ties in to their case."

"What makes you think I'll be of any use?"

"Well, I have reason to believe the Piedmont Pride is familiar with some of Mr. Slade's private doings."

"Such as?"

"What you might call homoerotic pursuits."

"Ben talked to your partner about that. I know nothing apart from what Ben wrote in the article he sent to Wiley Faulks. Nothing more, nothing less."

"Do you know Wiley Faulks personally?"

"No. I've met him a few times, but I've never spoken in depth with him."

"You just told me Faulks heard Slade call for the Defense of Dignity Bill. How did you know that? He must have told you."

"He did tell me. Look, I'm not lying."

"I didn't say you were."

"I said I've met Faulks, and he mentioned to me the last time I saw him that he was at Whitehall when Slade made that speech."

"Don't get all flustered. You just forgot to mention it is all," Lombard said.

"Well, I don't trust you!" Frost shouted. "You work for a murderer and a slanderer of decent people. Slade grew up in a culture that made him hate himself so much that he launched a campaign to destroy honest, decent citizens who simply want to live out their lives with integrity. Simply put, he's the most dangerous kind of obstacle to gay rights: the repressed, self-loathing homosexual. Only he burned both ends of the candle. And now everyone knows the truth, now that he's murdered an innocent gay man. With that Defense of Dignity idea, he came close to engineering a defense for himself!"

There were a few seconds of tense silence between them, and Lombard said, "You know, I think you're probably right about that."

"Don't patronize me, Ms. Lombard."

"I'm not." Lombard stood up. "I guess you want me to leave."

"Wait. Ms. Lombard, I have to ask you something."

Lombard paused and said, "What?"

"Are you gay?"

"Now, there's an interesting subject," Lombard said, pointing at Frost.

"What subject? It's a simple question."

"No, it's not so simple. It has to do with words and how they fit. The word *gay* just never has really suited me. I think of happy jolly giddy gay. It's not me. Lesbian, yes, life-long and full-tilt, but even that word sounds too poetic. I ain't no Sappho," Lombard grinned. "*Dyke* probably suits me best." She nodded with a resolved look. "Dyke, for sure."

"A simple yes would have sufficed," Frost said. "How can you work for Slade?"

Lombard looked reflective. "I used to ask certain lawyers that question, back in Charlotte. Never thought I'd see it turned around on me. 'How can you work for that murdering lowlife?' I'd say. Well, I didn't use those exact words. You know what they used to tell me?"

Frost stood in mute attention and shook her head.

"They usually said, oh, it was the Constitution and the right of a fair trial, and theirs was a noble cause, et cetera. This one lawyer impressed me, and this is what she said: 'I'm only one woman standing between the accused and the ruin of his life. What if everybody else is wrong, and he's right? I'm the one who has to find out. That's a hell of a lot of pressure to be under, and I don't need more than that. So get off my back.'"

3

LOMBARD WENT TO HER OFFICE AS SOON AS SHE returned to Asheville. Secure Services Inc., resided in an ugly little salmon-colored brick building on an extremity of Haywood Street between the Buncombe County Sheriff's Department and Interstate 240. Situated among a few look-alike neighbors that had been built in the heyday of post-1950s utilitarian architecture, the building had once housed an easy-loan office, and before that a dry-cleaning service. Lombard had chosen the location because of the building's cheap rent, its easy access for clients traveling by interstate, the free parking, and its proximity to downtown Asheville proper, only blocks away.

The first thing she did when she sat down at her desk was call Ross McKenna. Was Slade coherent yet? Why not? Why didn't they stop shooting him up long enough for an interview? McKenna reminded her that the Demerol was prescribed, and Slade was still in too much pain. She would have to wait. McKenna then asked her to convey his thanks to McLean for his valuable interview of Ben Hartley and told Lombard to keep him informed of McLean's progress. Lombard seethed when McKenna went on to commend her talent for delegation. By the time she hung up, she was boiling angry and suspicious of the delays. She wondered if Slade had spoken to his lawyer. She pulled the phone book out of her desk and flipped through the attorney directory. Then she picked up the phone and called Sig Mashburn's office.

Retta, the office manager, appeared at Lombard's door. "Loy, somebody's here to see you."

"Shh. I'm on the phone," Lombard whispered, swatting at Retta.

"It's a reporter."

Lombard pursed her lips. "Well, you know what to do with him. Or do you want me to… Hello?" she abruptly spoke into the phone. "This is Loy Lombard. I'm the investigator for Jasper Slade. I need Sig Mashburn." She turned to Retta while she was on hold. "Tell him I said to go to hell, and he can quote me."

"It's a woman. A lady reporter," Retta said dryly.

"I don't give a damn if she's from Court TV. Tell her I said no comment."

"She's from the TV news. She's hell-bent on talking to you, and I'm wore out trying to run her off. *You* tell her no comment," Retta said, and walked away.

Mashburn's receptionist told Lombard he was out and offered to take a message.

"I'll call back later," Lombard said, and hung up. She glared in the direction of the lobby. "Retta!" she shouted.

"What do you want?" Retta bellowed.

Lombard loped out of her office. The reporter stood up and smiled. Lombard recognized her from TV but didn't recall her name. She was a tall redhead, slender and poised. "I'm Hunter Lyle. I'm a reporter with…"

"Retta told me," Loy interrupted. "But I'm afraid you've wasted a trip. I'm very busy, and even if I weren't, I wouldn't have anything to say to you. I don't discuss my business with any stranger, let alone strange reporters."

Hunter Lyle said coolly with a charm-school smile, "May I speak now? I'm very pleased to meet you, Ms. Lombard, and only wanted to introduce myself."

Lombard couldn't help smiling back. "Now, I know better than that, Ms. Lyle."

"Could we speak privately?"

"We are speaking privately. Nobody in here but you, me, and Retta."

Lyle asked Retta, "Would it bother you if I spoke to Ms. Lombard in her office?"

Retta said, "I'd get more work done that way."

Lombard frowned at Retta and reluctantly invited Lyle into her office. Once inside, she motioned Lyle to sit. Lombard sat along the edge of her desk and glanced at her watch. "So."

Lyle reached into her shoulder bag and pulled out a hand-held tape recorder.

"Oh, no! No ma'am," Lombard said. "You just put that contraption back in your little pocketbook, sugar. I'm not about to be recorded."

Lyle looked unperturbed. "It's normal for me to record, for accuracy. It's routine, I mean. Most people don't mind."

"I mind."

"I only have a few questions, Ms. Lombard. You don't have to answer them."

"I thought you said you just wanted to introduce yourself."

Lyle's soft features grew rosy. "Why don't you stop being so hateful?"

"Because I don't like reporters." Lombard smiled at Lyle's evident anger, written in every feature of her pretty face. And it was only because of Lyle's beauty that Lombard added, "But I do apologize for being rude. And to make up for it, I'll answer any reasonable questions you have."

Lyle straightened her shoulders and crossed her legs. "I understand you've been retained by Jasper Slade's defense team as a private investigator."

Lombard gave a blank look. "Who told you that?"

"I don't name my sources."

"Oh? How noble. In that case, I don't know what the hell you're talking about."

Lyle's cheeks turned crimson. She said in a measured tone, "I suppose it's not confidential. Sig Mashburn. Slade's lawyer. I interviewed him earlier today at the courthouse. He confirmed that you are the investigator."

"Oh. So Sig Mashburn talks to *you*, huh? Wish I could get his attention. I guess that sweet smile and little wiggle come in handy with hot-dog lawyers."

Lyle stood up and glowered at Lombard. "This is going nowhere."

"Where's your cameraman?" Lombard asked, smiling broadly. "And the hairdresser and the makeup boy?"

"Go on, Lombard. Let go of every shot you've stored up since Charlotte," Lyle said, slinging her bag over her shoulder. "I knew better than to bring a camera here, because I know your history with reporters. I know how the Charlotte media hounded you and printed innuendo and helped ruin your career. I research my subjects. I thought I'd respect you and come alone to request an off-camera comment. I didn't know it'd like opening a vein. Sorry I defiled your inner sanctum here." Lyle pushed the door open and stormed into the lobby. "I pity you," she muttered as she blew past Retta's desk.

"Don't lose your cool, now," Retta yawned. "She's a soft touch, deep down."

Lombard chased into the lobby. "Ms. Lyle! Aw, I was just teasing, really…"

Lyle turned on Lombard. "I don't have time for teasing. I have a story to cover."

"I know," Lombard said, hunching her shoulders and holding her hands up in a gesture of surrender. "I guess I came off a little hostile." Lombard avoided eye contact with the smirking Retta. "The thing is, Ms. Lyle, I'm not ready to commit—I mean!— comment, not yet. I just got this case and I have to be careful. Now, don't quote me, but I…well, give me some time. No promises, but maybe I can talk later."

Lyle nodded. "Thank you. And I accept your apology."

After Lyle left, Lombard turned to Retta. "I didn't apologize."

"Nope. You didn't apologize," Retta grinned. "You kissed her ass."

"Shut up," said Lombard, looking out the front window with soft eyes.

———

Lombard trusted Sam McLean and Retta Scott. Retta had been a widow with three sons and a dire need for work when Lombard hired her to manage the office. She could scarcely afford an office manager at the time, but Retta had reminded Lombard of the person she had loved more than anybody, a now-deceased aunt named Anna Mae.

Lombard's mother had died and left her husband to raise their only daughter from the age of four. He had been alcoholic, though devoted to Lombard in his own way, before the bottle took him to his grave when Lombard was sixteen. By then Lombard was running with a rough crowd of dropouts. She had learned how to pick locks, pick pockets, and hot-wire cars. When she wasn't getting high or ripping people off, she read books and stole afternoons at the movies, romancing dreams of a better life.

Anna Mae straightened her out. On the night of her father's funeral, Lombard went to live at her aunt's house. Anna Mae had managed a butcher shop, gone through two marriages and two husbands' deaths, and raised five children almost on her own. She couldn't afford to take Lombard in, but she did anyway, because

Lombard was her blood. Anna Mae put her to work in the butcher shop. Lombard went to school every day, went to work after school, and studied at night. Anna Mae didn't spare Lombard a minute for drugs or petty crime. She drove Lombard to exhaustion with work and study, and stayed on her about graduating high school, which no member of the family had ever been able to do, with poverty always at arm's length.

When Lombard got her diploma, Anna Mae gave her $300, a suitcase packed with new clothes, and a kiss goodbye. Anna Mae told Lombard a woman grew strong by making her own way. Lombard was nineteen years old and more alone than she had ever been in her life. She had grown fond of the discipline and security of Anna Mae's household, and the only other place she could imagine finding the solace of order was the military. She headed straight for the Navy recruitment office.

It was then that Lombard was able to explore a side of herself that she had kept locked up for years. Tomboyish and athletic as a kid, Lombard had gotten along well enough with boys but had been hopelessly awkward around girls. She had never had a close girlfriend and had been mortified by the persistent sexual fantasies that filled her mind every time she found a girl she wanted to befriend. She didn't contemplate the fact that she was a lesbian until after she had joined the Navy. She knew it was dangerous, though, and feared dismissal from the Navy so much that she avoided sex until she was twenty-one and off base at a port in Italy.

That experience released her from all inhibition, save her fear of getting caught. It became a private game for her, closing off her true identity to satisfy the demands of authority and waiting until just the right safe moment to unravel her desire in the chase of a woman. By the time she left the military, she knew as though it were second sight when a woman was open to expose herself to a lesbian experience.

As Lombard sat waiting for Lt. Mike Church on the porch of the Rosemond Inn on Watauga Lane, she let her mind wander to Hunter Lyle. The journalist had made an impression on her, and Lombard felt an unwelcome attraction. She wished she had kept her mouth shut and not invited another chance of an interview. She realized that she had made the offer out of an unconscious desire to see Lyle again.

Lombard pulled her jacket tighter as a crisp April wind rushed over her. A car pulled along the curbside, and a man who looked like a middle-aged detective stepped out of it and onto the front walk.

"You Loy Lombard?" he asked.

"I am," she replied, standing up.

"I'm Mike Church."

Lombard glanced over her shoulder. "Mrs. Rosemond wouldn't let me in till you got here. I told her I work for Slade. I don't think she likes me."

"You should have told her you're a cop. I understand you were a good one."

Lombard smiled. "Word gets around."

"I've thought about quitting, going into private work," he said. "Been doing this for so long, though, I don't know what else to do. You get stuck. You get a wife, kids, and there's the mortgage. And long about that time, they promote you to investigator, and I'll be damned if that don't trap you for life. All of a sudden you're dug in." He gave her a wary look and shrugged. "Well, unless they run you off."

"Hmm. Too much word gets around," she said thinly.

"I followed that case in Charlotte. It was in the papers here. But what I know I like, standing up for your partner. Only thing is, now you're on the wrong side."

"I guess that depends on how you look at it."

"And I guess money makes a difference on how you look at it," he grinned. "Speaking of money, where's that lawyer, Sig Mashburn?"

"Late," she said, looking out at the street. "Let's wait inside, out of the chill."

They walked into the foyer together, and Church began to talk about the night of the homicide. Lombard listened to him intently, and very soon into his account she knew he was holding back something. He told her what the public already knew, what she had read in the papers and seen in reports on TV. He might respect her for her prior work as a real cop, but he wasn't talking to a cop now, he was talking to part of a criminal defense team. She understood. She was grateful he had at least arranged for her to see the murder scene.

There was a knock on the front door, and through the lace curtains of the window could be seen the figure of a man. Lombard started for the door when Mrs. Rosemond, a stout, nervous woman with silky white hair, pinched features, and a raspy voice, rushed in from the parlor. She was flushed and slightly perspiring, but Lombard suspected she was always flushed and perspiring, as though she had never quite shaken menopause.

"I'll answer it!" Mrs. Rosemond said. She glanced at Church. "Who are you? Did I let you in?"

"I'm Lieutenant Church, ma'am. The lead investigator for the police. We met out there on the front porch the night of…"

"Don't speak of it! I know why you're here. Just don't speak of it. I've had no end of nightmares." She opened the door and frowned at the man standing outside. This was Sigmund Blaise Mashburn, announced the card he handed Mrs. Rosemond with a large, tanned bear claw of a hand. Sig Mashburn towered over everyone at better than six and half feet. He looked to be the sort of man who had been lanky in youth but who had developed his girth through years of consuming Southern-fried food and cold beer. With large, kind dark eyes and thinning salt-and-pepper hair, he was not particularly handsome, but he had a disarming, wide grin full of large white teeth, and an infectiously wry chuckle. He was the kind of man people liked at first sight, and even after they discovered he was a lawyer. He was the man to whom people handed thousands of dollars to represent them without much more than a smile and a handshake as assurances of his legal acumen.

While Sig Mashburn introduced himself to Mrs. Rosemond, Church whispered to Lombard, "She was the one called the police. Heard a commotion and was standing right behind the police when the door opened, and all that blood...poor old thing."

That hadn't been in any reports, Lombard thought. It didn't matter. She felt more comfortable with the idea that the information Church kept to himself was trivial. "So it was her voice I heard on the 911 tape?" she asked softly.

"Yeah."

"What was it she heard exactly? The tape doesn't make that clear..."

"Loy Lombard! We finally meet," Sig Mashburn said gregariously. He gave a courtly nod and shook her hand firmly. "There's Lieutenant Church. We meet again."

"You two already talked?" Lombard asked.

"Not about this case. We've been on the opposite sides of justice many times. Me on the right side, of course." Mashburn beamed at Lombard and nudged Church. "Boy, I tell you what! Have you laid eyes on a better-looking woman all week?"

Lombard said dryly, "It's only Thursday."

Mashburn slapped Church on the back. "How's them bass treating you?"

"What I catch I generally throw back," said Church.

Mashburn laughed. "Well, I tell you what. I wouldn't mind us two getting together on my bass boat one of these days and me learning a thing or two from a real river sportsman. I'm just trifling with it."

Lombard interrupted. "Mr. Mashburn…"

"Sig," he said, shaking his finger at her. "Call me Sig."

"Sig, how about we go on up?"

They followed Mrs. Rosemond upstairs while she upbraided everyone for the inconvenience of the whole case. "I look forward to the day this is all over with. I haven't been able to rent that room, what with police and lawyers always threatening to come look at it. I doubt I'll ever have the nerve to rent it again. That's income, you know." She walked briskly ahead of them to the door and unlocked it. "I'll be downstairs. Don't come asking me questions either." She clipped past them toward the stairs.

Church showed them the bed and described the scene he encountered the night of the homicide. He described the position of the body, the nature of the injuries, and the state in which he had found Jasper Slade. Mashburn asked about the crime scene photographs, which he hadn't yet obtained from the DA. Lombard quietly patted her jacket pocket, inside which she had concealed a camera, just in case she needed it.

"What about the murder weapon?" Mashburn asked.

"We didn't find one, like the papers said. I don't know who spilled that, but we think Slade threw it out that bathroom window in there. We looked high and low all around the premises but never found it. We taped off the entire outdoor perimeter around the house, and I figure some busybody grabbed it and took off with it when there weren't any police around. It was damn dark, and by daylight anybody could have picked it up. Hell, maybe that old lady, for all I know."

Mashburn chuckled. "Reminds me of the time I was down in Florida trying this RICO case. This Good Samaritan type all of a sudden turned up—right in the middle of the trial—with a bag of cocaine he said he'd picked up off the street after the drug bust on my client. Somehow in the heat of things, a cop must have dropped it. Well, it was important evidence; you can imagine how much fun I was having with that missing. This Good Samaritan eyewitness had picked it up after the dust settled so no kids would get their hands on it, and he neglected to go to the police with it for fear of what they might accuse him of. Then his conscience got the better of him and he showed up at trial. Of course, the chain of custody was shot, and it couldn't come in. So maybe Mrs. Rosemond—or somebody else—did pick up the knife for safety."

"Maybe somebody ought to ask the old lady about it," Lombard offered.

It was like she wasn't there. They either didn't hear her or ignored her. Mashburn and Church were telling war stories now, trading fond reminiscences of cases they had worked, laughing at familiar stories of cases they had shared. Mashburn barely looked around the room, and Church seemed merely to relish the chance to get out of headquarters for a spin around the crime scene. It was a break for him and for Mashburn, a chance to see if anything was obviously awry, to get a notion of where things were placed, how they looked now as opposed to how they had looked that night. He would want to have a good look, of course, as a point of reference for his trial theatrics later.

The bed was neatly made. It had been one day shy of a week since the bloodshed, and the room was spotless. The walls smelled of new paint, and the floorboards had been polished. The scent of varnish and antiseptic cleaners permeated the whole room: The old lady had gone to task or had had somebody else work it over. Lombard critically inspected every neat corner, and she wouldn't leave until she had checked every inch of the room and the bathroom, until she was satisfied nothing remained undiscovered.

The men were now talking about the upcoming court hearing. Mashburn had been to Raleigh and had interviewed Slade. Lombard bristled at hearing this news. "When did you talk to Slade?" she asked.

"Yesterday," Mashburn said. He eyed Church. "Excuse us, Mike." He nodded toward the bathroom, and Lombard followed him inside. "It wasn't much of an interview," he said in low tones after closing the door.

"That lying son of a bitch told me Slade was too doped-up to talk."

"Well, he is doped-up. He's all thick-tongued, just like that little gospel-singing mongoloid girl on the Down syndrome telethon…"

"Stop stalling, Mashburn. What did he tell you? I feel like I'm working with one hand tied behind my back."

"Not here," Mashburn cautioned. "I'll talk to you about it later, after I talk with Ross McKenna."

"It's like McKenna's afraid of what I might find out!" Lombard hissed.

"No, it's about control," Mashburn said. "I'm normally the master of my defense team. Ross didn't like the idea of me being in charge of the defense investigation. He wanted the investigator to report to him directly, not through me. So he had to find somebody I didn't know personally. He did let me recommend somebody, and I picked you."

"Why me?"

"You remember Iman Casteel, surely."

Lombard looked sharply at Mashburn. "You didn't represent him. I'd recall that."

"No, that was Arlo Saperstein, of the Charlotte bar. Arlo is a friend of mine."

"That jackal? The way he tried to make it like me and Sam had something to do with Iman's dirty business." Lombard's voice shook with rage. "What do you mean he's a friend of yours? The hell with you if he is!"

"Arlo told me all about you and Sam. He never believed you-all were guilty."

"He damn sure pointed his spindly fingers at us, though, all through the trial."

"I know. There was bad blood between you. You put plenty of his clients behind bars. You were cocky and hard to get along with. You were in for the win, just like he was. He called you every name in the book when he talked to me about that case. He enjoyed casting blame on you. Said he was glad he helped to rid the Charlotte defense bar of you." Mashburn grinned. "But hey, he thought you were smart as whip."

"So you recommended me to McKenna because of what Arlo Saperstein said about me? Well, don't think I feel like I owe him or you anything. He can rot in hell right next to Iman Casteel as far as I'm concerned."

Mashburn chuckled. "He ain't dead yet. Arlo's got plenty of fire to let loose in this life." He opened the door and said, "Why don't you stay in here and cool off? One of these days, you'll like me. Everybody likes Sig Mashburn."

Lombard remained in the bathroom, looking out the window and seething. It made her hot, and she tried to push up the window, but it was stuck. She pushed up against the window again. It was an old window, hard to loosen from the sill. She gave it all her strength, and it abruptly popped loose and slid up the cords in the window frame. A cool breeze rolled over her and made her smile. Then she noticed there was no screen. There were chisel marks in the frame, and the exposed wood looked to have been recently cut. She ran her fingers along the outside edge of the window and felt the fresh splinters. She bent down and craned her neck for a look. The marks were consistent with someone forcing the window open from the outside with some sort of tool.

How could that be? Lombard was puzzled. This was the third floor, hardly making it easy for entry from the outside. She heard leaves rustle and looked out to the sturdy limbs of an old elm tree that had escaped the rot of Dutch elm disease, rooted in the earth directly below where she stood, outside the house by mere feet. One of the strongest branches ran to within inches of the window. She slowly walked to the door and peeked through the crack at Mashburn and Church, who were laughing about something. She quietly closed the door and locked it. Then she withdrew the camera from her pocket and aimed its lens at the damaged windowsill.

4

THE NEXT DAY, LOMBARD DROVE TO A SMALL OFFICE
building situated on a narrow lane that jutted off of Broadway.
The building was a 19th-century brick relic whose walls still bore
the weathered painted logo of a defunct bedding company. The
building looked abandoned; there was no indication at all that an
active, radical press was being operated inside.

Lombard pressed a buzzer for a reasonable length of time and,
getting no answer, pushed through the unlocked door to a musty,
hollow interior with opaque windows on the side of the building
facing an alley. The overall aspect of the place, windowless brick
walls on the other three sides, was grudging of sunlight and
devoid of apparent activity. Stacks of books and magazines and
yellowed newspapers rose up in dusty pillars all over the scuffed
heart-pine floor, except the portion occupied by a long, heavy
oak table. It too was cluttered with papers and books.

"Hello?" she called out.

A smallish man appeared on the landing of a staircase abut-
ting the wall opposite the windows. He was very thin, with bristly
gray hair and wire-rimmed glasses. His face was thoughtful and
placid, and he was wearing soft flannel pants, a shirt buttoned at
the collar, and a plum cardigan buttoned up to the rib cage. "Who
are you?" he asked.

"Loy Lombard," she said. "Are you Wiley Faulks?"

He said that he was, and she told him she was investigating the
Slade case. Faulks invited her upstairs to his apartment, as though
he might have been expecting her.

"I thought you ran a press," she said, "but I don't see one."

"That's down in the basement, with the other equipment. I have to keep all that safe, so I have an alarm down there on the basement door, at the bottom of these stairs. There's no basement access from outside, only from inside."

"Well, you don't even lock the front door," said Lombard.

"I do at night. I like to keep it open in the daytime for visitors. I'm trying to organize a library on the main level, and I envision a study center for questioning minds." He smiled on opening the door to his apartment. "And this is where I live."

Lombard looked around the loft. It was modest and immaculate—especially compared to the chaos downstairs—decorated in dark tones of maroon, old gold, and chocolate-brown. Tall bookcases lined the walls, the shelves stuffed with thousands of volumes. "Do you live alone?" she asked.

"Yes."

"So you keep an alarm on your basement, but not up here where you live, right?"

"That's right." A high-pitched squeal suddenly shot through the loft. "Oh, there goes the kettle!" He jumped and scampered over to an open kitchen.

"Look at all those books!" Lombard marveled. "Did you write any of them?"

"Oh, I haven't published any books," he said, bending over a stove.

Lombard got to the point. "I've read some of your material about Jasper Slade."

Faulks scuttled back toward the damask-upholstered Victorian sofa where Lombard sat staring around the room, and brought with him a bamboo tray of croissants and two steaming teacups. "I hope you don't mind green tea. Oh, look. You sat down without my having to ask. I'm glad. I hate it when people wait for permission to do things like that. Decorum is such a waste of energy." He sat down next to her and set the tray on a burgundy and gleaming-brass steamer trunk that served as a coffee table.

"Anyway, there's some question about Slade's sexuality." Lombard eyed the croissants and picked one up in a napkin.

"Clearly."

"I'm interested in what you know about it and why you care," she added, biting off a third of the pastry and reaching for the tea.

Faulks leaned forward and rested his elbows on his lap. He kept his eyes on his fidgety hands and spoke softly. "The answer to the latter query is obvious. I believe that hierarchical hypocrisy needs to be exposed, and that's part of what my press does. People need to know when their leaders are lying to them. It's hard to catch them in the relevant lies, but we expose them all, even the little ones that don't seem to mean much, because they all mean the same thing: You can never trust those who wield power." He drew a deep breath and sighed. He reminded Lombard of a priest in a confessional. "And in Slade's case, the lie was huge," he said, raising his voice a little. "It was the rare chance of snaring them in the act of a relevant lie. Here is a man who wants to crush sexual liberty—which any legal scholar worth his salt should construe as a fundamental right—and yet he was living out his own sexual desires with impunity. I had a duty to expose him."

Lombard was chewing on the remains of her croissant. "Are you a legal scholar?"

"I graduated from law school. I never pursued a career in law, though. I use my understanding of the law to fight tyranny, both corporate and government, which appear to have merged into one soul-crushing beast." He sat on the edge of his seat while he delved deeper into his mission. "Slade is an evil man. I was at Whitehall, you know."

"For the Defense of Dignity speech?" Lombard asked, impressed and a little baffled by his candor.

"I find it ironic, almost comically so, that he sought to devise a defense for homophobic slaughter and then committed the act himself."

"But he has denied making that speech. Why?"

"Politics. The speech practically promoted hate crimes. Even conservatives were shocked by it. Slade got carried away talking to that college assembly, but he was speaking from the heart, such as it is. Still, he'll deny it now, because he doesn't wish to appear bloodthirsty."

"Do you know anything about that boy he killed, Jay Hughes?"

"Only what I read in the corporate-controlled news media."

Lombard smiled on recalling McKenna and Mrs. Drinnon's characterization of the media as controlled by a gay-friendly intelligentsia. "I figured he might have had something to do with that 'dark pink secret' you wrote about."

"I never knew the identity of any of Slade's supposed lovers."

"Now, this other article interests me. 'Slade Rides Again,' it says. There was no byline. Who wrote it?"

"Ben Hartley. Am I passing your truth test?" Faulks smiled at her.

Lombard gave him a sidelong look, full of both suspicion and good humor. "You're a smart fellow, and honest. But come on now, surely Ben Hartley told you who Slade's lover was."

Faulks said calmly, "He told me he had spoken personally with Slade's lover. But he didn't name him when he submitted the article, and I didn't ask for the name."

"Do you think it was Jay Hughes? I mean, obviously that's who got killed. But was it Jay Hughes that Hartley was talking about in that article?"

"You already know it was Jay Hughes."

Lombard was caught in Faulks's quiet gaze. "How did you know that?"

"Ben Hartley told me yesterday. I've been expecting you, Ms. Lombard."

She frowned. "Was yesterday the first time you ever heard mention of Jay Hughes from somebody you know, somebody connected to this press you run here?"

Faulks's eyebrows arched as he stared off into space. "I believe so."

"Because to get to the truth about his relationship with Slade, I need all the facts I can get. And we are all interested in the truth, right?"

"I don't have any facts. I really don't know what kind of relationship the men had beyond Ben's amusing article and the fact that Hughes spent the last few hours of his life in bed with the senator."

Lombard's hands flew up, and she shook her head in frustration. "You never even heard rumors? Don't you socialize? Ben told my partner that Jay was a real looker, hung out at clubs, and stayed in the public eye. This is a small town, Mr. Faulks. People talk, don't they?"

"Why would I know anything about common gossip?"

"Because you're a gay man!" she shouted. "And doesn't the editor of the meanest liberal press in western Carolina have anything to reveal about the most talked-about murder victim in the nation?"

"I really don't. I don't socialize much. And I certainly avoid common gossip. It's shallow and a waste of energy. I like real ideas and issues. Hughes offered nothing like any of that until he died."

Lombard leaned forward and snatched up another croissant. "Mr. Faulks, you're the damnedest thing I ever saw. I mean that in a nice way."

"I'm also celibate."

Lombard choked on a crumb and groped for her cup of tea. "What did you say?" she coughed.

"You heard me," Faulks smiled. "Oh, it's not so strange, really.

I'm very open about my sexual orientation, but I'm totally committed to justice for all people, to the exclusion of my personal desires. My cause gets all my energy. So I have found that if I limit my social life, then I don't get tempted to compromise that energy. Does that make sense to you, Ms. Lombard?"

She stared at him for a moment, smiled and patted him on the leg. "Of course it does. You must be a saint, Mr. Faulks. The only saint I ever met in person."

"Oh, dear," he said, waving his hand in front of him, "don't even get me started on the church."

Lombard rolled her eyes and stood up. "Of course. Everybody's got something smart-ass to say about the church."

"Are you a Catholic?" Faulks asked with a surprised tone.

"Not anymore, but I get tired of hearing people knock it."

"Have I offended you? Are you leaving?" He sprang off the sofa and rubbed his hands together. "I hope I haven't insulted you."

"You haven't. I have to go the toilet. Do you mind? That green tea ran right through me."

"Of course! It's right over there." He pointed to a corner door of the loft.

Lombard walked into the bathroom, closed the door, and relieved herself, though she could have waited. She wanted to check out the bathroom. Bathrooms were always revealing, she had long believed and recently confirmed. After she flushed, she opened a wicker cabinet and quietly inspected the bottles and jars inside. Among them were a box of adhesive bandages, a tall brown bottle of hydrogen peroxide, a strange green bottle containing some kind of organic mouthwash, and a bottle of ibuprofen. Lombard narrowed her eyes as she gently pushed aside the contents with her fingers, wondering if she would discover a box of rubbers or a jar of lubricant and lay waste to Faulks's protestations of celibacy.

She fully expected to find some evidence of sexuality, something that would betray some connection to Jay Hughes, or at least to someone else who might have known Hughes. What she didn't expect to find was three little bottles tucked in the back of the cabinet, containing a clear substance and wrapped in prescription tape from Rex RX Drugs on Broadway. The sober script of the labels announced that liquid Demerol stilled within these vials, and next to them, stuffed inside a small, clear plastic sleeve with a button fastener, lay a syringe.

———

"My God, this has been a long week." Lombard was in her office, leaning back in her chair with her hands covering her face as she massaged her forehead. "I've had this bitchy little headache for hours." She and McLean had just wrapped up discussing her visit with Wiley Faulks. McLean had been at the medical examiner's office all afternoon to collect a copy of Jay Hughes's autopsy report and interview the pathologist.

"You should have got some of that Demerol you found in Faulks's medicine cabinet," McLean said dryly. "I hear it's good for migraines."

"I took some of the ibuprofen." She noticed the look McLean gave her. "I *asked* first," she added. "Anyway, it didn't help." She looked a little sad. "One week ago today was the last day of young Jay Hughes's life. I wonder what he was doing one week ago this very minute?"

McLean checked his watch. "It's almost 7. I bet he was having supper. That reminds me, Selena's frying up catfish tonight. We'd love to have you over."

Lombard shook her head. "No, thank you. Aren't you running late?"

"I always am these days. She'll feed the kids at 6 and wait for me to get home. She's gotten used to the hours. Come on over, Loy. We cook up some good catfish, batter-dipped and spicy. You'll like it."

"I'm sure it's good," Lombard said impassively, not believing for a minute that a McLean fish fry could compare to what she had grown up on, "but I'll be working late."

"Well, I'm not," McLean said firmly. "I've scarcely seen my family all week."

"Nobody's putting pressure on you," Lombard said irritably. "If you'd let me finish, I was gonna say I'm working late at home. I'm going to have supper there, and then I'll read this autopsy report." She pointed at the report, stapled together and sitting on top of her desk. "Have you read it yet?"

"Scanned it. They didn't have the copy ready until after 4."

"What does it say, in a nutshell? Did you talk to the medical examiner? What's his name again?"

"Dr. Sanger. Yeah, I talked to him before I got the report." McLean cut his eyes to one side. "By the way, Loy, I'm pretty sure he thought I was a cop. I'm afraid we're going to get in trouble for impersonating the police if we don't start being more up-front about who we are."

"Don't be such an old lady," said Lombard. "You didn't tell him you were a cop. You told him you were an investigator, which is the truth."

"He asked to see my badge, Loy."

"And?"

"I showed it to him." McLean looked dreadfully uncomfortable.

"So? It's a legitimate badge. If the idiot bothered to look closely at it, he would've seen that it's not an official badge. It's not counterfeit. There's nothing wrong with it."

"We're misleading people, Loy."

"Just tell me what the man said, Sam!"

"All right!" McLean frowned. "He said the boy basically bled to death. The fatal wound, he thinks, was a laceration of the femoral artery, this big old blood vessel in your leg, near the groin." McLean shifted in his seat.

"What about the slit throat? Lieutenant Church said his head was practically cut off," Lombard said.

"Sanger thinks Slade—I mean the killer—did that postmortem. The way he bled, the death blow was to the leg. The report explains it." McLean pitched forward, as though ready to spring out of his chair. "I need to get going."

"Wait," Lombard said, looking pointedly at him. "What's wrong with you? Something's on your mind, and it's not supper, and it's not guilt over that badge."

McLean fell back in his chair. "I've never seen torture," he said. "I don't like to think a human being could do something like that to another man, especially somebody he's supposed to care about."

"What else was there?" Lombard picked up the report and began scanning its diagrams and notes.

"Just what I said. Stabbing a man like that, cutting him up." McLean's face was screwed up in disgust. "Nobody deserves that. I just hope the other thing Sanger told me is true."

"What's that?"

"That the victim was loaded up on Demerol."

Lombard froze in her seat, and to her eyes it seemed like the lights turned down a shade except for a narrow halo of revelation surrounding McLean. "Demerol, huh?"

"Yes. A lot of it, thank God. So maybe the poor thing didn't suffer too much. Sanger said it wasn't enough to overdose him, hence the cause of death, but it was enough to make him loopy and listless at the time of death."

"Is that a popular drug of choice these days?" Lombard asked.

"I don't know. I wasn't surprised, of course. We already know Slade is hooked on it. Maybe he drugged Hughes before killing him. Maybe they were in a drug daze when things got out of hand."

"I don't see it," Lombard said. "Demerol is an opiate. I don't see people killing each other on downers. Speed is one thing. This doesn't make any sense at all." She looked crossly at McLean. "What do you make of those vials of liquid Demerol I found in Wiley Faulks's medicine cabinet?"

McLean shrugged. "Not exactly a bombshell. If he knew Hughes—despite what he told you—maybe they've done drugs together. Maybe that's how Slade got hooked."

"McKenna says Slade got hooked a long time ago due to pain."

"So it's the other way around, maybe, and Slade got Hughes hooked, and he in turn…"

"No, I don't believe it," Lombard interrupted. "I'd bet my front seat in hell Wiley Faulks isn't a doper. Not a chance. Even if he knew Hughes, even if he's lying about his sex life, I don't think he'd ever take any drug that hadn't been prescribed. And he wouldn't give it away. If he takes Demerol at all, he's private about it, and he takes it for a reason." She frowned. "I can't believe a fluke coincidence that close."

"It happens," McLean said.

"We can probably find out more about Faulks," Lombard said coyly. "It's Friday. What do you do after supper?"

McLean said, "Watch CNN and Fox, all my favorite talk TV programs. Have a tall cold one, and go to bed. Why?"

She smiled. "Sounds very pleasant."

"It is. What's up your sleeve?"

"Tomorrow night is Saturday. Lots of people go clubbing on Saturday night."

"You want me to go to the Grotto."

"Sam, we're running out of time. There's a court hearing in

less than two weeks. We have to show McKenna we've worked this thing over as much as possible up to the last minute. And that means turning over every stone we find."

"What can I realistically expect to find out? I don't know how to talk to gays."

"You're not talking to Martians, damn it. Jay Hughes hung out there. Ben Hartley said so. People there are bound to have known him. No doubt they're still talking about the murder."

McLean stood up. "I'll be dreading this all night tonight."

"Pray on it."

"With that hearing coming up," McLean said on a sudden thought, "you'd better be turning those pictures of the Rosemond bathroom window over to McKenna."

"I will as soon as he lets me talk to Slade."

"Do it now, Loy," McLean said as he opened the door to leave. "This is a job, not a game of wills."

Lombard looked distracted. "I wonder why there wasn't a screen in the window. All the other windows had screens."

"I'll find out tomorrow," said McLean. "I'm going to talk to Mrs. Rosemond. Look around the place, follow up your lead. Maybe get a look at the register for last Friday."

"Aw, Sam. Thank you. And on a Saturday."

"Might as well put in a full day," he said sullenly, "right on up through the night."

Lombard arrived at the McLean home at 8 sharp the next evening to discuss McLean's interview of Mrs. Rosemond, and also to help him dress appropriately for his night out at the Grotto. McLean had informed Lombard over the phone that his wife would have nothing to do with the mission, not even help him pick out socks.

Selena answered the door and gave a forced smile. She said little to Lombard and barely contained her distaste at having to be hospitable. After the usual beverage was offered and declined, she said crisply, "Sam says you're sending him to a gay bar."

"It's part of the investigation," Lombard explained uneasily.

Selena glared at Lombard. "Then I guess I'd better go get Sam."

Lombard overheard a muffled exchange in the hallway. It sounded like the McLeans were having a mild disagreement. Then she distinctly heard McLean say, "Just bring her on back to the bedroom, Selena! Dang!"

Selena reappeared. "Loy, would you mind following me back to the bedroom? Sam needs your help." When they were at the bedroom door, Selena said, "If you need anything, I'll be in the girls' room, going over their Sunday school lessons."

McLean was standing in his boxers and T-shirt next to his bed, on top of which were sprawled a half dozen shirts and pants. He put his hands on his hips and said abjectly, "I don't know what in the world I'm gonna wear."

Lombard was moved nearly to tears. Here was a man whose usual Saturday night was spent in the company of his pretty wife and pampered daughters looking forward to a quiet evening before church the next day and a Sunday dinner of fried chicken afterward. And here he was, trying to dress appropriately for an excursion to a gay men's club, without a notion as to how. He wanted to do it right, though, and that choked Lombard up. "Is Selena mad at you?" she asked.

"No, she's mad at *you*."

"Does she hate me?"

"She doesn't hate you, but she knows this was your idea. So go figure."

Lombard looked over the array of clothes on the bed. "Wear the jeans and the red shirt, tucked in. Put on some good shoes. The shirt will show off your blond good looks, and those jeans will show off that tight little ass of yours." She let go a sinister giggle.

"Loy, don't tease me at a time like this," McLean warned. "Now lemme dress."

"First, tell me what old lady Rosemond said."

"That won't take long. She said the window should have had a screen, but she never noticed it missing. She was so shocked she didn't check the room for days. She had housekeepers deal with the whole mess. She said even if she had noticed, she figured the police had it for some reason."

"But they didn't, did they?"

"I checked. I went around back of the house, underneath Slade's room on the third floor, and found a window screen lodged between some peony bushes. Mrs. Rosemond confirmed it would fit the bathroom window of Slade's room."

"The knife's probably lodged in there somewhere too," said Lombard.

"I looked for it. I sneaked all around the perimeter. Nothing."

"What did you do with the screen?"

"I told Mrs. Rosemond to call Lt. Mike Church and report the discovery."

Lombard looked puzzled. "Why did you do that?"

"What was I supposed to do? Conceal evidence of a crime? You know better than that, Loy. Anyway, if Slade pushed out the screen to ditch a murder weapon, why wasn't it lying beside the screen down in those peonies? I looked all over. If anything, that helps us."

"Hmm. Now they'll check the window and find those marks. I'd better get my pictures to McKenna," Lombard said. "Oh, what about the register? Did you get a look?"

"I couldn't get near it," McLean said. "The old lady wouldn't let me look. Now get out of here and let me dress. I want to get this night over with."

In a few minutes McLean appeared in the clothes she had prescribed. He looked very nice, she told him. McLean was handsome in a country-boy way, though he never seemed remotely aware of it. Lombard thought he would get a lot of attention at the Grotto, but all she said was, "Be prepared for men to want to talk to you. Now, they're going to think you're gay, and that's not unfair given that you'll be in a gay bar. Just keep your mind on why you're there, and find out what you can."

———

Later, toward midnight, Lombard was stretched out on the sofa in her living room watching Hedy Lamarr in *Algiers* on an old-movie channel. She was about half drunk. During the week she limited her drinking to a nightcap or two before bedtime. Weekends were different. She tended the house. She gardened at this time of year, and her rosebushes, flowers, and vegetables were the objects of her maternal devotion. At the end of the day she poured a glass of bourbon and sat down to watch a movie, the older and more romantic the better. When the glass was empty she filled it up again. She didn't consider herself an alcoholic, but she never let herself run out of bourbon.

She didn't brood about being alone now, but back in Charlotte she'd had a social life. She had partied and had good friends. She had been involved with a lot of women too—gay, straight, bisexual, the don't-label-me types. She'd had two serious relationships, the latter having ended right after she lost her job in Charlotte, when she discovered her partner had been having an affair.

The last thing on her mind when she left for Asheville was finding romance. She had known when she moved here that it was a gay-friendly town, yet she made no effort to establish any gay contacts. She hadn't tried to meet any women at all. She had kept her mind on building up her business, something she could hold on to and know inside and out. There was no mystery to it, and the risks were in the money, not in the heart. The only thing she would admit missing now was sex.

The movie ended, and she scanned the channels looking for Slade-related news. She hoped McLean was getting along all right at the Grotto. Maybe she should have gone to a lesbian bar, she thought, just to find out if the girls were talking about the Slade case. Maybe one of them knew something; Asheville was a small town. She yawned. "Maybe next weekend," she mumbled. She clicked the TV onto the local news, which was airing late due to a televised baseball game that had run into extra innings.

A report from earlier that day was replaying. Hunter Lyle appeared on the screen against the soft blue backdrop of the Carolina sky. It was something about a civic group's protest about property-use variances. Not about Lombard's case, though Lyle was covering it and boiling with determination to try that case in the local media.

Lombard watched Lyle's report and then clicked off the TV. It was time for one of two things: an all-out solitary drunk, or bed. She chose bed. As she drifted off to sleep, she recalled Lyle's promise of calling for a follow-up interview. Lombard hoped she would call soon.

McLean's misgivings about the Grotto were rooted entirely in fear, and he knew it. He didn't admit it to himself until he approached the door of the bar sometime after 11. His steps became heavier as he neared the Grove Street address, a windowless brick building with a black awning and a black steel door. When he finally got to the door, McLean looked up at the awning, illustrated with a wide-eyed, leering, horned idol and the club's proper name: PAN'S GROTTO.

Dots of perspiration beaded up around his hairline, and he felt clammy. He found it hard to swallow. He took a deep breath, swung the door open, and stepped inside with all the lightness of breezing into work. As he walked in, a flush-faced young man was hurrying out, muttering a curse word. McLean was momentarily distracted by how upset the young man seemed.

"Were you with him?" somebody asked.

McLean turned in the direction of the voice. There was a bouncer sitting on a bar stool near the door. He said, "I asked you if you were with that guy."

McLean pointed behind him. "The one that just ran outside? No. I just…well, he looked worried."

"He's not worried. He's pissed off because we were at maximum capacity. I couldn't admit him."

"Oh," said McLean, feeling relieved. "Well, that's too bad. Guess I'll have to check back some other time."

"Wait," said the bouncer. "We were maxed when that redneck was trying to get in. Are you a member?"

"No."

"Somebody's guest?"

"No."

The bouncer smiled. "Well, you'll be my guest, then. Never mind the cover. Go on in."

"Thanks," McLean said uncertainly. He casually glanced around the place as he sidled up to the bar. He wanted a drink as soon as possible, but he wanted to look comfortable. A few men turned to look at him, but their expressions showed more curiosity than interest, as if they were trying to place him. He had expected to see all manner of leather garb, gold chains, and body hair. Yet everyone looked pretty casual, wearing khakis or jeans and pressed cotton shirts. They looked to be young professionals in their twenties and thirties. McLean began to relax.

There was only one bartender, and he ignored McLean. The DJ had just switched from dance music to a slow tune, and a crush of men surged into the bar from the dance floor. McLean felt lucky to have a bar stool but was annoyed at the bartender's refusal to acknowledge his calls for a drink. One of the men who had just come off the dance floor pushed between McLean and the man sitting next to him, and the bartender immediately asked him what he wanted, looking right through McLean.

"Now, just a minute!" McLean shouted, leaning over the bar and pointing. "You're not gonna ignore me all night."

"I'll get to you," the barkeep snapped, not looking at McLean as he hosed a mug full of draft for somebody else.

"I've been here ten minutes!"

The bartender looked at him dead-on. "Look, you'll just have to wait."

The man sitting next to McLean spoke up. "Don't be such an asshole, Todd."

The bartender glared back at the man. "Shut up, Adam. You try tending this madhouse by yourself, instead of just sitting on your ass giving orders."

"It's your job," Adam retorted. "If you're not happy, do something else. Hey, do you hear me, dude? Get him a drink. What's your problem?"

Todd asked McLean what he wanted. McLean asked for scotch. Todd nodded and poured a double shot.

Adam spoke to McLean. "He's pissed off because the other

bartender has been out back smoking pot for the last half hour. He might even be getting blown, for all we know. Anyway, I'm Adam." He shook McLean's hand and smiled affably. He looked to be in his early twenties, with moody good looks and thick dark hair. He pointed to his glasses and said, "I used to wear contacts. But now I wear these to look smart. Wards off the morons, like Todd. He's such a rude loser. Just tell him what you want, and if he gives you any more shit, I'll talk to his boss, who I date. Gary doesn't put up with bad service from his employees."

McLean coughed over his glass and smiled, but his mind was still replaying "out back getting blown." At least, that's how he remembered it. He spotted a new face behind the bar and checked out his movements for signs of a high. He couldn't tell.

"That's Dustin, the other bartender I was talking about," said Adam.

"He doesn't look high to me," McLean said.

"Oh, he is, trust me. He smokes, like, all the time. Really primo shit too. Hey, what's your name?"

"Sam."

"Cool. I'm Adam. Good to meet you. Have you been here before?"

"This is my first time."

"I thought so. You from in town?"

"Yeah."

"Huh. Really? I've never seen you around."

"I don't get out much."

"Oh, I get it. Well, welcome to the scene, Sam!" Adam grinned broadly. "My boyfriend—you know, Gary, the guy that runs this place—he loves to show new guys around. You know, like we're into including people. Shit like that."

Adam ordered another round of drinks for the two of them, and began telling McLean all about his happy relationship with Gary. He talked about how they met, right here at the Grotto. He talked about how they made love the first night and how he had recently moved into Gary's mansion. He bragged about their travels abroad and how much he had learned from living with a rich man. "We dine in the best places. I'll never drink cheap wine again. That's being with a man of style for three years. Otherwise, who knows? I might have ended up with a druggie dropout like Dustin."

"Hey, Adam!"

Adam turned to the bar, where Dustin stood bewildered, shaking his head. "Shut your fucking mouth, Adam!" Dustin looked at McLean. "Hey, look, no offense, man. It's just that you're not familiar."

"Don't worry about it," McLean said.

"Look, can we get your friend another drink?" Dustin asked Adam, barely masking his disgust.

Adam rolled his eyes at Dustin and suggested to McLean that they move to a table. "He's such a girl, always worried. I mean, I'm very intuitive, and I know you're cool. There's a table in the back that's always reserved. Let's go."

A few minutes later, McLean was trying to steer his conversation with Adam to the subject of Jay Hughes. Adam had nearly brought up the issue by voicing a vague concern for his safety since the "big murder." But Adam was so intent on revealing more about himself and his friends that his reference to the most compelling gay-related story in the nation sank back into his subconscious almost as soon as it had surfaced.

Presently Adam was yammering about how jealousy is a bad thing and how jealous other young men were of his relationship with a sophisticated man. He also pointed out that he was monogamous, just in case McLean was wondering. "I mean, I know you're just here to meet people and get in the scene, Sam. But I think I owe it to you to tell you that I would never be with anybody else as long as I'm with Gary."

"I admire that, Adam," McLean said, finally getting a word in. "And you're right about me wanting to get in the scene. It reminds me of what you said a minute ago, about safety. I guess that's the reason why I don't go out much. You never know what danger is out there. Take what happened at the Rosemond Inn!"

Adam gasped. "Oh, God. Was that not ugly? That man was a senator, wasn't he?"

"Uh, yes. Yes, former Republican U.S. senator Jasper Slade."

"Gosh, and I didn't even know he was gay until he killed Jay. Or at least it looks that way. The papers say they were both naked, so let's call a spade a spade."

McLean immediately noticed the familiar use of Jay's first name. He wondered why Adam hadn't mentioned it till now. A gossip like him would surely have seized on the hottest topic in Asheville right away, especially if he actually knew something. Maybe he'd been told not to talk about it.

"It's a tragedy about Jay," McLean said, gazing mournfully into his glass.

"Well, *you* didn't even know him. Tragedy is right," Adam said. "I'll be honest. I had no idea he was dating a big-time politician. I mean, he always made eyes at Gary, like everybody else, so I just assumed he was lying when he spouted off about his rich boyfriend, you know, trying to be all important. He never brought him around here."

"I guess we know why."

"Well, duh! Hello? I mean, major top-secret shit going on there!" Adam shook his head. "But there was one thing that made me think maybe Jay was telling the truth about having a famous lover."

McLean said nothing, just stared in apprehension.

"He was terrified that he, Jay's mystery man, would find out about Jay's past. I mean, it was pretty nasty shit. He worked the streets in Knoxville, Tennessee, when he was a teenager, and that was just a few years ago. I was so, like, not respecting him after I heard that. I also heard he left Knoxville and moved to Atlanta and got into God knows what down there. I think that's where he hooked up with Slade, because pretty boys like Jay are easy pickin's in Atlanta, if a man is rich enough."

"So he brought Jay back to his home state and set him up in a nice quiet bedroom community," McLean guessed.

"Bedroom is right. By the way, I knew Jay, but the stuff I told you about his past, I heard that from somebody else. *I* do not learn these things firsthand. They are so beneath me. Jay just hung out here. I had no idea what trash he was until long after I met him."

"Who did he tell about his past? Somebody here?"

Suddenly Adam looked suspicious. He glanced across the room, and his confident air evaporated. "Gary's here. That's a bad sign," he said as though he were talking to himself. "Look, I have to go."

McLean glanced in the direction Adam was looking and noticed a large, elegant man in his forties staring at them.

"You're not a cop, are you?" Adam asked teasingly.

"Sort of," McLean said.

Adam winced. "Shit. Look, I don't know you. I…"

"Calm down. I won't tell anything. I just need to know who has this information."

Adam shook his head. "I don't know."

"Don't lie to me, Adam. I know when I'm being lied to."

Adam breathed deeply. "Okay. Look, I totally blew it talking to you about this. I promised I wouldn't talk about it. It's just that…I don't know. I get to running my mouth, and…"

"Just give me the name," McLean snapped.

"Are you guys gonna raid the bar? Oh, God. I was lying about the pot. Gary doesn't know about Dustin…"

"The name, Adam. And I swear nobody will bother your club

or your neat little life. Tell me before Gary gets over here. And don't you dare lie."

Gary was moving toward them. "Tyler Rhodes," Adam said.

McLean's next move was to find out how to reach this Tyler Rhodes, but Gary arrived and hijacked the next twenty minutes welcoming him to the Grotto and, McLean sensed, quashing any designs he might have had on Adam. There was another round of drinks, there were jokes and lighthearted conversation, and finally a lull that allowed McLean to excuse himself to the bar.

Dustin was chatting with a club patron. McLean edged up and folded his arms along the bar. He stared at Dustin intently, sending a silent signal that finally caught Dustin's attention. Dustin was laughing about something when he glanced at McLean, and his smile faded.

"That was scotch, right?" Dustin asked.

"Not now. I need to know if you've seen Tyler in here tonight."

"Who?"

"Tyler Rhodes."

"Who's that?"

McLean looked Dustin squarely in the eye. He reached in his back pocket and pulled out the wallet with the fake badge. "Now, you know Tyler, right?"

Dustin nervously shook his head. "No. I don't know who you're talking about." He sniffed and averted his eyes.

McLean sensed Dustin was lying. "You know, that Adam sure runs his mouth."

"What does that mean?"

"It means I know you're a drug dealer, and I might have to focus my attention on you unless you help me out."

"Bullshit."

"I know you were outside selling dope. Don't think you can hoodoo me. You don't smoke while you work, and that explains why you weren't high when I saw you right after Adam said you were out back smoking a joint. It explains why that other bartender was pissed off working the bar alone. You were out back dealing. That 'primo shit' Adam says you smoke is what you peddle, and if I have to get a search warrant, I'll do it. Now answer me. Where is Tyler Rhodes?"

Dustin set his jaw tight. "He hasn't been in here for a while."

"In how long?"

"It's been a couple of weeks, at least. Look, I'm busy." Dustin wrote an address on a napkin and handed it to McLean. "Meet me there after my shift. I promise I'll be there. I don't want to get busted, right?"

———

The address on the napkin led to a diner. By the time Dustin arrived it was crowded and loud, crammed with late-night partyers, most of them college students. When Dustin slid into the booth where McLean had been waiting for him, McLean said, "Listen. I'm not trying to make you nervous. After we leave here, you'll probably never hear from me again."

"What do you want from Tyler?" Dustin asked.

"Information about Jay Hughes. Adam told me Tyler knew him pretty well."

"So what? I knew Jay."

"Did you know Jasper Slade?"

Dustin's eyes widened. "Jesus. You know something? I knew you weren't gay the second I laid eyes on you. Adam is such a stupid shit. I pegged you as a cop at first glance." A waitress arrived, and McLean ordered coffee for both of them. After the waitress left, Dustin lit a cigarette and said, "Of course I didn't know Slade. I don't know if Tyler knew Slade either. So I don't know what you want from me."

"Why so secretive about Tyler Rhodes?" McLean demanded.

"There's no secret!" Dustin said emphatically. "Look, the Grotto is a private gay club, and bartenders don't just hand out information about the members to straight-looking strangers who walk up to the bar. It's that simple, man."

McLean nodded. "Fair enough. What do you know about Jay Hughes?"

"Less than Gary and Adam, probably," Dustin said, exhaling.

"Then tell me what you know about Tyler."

Dustin rubbed his eyes and sighed. "Okay. I know Tyler, just as a club member, though. He's a lawyer activist, but not for gay rights. He's gay, but his thing is Green politics. His family's rich, but he rebelled. He has this obsession with corporations, mainly. Like he has it in for the tobacco industry. Can you believe that? In North Carolina he would be pretty unpopular, if anybody knew who the fuck he was." Dustin shook his head and took a drag. "Not many people do. He runs with a radical crowd, and he's pretty smart. He comes around the Grotto to get laid every now and then, but he looks down on everybody there. After a few drinks he'll start spouting off about how we're all pawns of corporate America, and then he'll start telling us all how shallow we are." He took another drag. "You wouldn't think he'd get far with the boys after telling them how stupid they are, but he's a fine looker, so he gets them anyway. That proves he's right about them being stupid, I guess." Dustin crushed out his cigarette and stared wistfully into the ashtray as he shook his head. "Not me, though. He knows better than to hit on somebody who can match wits with him."

The waitress arrived with their coffees. McLean asked, "Ever heard of Wiley Faulks?"

"The Monk? Yeah, I know who the Monk is. Look, if you want to know anything about the Monk—nobody except Tyler calls him Wiley—then Tyler's your man. He worships the Monk. Talks about him all the time, how great he is. He brought him to the Grotto once, but the Monk just sat there and drank water."

"So what's Tyler's connection to Jay Hughes?"

Dustin raised his coffee mug to his lips. "He fucked him."

"How do you know?"

"*Everybody* knows that. They were an item for something like a month."

"When was that?"

"I don't know. A few months ago, maybe? Wait. Do you think Tyler has something to do with the murder?"

McLean rubbed his forehead and yawned. "I don't know what to think."

Dustin said, "Well, it's not like that. If Tyler could kill anybody, it would be Slade, not Jay. He hates Big Tobacco, and he bitches about Slade's power when he starts holding forth on politics. Jay was real sweet, and Tyler was sweet on Jay. Everybody liked Jay, even me. It would take a monster to cut him up. And Slade was literally caught red-handed, right?"

"Where can I find Tyler?"

"He's a lawyer. Shouldn't he have an office? Or try the Grotto again some night."

McLean pulled money from his wallet for the bill. "Just one more thing, Dustin. Do you know a man named Ben Hartley?"

"No," said Dustin. "I might recognize him, but I don't know everybody who walks in the bar. I'm familiar with Tyler and the Monk because they're crazy. They're total radicals. I mean, they're like militia types, honey. They freak me out."

"Why do you keep calling Wiley Faulks the Monk?"

"He gave some crazy-ass speech about celibacy at a *Pride*

rally, dude. He doesn't have sex, right? He was saying how the leaders of the gay rights movement should be celibate, like him. He's clueless!" Dustin chuckled. "So that's when people started calling him the Monk. But never around Tyler." He lit another cigarette. "You don't say anything unkind about the Monk around Tyler Rhodes."

5

THE PHONE BEGAN RINGING AT DAYBREAK, BUT LOMBARD let the answering machine pick it up. She rolled over in bed and glanced at the alarm clock. It was only 6:30 on a Sunday. It was probably important. If it was terribly important, they would call her cell phone. She closed her eyes. Within seconds her cell phone warbled inside her shoulder bag. Somewhere between hung over and dead tired, she reached out and dragged the bag to her bedside and fumbled with its contents until she caught the phone.

"Lombard," she mumbled, half-awake.

"Where are you?" Ross McKenna asked, his voice quavering.

"At home." She sank into her pillows and closed her eyes.

"I've called your house repeatedly."

"Sorry. I was asleep. What is it?"

"I have shocking news. Realizing how badly you've wanted to interview Jasper, I thought you should be the first person I called."

Lombard snapped awake. "Is he fit for it? I'll get on the road right away."

"No. You won't have to come here for an interview."

Lombard assumed he meant that Slade was in Asheville, and that could mean only one thing. "If the sheriff has picked him up, something's happened to his bail bond. I don't know what, but I'll be at the jail in an hour. In the meantime, you should call Sig Mashburn if you haven't already…"

McKenna said, "Jasper's dead, Miss Lombard. Della found him before dawn."

A splitting headache suddenly overtook Lombard. "How?"

"Hanged himself in his room."

"Any note?"

"Nothing."

Along with the thumping pain in her head, a wave of numbing disappointment rolled over her heart. She was losing the Big Case. It was gone in the instant it took a desperate man to kick a chair out from under his feet. She thought, *What a weak, pathetic loser. Damn him to hell,* but she said, "I'm very sorry, Mr. McKenna."

"I know you are, but you can cheer up. The case is still open."

Lombard tried not to sound relieved. "How's that?"

"I paid you to clear Jasper's name. I still want you to do that. It's more important now than ever. This suicide will make him look guilty. Of everything."

"Yeah. We still have a lot of loose ends," she said wearily.

———

The suicide was explosive news. Lombard, who ordinarily kept the TV on at home and in her office for every breaking story about Jasper Slade's public and private life, was growing sick of it. Talk of the suicide rankled her; she felt depressed about it, despite McKenna's reassurance that from his standpoint the case was still open. She grew more suspicious that Slade's death—and its foreclosure of any communication with the senator—had ruined her investigation. Her best witness had slipped through her fingers.

On Monday morning Lombard arrived at the office earlier than usual. The only person she expected to see was the night dispatcher, a gruff, retired Buncombe County deputy named Jeb Granger.

"You're early," he said on seeing Lombard. "I've been meaning to tell you that you're in the novel I'm writing, as a minor character, so don't get a big head." Jeb had taken the night job at Secure Services because other than checking on the guards by radio at the top of every hour, there wasn't much else to do but work on his detective stories, many of which he had published. The office gave him a quiet place to work and a little extra cash. "You want to look it over? You'll have plenty of time now that Slade's dead."

"Not so fast," she said, heading for her office. "The case is still open."

"How so?" said a woman sitting in the shadows.

Lombard spun in the direction of the voice. She was both annoyed and pleased when she saw Hunter Lyle sitting on the lobby sofa.

"Oh, her," Jeb grunted. "I was just about to tell you this reporter came in at the crack of dawn and wouldn't leave." He looked at his note. "Name of Hunter Lyle."

"I know," Lombard said. "The early bird gets the worm."

Lyle stood up and smiled tentatively. "There's bound to be a few others like me roaming around here today. Everybody knows you covered the case."

"Thanks to your reports on TV," Lombard said peevishly.

"I know it's early, but I'm off the clock. I don't report to work till noon."

"So?"

"So this is off the record, like I promised before. And you promised me an interview."

Lombard said, "I never promised an interview."

"Okay, comments. Something. No cameras. You have no idea how unlike me it is to go anywhere without my cameraman, and I've come to you like that twice now."

Lyle started in on Lombard as soon as her office door shut behind them. "Loy. Oh, may I call you Loy? About my TV reports, I thought you wouldn't mind a little publicity. I bet PI's all over the state were green with envy over your getting the Slade case. It's bound to bring in lots of new business."

"Sit down, Hunter, please." Lombard sat behind her desk. "I don't care about the press coverage, one way or the other. That's your job, so fine."

Lyle sat in a chair and crossed her legs. She was wearing a peacock-blue suit with a V-neck jacket that gathered at the waist and covered the length of her mid-thigh-length skirt. Lombard noticed she had curled her red hair, which had been straight the last time she came to the office and in the TV spots Lombard had seen since.

"Jeb," Lombard yelled so he could hear, "do you mind bringing us some coffee?"

"I'll bring it, but you'll have to cream or sugar it yourself," Jeb thundered back.

"You know I take it black, Jeb." She turned her attention back to Lyle, starting with the slender bend of her knee. "What about you?"

"Nothing for me, thanks. I only drink coffee with desserts."

Lombard watched Lyle's foot flex and silently observed that a woman with legs like that probably passed on most desserts.

Jeb swung the door open and plodded in with two steaming mugs. He set them down on Lombard's desk and turned back without speaking.

"Thank you, Jeb," Lombard said. He grumbled and shut the door behind him.

Lyle began. "What's your reaction to Slade's death?"

Lombard yawned. "Sad thing, this suicide. Tragic, shocking news."

"Hmm. You don't seem too torn up about it."

"Sure I am. My heart goes out to his family, and to all his followers." Lombard grinned and picked up her coffee mug. "He'll be missed."

Lyle smirked and shook her head. "Your sincerity is really moving, Loy. Tell me, why is the case still open?"

"That's not open for discussion right now." Lombard damned herself for running her mouth earlier.

"But the case *is* open," Lyle smiled.

"Hunter, do me a favor. Don't report that. I know it's your job. And you can report anything you want. But I will tell you this: If you let it out that I'm still on the case, you'll never get a shot at my comment again. If I break something—and that is very likely—and you've let this out, I'll give an exclusive to the first wet-behind-the-ears paperboy comes to me for a word, but I won't know you exist. Understand?"

Lyle retracted her smile and leaned back in her seat.

Lombard said, "You won't be sorry. I will break this case. That's off the record, of course."

"Of course." Lyle stood up and grabbed her shoulder bag.

"Hunter, you realize I hate reporters, but only generally, right?"

"Whatever." Lyle paused before opening the door. "Thanks for the tip."

"So don't take this personally, but I won't be surprised if I hear everything I've said voiced-over on the news tonight."

"You won't. Watch me."

———

Lombard lay on her stomach, on a white sandy beach of the Florida panhandle, under a pale blue sky and platinum sunlight. She kept her eye on the indigo and turquoise stripes of the Gulf water, while a lithe redhead wearing a large straw hat and not much else rubbed oil on her back. A seagull landed on the ground in front of her and snorted.

But seagulls don't snort, she thought as she started out of her dream and found herself coming to at her desk, her head crooked to one side, her mouth wide open and dry from evident snoring.

McLean was standing in the doorway. "You sure do saw a log," he said. "I was almost afraid to knock."

"Oh!" she winced, rubbing her neck. "I got a crick. What time is it?"

"Almost lunchtime."

She scowled at him. "You interrupted a damn promising dream."

He threw a stack of envelopes on her desk. "Your mail, including tidings from Sig Mashburn, hand-delivered by his clerk." He shoved the ocher envelope across her desk.

"It's addressed to both of us," she said, shoving it back. She glared at McLean. "Where were you yesterday? I tried calling all day to tell you about Slade and to get the scoop on your big gay night on the town."

"I slept late. Missed church," he said reproachfully, "but I made it to the church picnic the kids had been looking forward to all week."

Lombard pointed a letter opener at McLean. "And you didn't call me even after you'd heard about Slade's death. It was all over the news."

"I needed a break, Loy!" McLean shouted. He pursed his lips and stood quietly for a moment. "*One* day with my family. Slade was dead, so was the case, and that was that and we could talk about it this morning." He sank into a chair and avoided eye contact with Lombard.

"It's noon," she said, "and the case, Sammy boy, is still open."

Lombard told McLean about McKenna's phone call to her the day before. "He says we have to prove that Slade wasn't a killer and that he wasn't queer. We've got to save the good name of the AFFC."

McLean told her about his visit to the Grotto and his interviews of Adam and Dustin. "So out of all that I got one lead, this lawyer Tyler Rhodes, who is evidently connected to both Jay Hughes, who was his boyfriend of sorts, and Wiley Faulks, who's his best friend and mentor, to hear Dustin tell it."

"Well, that's progress, Sam," Lombard said brightly. "That lunatic Ross McKenna's gonna be tickled pink! He gave us no more than a newspaper clipping and a half-assed crazy theory, and you've tied Wiley Faulks directly to the murder victim."

"Maybe." McLean grabbed the envelope from Mashburn's office and opened it. He pulled out a card and read aloud. "Dear Loy Lombard and Sam McLean of Secure Services Inc., Please accept my cordial invitation to dinner at my home this Friday, April 23 at 8 P.M. The party is small, but the dress is elegant. Looking forward to an intimate evening with new friends, I remain, Yours Sincerely, Sigmund Mashburn." McLean smiled. "Well how 'bout that? That might turn out to be fun."

Lombard shook her head. "I don't want to go to any damn lawyer's party."

"Why not?"

"I'm allergic to bullshit."

"We have to go," McLean said. "If the case is still open, we ought not to snub Slade's lawyer."

"Former lawyer," Lombard reminded him. "I don't want to go, but I will. I have to talk to the one man who interviewed Jasper Slade before he died, and that's Sig Mashburn."

McLean sat idly while Tyler Rhodes's secretary tapped on her computer keyboard and skittishly whistled along with whatever tune was playing on her Walkman. The lobby was dark and sumptuously decorated in traditional walnut tones and leather upholstery, its gleaming wood floors ornamented by antique oriental carpets. When Rhodes finally came out of his office, McLean stood up and began to introduce himself.

"Sam McLean?" Rhodes asked breezily. "I'm Tyler." He reached out and clasped McLean's hands with a strong grip. Rhodes was exactly what Dustin had described, a real looker. Salt-of-the-earth guys like McLean rarely pretended to take notice of a fine-looking man, but it was hard not to notice the long, chiseled features and tousled dark hair of Tyler Rhodes. He was trim and fit and had the looks of a classical Greek athlete, with large, sinewy hands and beguiling bow lips that curled naturally in a smile when he closed his mouth. His deep-set black eyes flashed in the frames of his dark-rimmed eyeglasses.

"Pleased to meet you," McLean said. "This is a very fine looking room," he added, glancing around the lobby.

"Thank you," Rhodes smiled. "It is, isn't it? The lobby is mostly Maitland-Smith and Brunschwig & Fils."

"I beg pardon?"

"The furniture. Step lightly on the rugs." Rhodes motioned McLean to follow him, whispering, "They're Aubusson. Very old."

They entered Rhodes's office, and Rhodes asked McLean to sit. McLean gave an officious cough. "I'm an investigator on the Jasper Slade case."

"I know why you're here. I heard your name on TV, during one of the news reports. They mentioned your firm and…what's that woman's name? Lois Limbaugh?"

"Loy Lombard. She's my partner."

"That's right. Well. All due respect, Sam, I would think the urgency of your investigation may have waned after the, uh, weekend's *turn* of events," Rhodes grinned.

"Not necessarily. All too often a suicide leaves a slew of questions." Rhodes leaned back and crossed his legs. "So you think it was a suicide?"

"Well, he was found hanged."

"That's what they say." Rhodes broadened his smile. "Oh, here's Ben." Rhodes looked past McLean to the door behind him. "Ben, I want you to meet Sam McLean."

McLean turned around and raised his eyebrows. "Ben Hartley," he said.

"You two have met?" Rhodes asked.

Hartley looked pale. "Yes. In Raleigh. Mr. McLean spoke to me at the Pride office. Oh, Tyler. I didn't mean to interrupt. Jenny said to come on back, so I…"

"No big deal," Rhodes shrugged. "Ben and I just had lunch together," he told McLean, then to Hartley, "I thought you were off to Raleigh, Ben. What's the holdup?"

Hartley glanced at McLean. "I…I just forgot something, you know. To tell you."

"Well, can it wait till after my chat with the inspector here?"

"Yeah, I'm sorry." Hartley moistened his lips. "I'll wait out front."

"Okay. I don't think Sam will be long. He's got some loose ends to tie up in the wake of Slade's final swing." Rhodes chuckled. He waited for Hartley to leave the room. "Terrible pun. Sorry. I shouldn't seem so delighted. But you see, Sam, the only thing I regret about Slade's final weeks is that an innocent man was murdered. The rest of it—Slade's secret getting out, his subsequent humiliation, the AFFC's panic, the scandalized American public, and Slade's ultimate kickoff to Judgment Day—I have found very gratifying, even amusing."

McLean looked around the beautifully decorated room. "Not

bad digs for a self-proclaimed radical." He patted the armrests of his chair.

Rhodes laughed. "Comfy? The chairs are all Edward Ferrell, my tribute to the North Carolina furniture industry, in the ascent of which my forebears played no small part. I'm an incurable rich boy with a heart of gold. I like nice things, and I want nice things for the disadvantaged. I've figured out that there's no reason why every person on earth shouldn't live like me. There's plenty for all. It's greed and competition that put the people under the feet of the powerful. I want everybody to have enough to eat, but I also want them all to have tastefully furnished dining rooms and decent china."

"Well, I'm all for that, I guess," McLean said. "Let's get back on point."

"And what's on point?"

"Whatever you can tell me about Slade's sexuality, for a start."

"He was homosexual, but don't think I want to believe it."

"But he was a widower. He'd been married for many years."

"Plenty of gay people get married and have children. We're socially engineered from childhood to seek that way of life. Sure, most people are biologically predisposed to the norm, but a few are not. We get caught in the crosswind."

"You have children?"

"No. I speak in the royal 'we.' I never had any illusions about my orientation."

McLean nodded. "I wonder how you're so sure Slade was gay."

"I knew his lover. I knew the deceased, Jay Hughes." Rhodes's smile vanished, and he stared at McLean with razor-sharp eyes.

McLean shifted in his seat. "How's that?"

Rhodes stood up and walked to the window near his desk. He put his hands in his trouser pockets and looked outside to the street below. "Jay Hughes was a nice young man. He was gorgeous too. You've seen his pictures?"

"Yeah. In the paper. And the crime photos."

Rhodes turned around. "I don't want to hear about those. Here's what you may not know about Jay. He was sweet and loving and mad to please. Men fell in love with him, but he wanted to be taken care of. He would give himself entirely to the whims of a moneyed man, whether there was love in the offering or not. There usually wasn't when it came to the men Jay was attracted to. He did some very stupid things. I don't know if it was his country-boy naïveté or what. When I think about the things he told me he had done, I'm surprised he didn't destroy himself sooner."

"What do you mean by 'destroy himself'?"

"Oh, I'm not implying anything, Sam. He fell in love with Slade. That was self-destructive. It could only lead to misfortune, though I wouldn't have predicted death."

"Were you in love with Jay?" McLean asked.

Rhodes narrowed his eyes. "What is that supposed to mean?"

"You were involved with him, based on other witnesses' accounts.".

Rhodes glanced in the direction of the lobby. "Did Ben tell you that?"

"No. I asked around at the Grotto."

"The Grotto? Now, there's a reliable pool of information."

"So you deny it?"

"No. I admit it. So what? I picked him up there and we had a fling. That's how I got to know Jay so well. It was more than just sexual. I was interested in him."

"But not in love."

"What difference does that make to you?"

"Well, you just said a minute ago that men fell in love with him, but he got all tangled up with guys that had money and didn't care about him…"

"That's not what I meant exactly. Well, yes, it is, as far as most of his dalliances went. I wasn't in love with him, but I did care about him. I didn't use him or lead him on or give him any impression that there was more to it than there was."

"Was this before or during his involvement with Slade?"

"During. Tell me, what did the boys at the Grotto say about me and Jay?"

McLean shrugged. "Not much. Just that you had a sexual relationship with him."

Rhodes smirked. "I'm sure there was more gossip to it than that. The Grotto isn't exactly where you go for stimulating conversation. Gossip is about as deep as most of those boys' minds get. Whatever they told you, this is all I know." He walked to a barrister's bookcase near the door and glanced out at the hallway. "When I met Jay I found him to be shallow, but not like the others. He was incredibly charming in a daft, airheaded way, and he was, as you know, beautiful. I was taken with him." Rhodes closed the door and turned to McLean. "We began an affair. It wasn't all sex. I was affectionate with him. He liked to talk and learn things. He listened to me. He never gave much thought to anything beyond what it took to look good, have fun, and get a rich man, but he liked to talk to me about my interests, and that pleased me. Soon enough, we were confidants as well as lovers, and he told me about his relationship with Slade and how Slade treated him. I bet you don't know about that."

McLean shrugged and shook his head.

Rhodes sat down at his desk. "Slade was verbally abusive. It's a classic case of a repressed queen taking his self-loathing out on his partner. Jay once cried to me about it. He was in love with this domineering, hateful politico, who fucked him for his own pleasure and then talked to him like an animal. Jay didn't enjoy that. He hoped Slade would change."

"If he was in love with Slade, why was he in bed with you?"

"He was lonely. Slade was gone most of the time. Jay bored easily."

"You have any idea how he met Slade?"

Rhodes sighed. "Jay was from Tennessee. He left home for the closest thing to a big city he could think of, Knoxville. He ended up hustling in the evenings near the public library. But like I said, he was beautiful, so it wasn't long before he got his chance to get out. Some fat-cat impresario visiting from Atlanta picked him up and took him home for a weekend. Jay moved to Atlanta, and by the time the fat cat dumped him, he was out working the clubs and making films. You know the kind of films I'm talking about?"

"I can only imagine," McLean said.

"A lot of rich gay men in the South go to the South's largest city to find pet boys. Slade was no different. He operated quietly, like a sinister vampire, if you ask me. Jay had the bad luck to catch Slade's attention. I don't know exactly how they met, just what Jay told me, that it was at a party for some closeted man from Birmingham. Now, Jay told me things in confidence. He trusted me, and I've never told anybody any of this. This party was attended by big-timers, gay men in oil companies and the like. Energy chiefs, corporate bucks. Slade ran with a strange crowd."

"It doesn't make much sense to me. Conservative types acting that way."

"Conservative is a state of mind," Rhodes said. "Nature is the real dictator, Sam, and it doesn't give a damn how you vote. A rich, closeted queer knows that as long as you've got the money and the power, you can do whatever you want in private, as long as you keep it private. That was Jasper Slade's problem: His secret seeped out, and he went nuts. His intolerance and insane egotism erupted that night at the Rosemond Inn, and he cut a poor dumb angel to pieces, out of fear and panic."

"How did his secret seep out?"

"How would I know?"

"You used the word 'secret.' I take that to mean 'dark pink secret.' Didn't Wiley Faulks write that piece?"

"Yes, he did."

"And Ben Hartley. He wrote an article...what was it? 'Slade Rides Again'?"

"Yes. So?"

"Did you tell Ben or Wiley about Jay and Slade?"

Rhodes's eyes went cold. "No, I didn't tell anybody anything. I told you Jay could trust me! Are you implying I betrayed his trust, and that led to his death?"

"No. I'm just asking." McLean scratched his chin and cautiously began the next question. "Lemme ask you this. Did you ever meet Slade?"

"No."

"When's the last time you saw Jay Hughes?"

"About a month before he died. I travel a lot, you know. I was in Alaska fighting big oil and its threat to wildlife the night Slade murdered Jay."

"I wasn't asking for an alibi."

"It's hard to tell what exactly you do want from me, but it's not just friendly information, that's clear enough."

"But you do believe that his secret getting out is what provoked him to go into some kind of rage. You just said so." McLean pointed to the door to the lobby. "And yonder sits the man let the cat out of the bag. Wonder where he got his information?"

"You'll have to ask him."

"I will." McLean thanked Rhodes for his time and excused himself. He looked around the lobby for Ben Hartley, but only the secretary remained. "Is Mr. Hartley still around?" he asked her.

"He left as soon as he came out of Tyler's office," the secretary said.

"Did he say where he went?"

"No. My guess is he's gone back to Raleigh."

The town of Ramp Hollow was situated deep in the Smoky Mountains, about eighty miles from Asheville across the Tennessee border. It didn't appear on the road atlas or any other map Lombard had consulted before making the trip. Once she turned off Interstate 40, a few miles southeast of the nearest dot on a map—a place called Newport—the road narrowed into a dense forest, winding around hillside curves along a rain-slicked mountain path that undulated with the stoic constancy of the Appalachian range. The rain had subsided and left in its wake a heavy mist. Just short of ten miles down the road, a white frame church bearing the sign RAMP HOLLOW PRIMITIVE BAPTIST CHURCH signaled Lombard that she had arrived in the birthplace of Jay Hughes.

The Hughes family wasn't expecting her. She had traced their address with the help of police reports and a county directory. It wouldn't be too much of a surprise; news reports about Hughes's hometown had already circulated, and journalists had attempted—unsuccessfully—to interview family members. Lombard disliked the idea of disrupting the privacy of a bereaved family, but it was necessary. In her line of work, necessity and good manners rarely coexisted.

The house was gray with white trim, humble and sweet, with all the trappings of poor folk wanting to make their lives a little more beautiful. A red swing hung on one side of a large front porch, and pots of geraniums lined the stoop. In the mist, the colors were stark and unsettling. A flower garden in the front yard bore witness to spring: Purple and gold tulips sprouted up among daffodils and irises, and pink-and-white–blossomed dogwood trees belied the foulness of the day. Lombard parked her Pathfinder in a gravel driveway and looked around the rolling hillsides surrounding the lone house.

A thin, middle-aged woman answered the door. She looked tired but cordial. "I don't want to talk to any more reporters," she said wearily.

Lombard gathered all her sensitivity. "Mrs. Hughes?" she said softly.

"I'm Mrs. Hughes, and I mean it. I'm over being bothered. Go on now."

"I'm not a reporter." She dismissed a passing notion to produce her fake badge. "I'm Loy Lombard, an investigator on your son's case. More to the point, I was originally hired to do private investigation work on Jasper Slade's case."

"He's dead, ain't he?"

"Yes, ma'am. But I want to talk to you about your son."

Mrs. Hughes looked suspicious. "Only if you promise to tell the truth about him."

"You have my word."

Mrs. Hughes opened the door and motioned Lombard inside. "What did you say your name was?"

"Loy Lombard." She followed Mrs. Hughes into a small living room and sat down on a tidy couch wrapped in a plastic sofa cover.

Mrs. Hughes sat in a reclining chair near the TV, on which a game show was blaring. She turned it off and said, "Your first name's Loy? That sounds like a man's name." She leaned back in the recliner like she was exhausted, closing her eyes and resting the back of her right hand across her brow.

Lombard smiled. "My real name is Aloysia, after a saint. Well, it was also my mother's name, only she went by Lola. I got the nickname Loy."

Mrs. Hughes's hand fell down in her lap. She stared at Lombard, studying her for a moment, and averted her eyes to the blank TV. "You want something to eat or drink?"

"No, ma'am. I won't stay long. It took me a while to find the place, and I couldn't stay if I wanted to. If you don't mind, what in the world kind of name is Ramp Hollow?"

"That's after the ramps."

"The what?"

"Ramps. They're a root. Grow wild all around these parts. Kind of like onions."

"I love vegetables. And I love to cook."

"Well, you ought to go to the Ramp Festival down in Cosby one of these days and pick you some. Jay used them, you know. He was a good cook and a wonderful baker."

"Is that a fact?" Lombard wanted Mrs. Hughes to talk about her son, and let her start any way she pleased.

"Why, he could make a pie crust so flaky, it melted right in your mouth…" Mrs. Hughes's voice trailed off. Her eyes became moist. "Light as butter, but he made them from lard, like you're supposed to. He should've been a baker. I thought when he moved to Knoxville he would go to work for a restaurant or something."

"When did he leave home?"

"Couple of years ago? It's been a while."

Lombard noticed a framed snapshot sitting on top of the television. It showed a balding man holding a shotgun, standing next to a young blond boy. "Is that little Jay in that picture?" she asked.

Mrs. Hughes eyed the photograph. "Yes, that's Jay." She smiled. "I'd say he was eleven or twelve in that picture. That's his daddy, my husband, Jack, standing there next to him." She leaned back and sighed. "He was hard on Jay."

"How so?"

"Jay was a sensitive boy. He didn't care much about hunting or guns like Jack. I'll never forget the day Jay came to me early one morning after Jack had gone off hunting. He told me he loved me but he couldn't stay at home. It was still dark, and I begged him not to go. He said he was going to Knoxville and stay with friends till he could find a job. He called me once after he moved, but Jack got on the phone and talked to him like a dog." Mrs. Hughes reached for a tissue. "Jay never came back home, not even after the accident." Suddenly Mrs. Hughes was crying, but in a soft, almost controlled manner, as though she was used to it.

"What accident?"

"Jack. His truck went off the road and hit a tree. He was a drinker. I never tolerated drinking in the house. So Jack went out to these card games at roadhouses. Maybe if I would have…"

"Naw, Mrs. Hughes. Don't go blaming yourself." Lombard waited for Mrs. Hughes to compose herself. She needed to keep her focused on Jay. "Did Jay stay in contact?"

"Yeah, but I didn't know where he was. But I'm sure Tracy did."

"Who's Tracy?"

Mrs. Hughes looked crossly at Lombard, as though she ought to know. "His sister."

"Oh. Where's she now?"

"In her room. They gave her a couple weeks off from school." Mrs. Hughes pointed behind her, to a back corner of the house. "I'll not have her mixed up in all this, though. She's too young to be grieved like this."

"Mrs. Hughes, I respect your wanting to keep Tracy out of all this sad business, but she could help me figure out what happened to Jay."

"What happened to Jay is clear enough," Mrs. Hughes said sharply. "She's only seventeen. If she could help you bring him back, maybe. But I don't want her any more upset by all this than she already is."

"Was she close to Jay?"

Mrs. Hughes sighed. "They were thick as thieves. Into all kinds of meanness."

Lombard was now determined to talk to Tracy. She was bound to have been privy to secrets Jay wouldn't have dared told his mother. "Did she talk to him often after he left?"

"Every now and then. After he moved to Atlanta, he got some kind of job making good money, and he called more often. He would tell me he was doing okay, making a living, and not to worry, but he was always in a hurry to gab with Tracy. They'd talk for hours. I wondered how high his phone bills must have been." Mrs. Hughes suddenly lurched forward and buried her face in her hands. "I never saw my baby boy again after he left home," she sobbed. "He promised to come back. He promised me he would come back when he could."

Lombard had always had difficulty comforting sobbing women. Rather edgily, she said, "Mrs. Hughes. Shh, now. I'm so sorry to cause you more grief."

Mrs. Hughes grabbed a fistful of tissues and dabbed her tear-streaked face. "I don't know why I should talk to you, being as you were hired to help that evil man. But you're the first person come to talk to me about my son. All the others wanted to know was, did I know he was gay. Well, I didn't! I read it in a newspaper, and then people came wanting to know if I knew. You're the only one that asked to know the truth about what kind of fine boy he was." She rose up unsteadily. "They make him sound so vile in the papers and on TV. My boy was not like that. He was just confused, and I don't know what else made him go to that place in Asheville. Somebody drugged him or something. That awful man, that Slade, he must have drugged my boy."

Lombard stood up. "Again, I'm very sorry, ma'am, for your loss. I think I should go now. Just, please relax." The grieving woman gave Lombard a look that bespoke a desperate need to be left alone.

"I'll just see myself out," Lombard said. "Thank you for your help."

Lombard walked briskly out to her car, stopped at the driver's side door, and turned around to give the house a long look. She racked her brain for some sensible means of getting to Jay Hughes's sister, who was bound to have known him better than anybody. The girl might tell Lombard to go to hell, but Lombard wanted to hear it from her. Suddenly, while Lombard was just giving up and getting into her car, a girl appeared from around the back corner of the house. She paused when Lombard saw her, then resumed a slow walk toward the car. She was a thin, pretty girl with long straw-colored hair. She looked like she could be Jay's female twin.

"I'm Tracy," she said as she approached the car.

"My name's Loy Lombard. I'm a…"

"I know. You're a cop."

"No, I'm not."

Tracy climbed into the front seat. "I don't care what you are. Just get me out of here for a few minutes, okay? I'm dying for a few fucking minutes away from here."

When they had traveled a few yards, Tracy said, "I'm lucky Mama's laid out on her bed crying her eyes out. I wouldn't have made it past the back door. She wouldn't want me talking to you." Her tone was weary and flat.

"She just wants to protect you," Lombard said.

"From what? Jay's dead. What's she going to protect me from? He's the one needed protecting."

Lombard parked the car in the deserted parking lot of an old, abandoned gas station. "Do you know why I came to talk to your mother?"

"I don't care." Tracy looked at the rusted gas pumps and murky windows of the gas station. "This place is dead too. Ramp Hollow, I mean. Dead and nothing to do. Jay wanted to get out of here because it was so dead. Now look at him. He's buried yonder in Lyon's Creek Graveyard. Dead as this old filling station."

"He sure is," Lombard said.

Tracy looked sharply at Lombard and laughed. "Damn, you're cold! Most people's always telling me how sorry and sad they are for me."

"I know what it's like to lose people you love. You get tired of pity, if you're tough."

Tracy nodded. "Damn right. So you're not a cop? What are you? You can't be a reporter, or Mama wouldn't have talked to you. Unless you're lying."

"I'm a private investigator. I was working on Slade's case."

"For who?"

"For Slade."

"Well, shit. What for?"

Lombard looked through the windshield at the battered garage doors of the gas station. "I don't know anymore," she said. "I want to find out about your brother. I want to know what he was like. I want the truth, not the rumors or the dirty stories."

Tracy shrugged. "You mean like, if he was gay?"

"Not just that."

"I don't care to talk about it. It's all anybody else gives a shit about. Why should you be any different?"

Lombard gave a long sigh and sank back in her seat. "That's not all I care about, Tracy."

"I'm just telling you, because it does have a lot to do with why he died, don't it?"

"I suppose so," Lombard said, nodding.

"He told me a long time ago. He and me even liked the same boys sometimes. But Jay couldn't live here and be happy. One time when he was in school he let on like he liked this boy, and a gang of 'em beat the livin' shit out of him. He told Mama and Daddy he got in a fight, but he told me the truth. I hated those boys after that. I know who done it too, beat him up like that. I slashed their tires, fuckin' jerks."

"Did he talk to you often after he left?"

"Like about what?"

"Like about what he was doing, out on his own."

Tracy yawned and pulled her hair back. "He never told me what he did in Knoxville, but he never had a solid place to live, so he must have been hard up. Always said he was with friends.

He wouldn't let me call him till he moved to Atlanta. He was with some rich guy for a little while—I forget what his name was—but he dumped Jay, and Jay had to find his own place. He said he made good money working in fancy nightclubs, but doing what, I don't know. He didn't finish high school, had no skills or nothing. Couldn't even change the oil in his car. Tell you the truth, I don't think he had a job. I think he got kept, you know, taken care of."

Lombard was surprised and looked it. "What does a girl your age know about things like that?"

"I'm not stupid, lady. He lived with a rich guy, never talked about a real job, and I know all about him and Jasper."

"Hmm. Were they an item?" Lombard asked.

"Yeah. Jay was in love with him. He talked about him like he was God. He'd go a while without calling and then tell me he'd been to some little hideaway somewheres." Tracy snickered. "They went to a place in Canada just to go skiing. Jay on skis. Now, I would have liked to seen that. Jasper flew him all those places and met him in secret. Jay always said, 'Tracy, don't tell anybody. It's a big secret. It could ruin him, and then I'd be ruined.' So I kept it to myself, like he knew I would. He said one day he'd build Mama a big house and send for me and make me over like a movie star, and I'd marry a rich, handsome man. He was a dreamer, Jay was. I knew it was crazy talk."

"When did they start seeing each other? Did he tell you that?"

"I don't know. A year ago, maybe?"

"Just a year?"

"Not even that. Jay moved to Asheville last summer, and he hadn't known Jasper long."

"Tracy, did Jay ever talk about problems with Slade? Did they ever fight?"

Tracy shook her head. "Jay never mentioned if they did. He said Jasper was good to him. He said that every time I talked to him. Got him an apartment in Asheville so they could be closer, but Jay said Jasper never came to the apartment because it was too risky. They met at the places where Jasper was staying when he was in town. They had to be real sneaky."

"Did you know about Jasper's political life?"

"Yeah. Jay told me he was a big-time politician, and about the AFFC."

Lombard's surprise showed. "You know about the AFFC?"

"Yeah. Jay told me about it the last time I talked to him."

"When was that?"

"A few days before he died."

"What did he say?"

"He just said Jasper wanted out of it. He wanted to get out of politics and felt like he was gonna have a breakdown with all the pressure that was on him. He wanted to take Jay to a foreign country and just escape. That's how Jay put it."

Lombard was astounded. "Tracy, how much have you been reading about all this in the papers?"

"I don't read that shit."

"I mean, how much do you know about the AFFC?"

"I don't know nothing about the AFFC. I don't even know what it stands for. Just that Jasper was big into it. Some political something or other."

"Are you sure they only met less than a year ago?"

"No, I'm not sure," Tracy said irritably. "Jesus, lady. It couldn't have been that long. He'd just turned twenty when he died."

Lombard faced the windshield and held the steering wheel for a few silent seconds before starting the car. Neither she nor Tracy spoke on the drive back to the Hugheses' home. Lombard pulled along the side of the road in front of the house, and Tracy pulled the latch on the passenger door. "Tracy," said Lombard, "before you go, I feel like I should say something, though it might not be any of my business to say it."

"What is it?" Tracy asked.

"I'm not sure how to put it. I just know how it is to be your age and in your shoes. That's all."

Tracy shrugged. "Okay," she said dismally.

"It gets better, you know," Lombard said.

"Yeah. It will once I get out of here." Tracy slid out of the car and shut the door without looking back. Lombard watched her all the way, until Tracy had disappeared behind the front door of the house.

6

SAM MCLEAN WAS BEHIND THE WHEEL OF HIS PRIDE and joy, a baby-blue Mustang convertible he had bought years ago, before he'd gotten married. On the rare occasions he had an opportunity to drive it—when the weather was warm and clear and the kids had a sitter and Selena felt like going out—he marveled at how a machine this simple could bring such joy to a man. Sometimes he took it out alone and pretended not to notice the looks he got from young women, and in weak moments he might let himself imagine one of them sitting next to him in the car, though shame and guilt immediately displaced the notion and sent him reeling back home with flowers and candy for his family.

He was driving too fast and loving it, headed to Chunn's Cove Road and Sig Mashburn's party, the wind coursing overhead, a country music station blaring from the radio, a setting sun and the moon hanging in the warm glow of a fragrant spring twilight. The only thing that could possibly spoil his ride was sitting next to him.

"You're ignoring me, Sam," Lombard shouted over the wind and the radio. "Turn that crap down and listen to me. This is business."

"What did you say?" he hollered, beaming at her.

"I'm trying to talk business!"

"I'm trying to have fun! Looks like I'm driving too," he said.

Lombard pulled a scarf out of her handbag and tied it around her head. "The wind's chilling me to death. It's still cold at night in these mountains. And it's mussing up my hair."

"Your hair?" he laughed. "It's mussed up all the time."

"I can't help it! It's too damn thick," she said, checking her face in the mirror. "God, I look like an old lady." She pulled the scarf off. "Pull over," she commanded.

"I'm not putting the top up."

"I'm not asking you to. We have to talk about those inconsistent statements."

McLean veered the car into the parking lot of a shopping center and faced Lombard. "You have two minutes," he said. "Then we're going to that party."

Lombard said, "We have to go back to Raleigh to grill Ben Hartley."

"Is that all?"

"Tyler Rhodes told you Slade was mean and hateful to Jay Hughes. Hughes's sister told me the opposite. They both claim to have been confidants of Hughes. Somebody's lying."

"Maybe Hughes lied to one of them."

"Ben Hartley might know. Hughes talked to him. I'll find out who's lying as soon I find Hartley."

"Okay, it's settled. We'll look for Hartley. Can we have fun now?"

"At Sig Mashburn's? Sam, he's a lawyer, and it's his party, which means a lot of role players with airtight assholes and no idea how to have a good time. I'll have to drink plenty just to ease the boredom. So if I get trapped by some lawyer's wife wanting to chatter about home decorating or the Junior League, I can't be held responsible for what I might say to her."

McLean tugged the hem of her sleeve. "So why did you get all dressed up?"

Lombard was wearing a silk tunic and matching pants of an eggplant color that bordered on black but for the flecks of purple that shone in the light of the sunset. "I've had this for years. You know, sometimes you've got to dress up and there's no way around it. That's what this is for. You know, practical."

"What about that makeup?" McLean smirked.

"I always put on a little bit when I go out nice places, you smart-ass."

"Nothing wrong in wanting to look nice," McLean said, shifting gears and turning back into traffic. "I wish spouses had been invited. I love it when Selena gets all dolled up."

"Is Selena mad about you going to this thing without her?" Lombard hollered over the wind, now whipping at McLean's soft locks as he sped up, while Lombard's two-inch black carpet of hair stood on end.

"I think she's relieved it's Sig Mashburn's and not a gay bar."

Lombard laughed. "What about you picking me up and taking me?"

"She trusts me around lesbians."

"Aha! She knows," Lombard shouted. "*That's* why she doesn't like me."

"No, that's not it," McLean said. "Selena's not homophobic. She just doesn't like *you*, Loy." He regretted the remark in the instant it slipped. All the color and expressiveness of Lombard's features vanished. She looked paralyzed. McLean gave her a double take. "Did that hurt your feelings?" he asked, a little shocked.

"No," she said briskly.

"I should have kept my mouth shut. I swear to God I never thought you cared what Selena thought."

"Well, of course I care. She's your wife. You're my partner and friend. I want her to like me." Lombard said sulkily, "I've always been nice to her."

"Loy, I was half joking. Selena's easily intimidated, and you just hit on something when you called me your friend. Maybe she doesn't altogether trust you. You know how it is with women."

Lombard feigned a look of bewilderment. "No! How is it with us?"

McLean's car began climbing the shady path to Mashburn's hilltop neighborhood. "Your two minutes are up. Time to have fun," he said.

———

Sigmund Mashburn's house was roosted on the edge of a ridge overlooking downtown Asheville. The road to his house was narrow and bent by hairpin curves winding up the steep slope of a hill. Lombard and McLean grew silent as they ascended the hill, its sides buttressed by thick woods, but over the leafy branches of trees they could observe the humble radiance of the town at dusk. Beyond the town loomed the dull purple outline of distant mountains, rimmed by a hazy orange sunset.

Mashburn's house was plainer than the view behind it. It was a chalet made of stone and cedar, intersected by wide, floor-to-ceiling windows. A single level of the house faced the driveway, while the rear of the house descended three stories into the precipitous hillside overlook.

Mashburn greeted them warmly. He apologized for not having a pretty wife as a hostess and made a joke about not being able to afford one after his third divorce. "Got a passel of kids too, but the ex-wives got 'em all. It gets lonesome up here on Sig Ridge." He led them into the living room, introduced himself to McLean, and offered them each a drink.

Lombard asked for bourbon and glanced around the room at the few guests, and when she spotted Hunter Lyle perched on a black leather sofa near the fireplace, her heartbeat picked up.

Lyle's beauty required little adornment, and though she was

Southern, she lacked the Southern woman's peculiar taste for teased hair, layers of makeup, clusters of rings and bangles, and evening wear loaded with sequins and lamé. Lyle's porcelain features glistened with a natural freshness, accented with the merest application of cosmetics. For jewelry she wore only a pair of turquoise earrings, a thin silver watch, and an antique cameo ring on her right-hand ring finger. Her emerald-green dress, cut mid-calf, would have seemed modest if not for the neckline that plummeted in a narrow V to the hollow cleft of her small breasts.

Lyle was chatting with another guest, and Mashburn introduced McLean to Mike Church. Lombard wasn't surprised to see him here, given the good-old-boy jawing she had observed back at the Rosemond Inn. It seemed everyone here had had a part in the Slade investigation, even Lyle. The one odd bird was that stranger Lyle was talking to. He had a rough, ruddy complexion and thick white hair. His stiff suit and necktie looked cheap and hastily thrown on. Lombard thought he looked like a professional wrestler.

"Grendel!" Mashburn shouted. "You haven't met Loy Lombard and Sam McLean." Mashburn handed Lombard and McLean their drinks. "Grendel Roper is the meanest, toughest son of a bitch in the Carolinas. Just ask him." Mashburn laughed. "Tell them where you've been the last week, Grendel."

Roper spoke with a low, piping voice. "Camping."

"All week by himself," Mashburn said. "He's a real outdoorsman, that one."

"Every chance I get," Roper said.

Mashburn asked everyone to move on to the dining room, where a pair of caterers dressed in white shirts and black trousers kept the swinging door to the kitchen in a constant state of batting back and forth between courses and bottles of wine. Mashburn seated Roper and Lombard at opposite ends of the table, with Lyle on Lombard's left and McLean on her right. Mashburn took a seat next to Lyle, and through the duration of the meal he made a small spectacle of murmuring comments in her ear, out of the hearing of the other guests, and gently patting her thigh when one of his sly remarks made her chuckle.

"I tell you what," Mashburn chortled halfway through the meal, "this old gal just about wore me out during that Slade deal. She's one determined professional when it comes to working a case. I never had the pleasure of making her acquaintance before, but I'm glad I got at least that much out of the whole mess."

Here the conversation turned to the inevitable topic of Jasper Slade and the aborted criminal case to which they had all been connected, with the seeming exception of Grendel Roper. After several minutes of speculation on what drove Slade to suicide and further ruminations on how the case would have come out—with some good-natured ribbing between Mashburn and Church—Mashburn announced that Roper had had his own stake in the controversy. "Grendel is the only person in this room who knew Jasper Slade personally," Mashburn said. "Oh, I talked to Slade, but Grendel really knew him."

"How did you two hook up?" McLean asked Mashburn.

Lombard ate quietly and waited for Mashburn's response. She had scarcely offered a word the entire meal. Mashburn deferred to Roper.

"I used to be with the State Bureau of Investigation, in the division fighting gambling and vice," Roper announced, and Lombard very discreetly rolled her eyes. "I went to work for the American Family Freedom Campaign when I took early retirement. The AFFC spoke for my values, and I don't know nor give a big hoot nor hell what that means to any of you. I got in it for the good of the country, which is what Jasper Slade stood for."

McLean asked, "So were you connected to the homicide investigation?"

"No. Just kept my eye on things. I was kind of like a go-between from here to Raleigh, so Mr. McKenna wouldn't have to travel so much."

"That's how come I got to know him," Mashburn said. "He's been hanging around Asheville ever since I got the case."

"After the senator's demise, I took a little R&R," Roper sighed. "I needed it."

"So I invited him to dine with us this evening, enjoy a little. It's been a trying time for all of us."

"I know one thing," Church said over his fourth drink of the evening. "I wish me and the boys at the station house had all this outside support, running interference for each other. Any time we get mixed up with outside agencies like the state police or the FBI, it's everybody trying to show how he's got a bigger dick than everybody else."

Mashburn laughed nervously. "Mike, there's ladies present." He beamed at Lyle. "And they are quiet as church mice tonight. I'd hoped you girls would carry on and miss the boorish behavior of the gents."

Lyle asked Lombard, "Do you smoke, Loy?"

"I quit two years ago."

"Well, I'm going outside for a smoke," she said. "Will you 'gents' excuse me?"

Lombard smiled at her bad luck: her one good excuse for a few minutes alone with Lyle, busted. Mashburn leaned toward her after Lyle had gone outside to the deck. "I think I'm in love," he said, holding a hand over his heart. "Only I don't know her too well yet. Think she'll go for me?"

Lombard said, "I sure as hell hope not."

Mashburn burst out laughing. "I like you, Loy. Come on. I'll give you the two-dollar tour of the Sig Chalet."

Mashburn escorted Lombard to a large room with garish maroon leather furniture and a billiard table, and buck heads hanging about the walls. Enormous windows overlooked the ridge, and Lombard was immediately taken with the view of Asheville below. "For a little town, it sure is pretty," she said.

"Yeah. It's something," Mashburn said. "Say, I mean to show you the house, but I have ulterior motives for getting you alone."

Lombard grinned. "Aw, are you in love with me too?"

Mashburn chuckled. "My heart's not easily divided. Truth is, it's about business. It's about Slade, more to the point."

"Good. That's the principal reason I came tonight, Sig. You promised me you would talk to me about your interview with Slade."

His smile vanished. "I figured you counted on that. I know the case is still open and you're still on it. Grendel told me. But me? I'm out. I'm out, and I'm pissed off."

Lombard looked out the window, craning her neck for a view of the deck and Lyle, to no avail. "Nobody can help Slade hanging himself."

"I wish I could be sure of that."

Lombard turned around. "What do you mean?"

"Bastards were coming at him from every direction is what I mean." He knocked back the rest of his wine. "I plan on pulling a drunk tonight."

"You'd better take it easy on the liquor if you plan on much else," said Lombard.

"Oh, Hunter? I got a snowball's chance in hell with her. She showed up to be polite, or political, but I can tell when a woman's interested. And Miss Lyle *ain't*."

"So you're pissed off. About what? The missed chance of a high-profile trial?"

Mashburn fell heavily into a suede recliner. "You don't like lawyers, do you?"

"I never cared one way or the other before Sam's trial. I got to know a few in Charlotte. Some of them were in it to do good, some of them were in it for their egos, but I got the idea most of them were in it for the drink at the end of the day."

Mashburn laughed. "And some of us are in it for all three! Come on. I'm interested to know what you think of me, Loy. Lemme have it."

"You want the spotlight on the news at 6. That's why you're pissed off. You were counting on defending the case of the century, and Slade blew it for you."

"You're almost exactly right."

"Then tell me what I missed."

"I can't."

Lombard frowned. "Then why the hell did you bring me aside like this?"

"I want you to work for me."

"I run a business. I got over having a boss the day I left Charlotte."

"I don't mean permanently. I want you to work the Slade case on my commission, not Ross McKenna's. Leave him and work for me."

Lombard asked, "If you know so much about what happened to Slade, why do you need me working for you?"

Mashburn stared at her with a flat smile.

"It's because you don't know enough," Lombard said. "Stop trying to manipulate me, Sig. I have no reason to trust you. You dangle that interview in front of me like it's bait. How dare you treat me like a child?"

"I'm on to Ross McKenna, Loy. You can help me blow the lid off this case."

"No. You're lying. Just like Arlo Saperstein, your buddy that tried to get me indicted back in Charlotte. You're all alike, the big-shot lawyers with inflated egos. You just want to stay on the front pages, and you'll tell me anything to help you get in through the back door."

"I have that interview…"

Lombard let go a laugh. "I'm barely curious at this point. Slade was a doper. Even you admitted he was on something. Whatever he said is about as reliable as your word."

Mashburn looked smug. "Do you like chartering guards out to waste management plants? Is that your limit of ambition, Loy? I'm giving you a chance to work for me and make a name for yourself. Where will you be after Ross is done with you? Staking out seedy motels for a snapshot of some jealous wife's cheating husband. You talk about the spotlight like it's something to be ashamed of. Well, I'd be ashamed of mediocrity. I avoid it. I can't imagine what it must be like to live for it. Tell me, what's it like?"

Lombard's eyes narrowed to black, smoldering slits. "We'll see who's mediocre, you arrogant son of a bitch. I'm still on the Slade case. You'll be back to representing jealous wives who *kill* their cheating husbands."

"Right now you're on a dead-end path, I swear to God."

Lombard shook with anger. "So you'll resort to invoking the Almighty just to get to me? I'm flattered. Did you pray for Hunter Lyle to show up tonight?"

Mashburn laughed. "You know what? You're meaner than a striped snake. I still like you, though."

Lombard gritted her teeth and stormed to the hallway. "By the way," she said on a sudden thought, "if you think that white-haired narc is gonna work for you, you're a gullible fool. He's AFFC all the way. I wouldn't be surprised if he's wearing a wire. Do you really think you can hire one of Ross McKenna's goons away from him? I've been studying that outfit for less than two weeks and even I know better. The AFFC is like a religion. Don't you get that?"

"Money talks," Mashburn grinned.

"It doesn't for everybody," she said, turning her back. She

made a beeline for the living room and found McLean standing with the other guests at the broad windows overlooking the ridge.

Mashburn came in behind her. "What are y'all staring at?" he asked.

"Hunter spotted a big fire," Church said, his eyes fixed on bright spot downtown, over which a thick cloud of black smoke rose up in the indigo sky.

"I noticed it while I was having my smoke," Lyle said. "Look over there."

Lombard observed a miniature torrent of orange and yellow in the dark distance and tried to speculate on the location. "Is that near Broadway?" she asked.

"Could be," Church said.

"You work arson cases?" McLean asked jokingly, nudging Church in the arm.

"No. Just homicides," Church said. "With my luck, it's arson, and there's probably some poor son of a bitch trapped inside, and I'll get paged and be up all goddamn night smelling burned-up bodies, interviewing drunk witnesses. Shoo."

Lyle mumbled something. Lombard didn't catch it, and looked at Lyle as she stared out at the flames. Her eyes were sharp and determined. Lombard asked, "You see a story down there, don't you?"

Lyle said, "Oh, no. Well, maybe. But the night crew will get it. I don't care." She smiled at Lombard. "I'm having a good time. Let somebody else have it. Just an old building with bad wiring, probably." Her smile fell, and she looked at Lombard with the same determined eyes. "Let's go sit down. I want another drink."

After they had poured a couple of drinks, the two women sat together on the sofa. The men had gone out on the deck, and Lombard forgot about how furious she was at Mashburn. She was listening to Lyle's thoughts on journalism and its role in advancing trust between the public and the police. She made a vague reference to Lombard's experience in Charlotte and remarked that she thought the media's treatment of the case had been vulgar and unprofessional.

"How do you know so much about that?" Lombard asked.

"I told you I always do research. I like to know about the people I interview before I ask them to reveal anything about themselves or what they're doing. If you don't mind my saying so, I respect how you handled yourself in that graft trial. Not many people would have had the nerve you had."

"It was a witch-hunt. They wanted to sacrifice some cops because they couldn't get to the big dogs, the real criminals Iman Casteel was afraid to rat out."

"Now, this is unusual," Lyle said. "You just talked about yourself. I thought I was going to go on all night without a single comment from you."

Lombard smiled. "I don't mind as long as it's all off the record."

McLean suddenly appeared and nudged her. "It's after 11," he said. "I promised Selena I'd get home way before midnight."

Lombard said, "Well, you best be moving along, then."

"How are you gonna get home?" McLean asked.

Lombard looked at him scathingly. "I'll call a cab."

"Oh, pooh," Lyle said. "You don't need a cab. I'll take you home."

"Aw, that's too much trouble," McLean said. "Loy lives way out in the country."

Lombard gritted her teeth through a smile. "Sam, I'll take a *cab*."

McLean brightened, as though Lombard's meaning had dawned on him at last. "Oh! Okay. Hey, that's great. Gives me the chance to cruise at top speed with some Steve Earle blasting out the radio. We'll see y'all later. Be careful on those dark roads."

The party lasted until well after midnight. McLean had been

gone for more than an hour, and Church had departed a few minutes after that. Lombard was so engrossed in talking to Lyle that she lost track of time. She was just explaining her decision to move to Asheville when she spotted Grendel Roper out of the corner of her eye. He and Mashburn were outside on the deck having what looked like a heated discussion, but the heavy glass doors and indoor music muted them.

"What are you looking at?" Lyle asked.

"The men. They're talking up a storm." She leaned forward to snatch her glass off the coffee table and deftly drew closer to Lyle as she leaned back to take a drink. "Where was I? Asheville. I like it here. Liked it the first time I visited here years ago, and I knew this was the place to move to when I left Charlotte. I had to get out of Charlotte, of course. I felt bad, angry."

"Are you happy here?"

Lombard stared into her glass. "Yeah. This town's got a good heart. It welcomes anybody and everybody. It's like New Orleans in that respect, but only in that respect."

"Do you ever think about going home, back to New Orleans?"

"No. Well, not to live. That was another lifetime. My parents are dead, and I don't have any other relatives, except for a few cousins down there, good people. But we're not really close, not like I was to their mother, my aunt Anna Mae. But she's dead now too."

"You're all alone?" Lyle looked perplexed.

"Pretty much," said Lombard. She noticed the look on Lyle's face and smiled. "Aw. You feel sorry for me. Don't, though. I'm content being alone. I'm used to it."

"Come on. You have to have somewhere to go on Christmas. Everybody does."

"I've got plenty of invitations every year, don't worry," Lombard said. "Sam, Retta, a few of my old friends in Charlotte, and all my cousins, they ask me every year. The truth is, I'd rather be alone. Last year I did go to midnight mass at the basilica, on a whim. I've never been very religious, but I am superstitious. See here?" She pulled out the long gold chain she wore around her neck under her clothing and showed Lyle the Saint Theresa medal fastened to it. "Anna Mae gave it to me, bless her heart. Theresa's my confirmation name, and she couldn't find any Saint Aloysia medals. I wear it for protection, though I'm not really sure it will protect me. It's hard to explain. I don't have faith. I just, you know, hedge my bets."

Lyle gave Lombard a puzzled smile, and Lombard found herself caught for a few awkward seconds in her gaze. It embarrassed Lombard, and she looked away, through the glass doors to the deck, and said, "I think we should go soon."

"Shouldn't we say goodbye to Sig?" Lyle asked.

Lombard shook her head. "No. I know it's rude, but after the row I had with him, I'd be a hypocrite to act gracious. Anyway, look at him and Grendel. They probably think we've already left." She touched Lyle's hand. "Let's go."

They barely spoke as Lyle drove down Hendersonville Road out of Asheville. Lombard told her where to turn off the main highway and gave her terse directions on which roads to turn onto to get to her house, situated on a lonesome, forested stretch of a country route.

All during the drive, Lombard privately debated whether what she was about to do was a mistake. Getting Lyle into her bed was a foregone conclusion; she was going to do it, and she knew Lyle wanted it. Lyle was no ingenue, Lombard had decided. She was a cunning woman, at ease flirting with Lombard, but that bothered her. Lyle might be interested in her, but she was at least as interested in what she could get out of Lombard. She hoped she wouldn't do something stupid like fall in love with Lyle. As pragmatic as she was, she had a terrible history of letting her heart deceive her head. She gave Lyle a long look. Damn, Lombard thought, was this a lucky break or what? A fine reward for two years of celibacy, and two years had been long enough.

Lyle parked in Lombard's driveway and turned off the ignition. "That wasn't such a long drive," she said.

"Not much traffic out here, even in daytime," Lombard said. She glanced at Lyle, who smiled roguishly and gently tugged her skirt above her knees. A wave of desire rolled over Lombard, and she looked away.

Lyle asked, "Do you want me to leave?"

"No. I want you to come inside."

Lyle leaned over to within inches of Lombard's nose. "For a nightcap?"

Lombard smiled, a little bashfully. "If you want," she said. She leaned forward and kissed Lyle, slowly and easily, pushing Lyle against her seat and sliding her right hand under Lyle's skirt. Lyle groaned softly, and Lombard pulled away.

"Why did you stop?" Lyle breathed.

"I swore when I got out of the Navy I'd never do it in a car again," Lombard said. Lyle giggled and followed Lombard out of the car. They went to the front door, where Lombard pulled Lyle to her and kissed her again, more ardently than before, as she stabbed the lock with the key and pushed the door open with her foot. She moved her hands along Lyle's body, turning her around to feel up her breasts and caress her neck, realizing without thinking that they wouldn't make it to the bedroom. They fell onto the sofa, sparing not even the second it would take to shut the front door. Lombard drew Lyle's skirt up to her hips and smiled, nearly chuckled, when she saw the garters drawn around Lyle's stockings, and nothing north of them in the way of underwear.

"You always this well prepared, Hunter?" said Lombard, pulling Lyle's legs apart and stroking her.

Lyle's eyes were closed, and she was breathing heavily. "Stop stalling," she said.

"I'm not," Lombard mumbled, kissing her inner thigh. "Don't be pushy. We have all night."

A few seconds later, Lyle's eyes opened wide and bright as two shooting stars. She reached between her legs and grabbed the hair on Lombard's head, drew a sharp breath, and cried, "Oh! Oh, my God! Oh, darling Loy. Oh, that's, that feels just gorgeous. Don't stop, or I'll kill you."

7

LOMBARD AWAKENED SUDDENLY THE NEXT MORNING, ON
a rush of adrenaline that caused her shoulders to tense and her
eyes to open. Her ears were on alert. A second later she heard a
footstep in the living room. She rose up on her elbows and looked
at Hunter Lyle, sleeping quietly beside her. A tentative second
footstep followed, and Lombard braced herself for a confronta-
tion with an intruder.

She suddenly remembered leaving the door open the night
before. The throes of lust had compelled them both to bed and blot-
ted out mundane considerations such as a door left hanging wide
open. She had made love with Lyle all night, until the first predawn
glimmers filtered through the window and exhaustion forced them
both to give in to sleep. Had they been followed? Had someone
watched them? There wasn't time to think it through; the hardwood
of her living room floor creaked again. The steps were spaced seconds apart; the intruder was clearly taking care to be quiet.

She turned on her side and gently nudged Lyle, who awoke as
Lombard raised her index finger to her lips. She whispered
almost inaudibly in Lyle's ear, "Somebody's here. Slide down off
the bed and hide next to it." Lyle frowned and started to say
something, and then footsteps fell on the hallway floor. She carefully slid off the bed.

The steps were heavier, closer. Lombard reached into her
bedside table and pulled out the revolver she kept hidden there.
The intruder was nearly right outside the bedroom doorway.
She got out of bed and glided to the blind spot next to the door,

her back pinned against the wall, her head turned to the doorway. She held the revolver pointing up until she heard the steps stop inches away.

The intruder moved quickly, sweeping inside the room and pivoting sharply to where Lombard stood pointing a gun straight at his head. She cried out, "Sam! What are you doing here?"

McLean looked horrified, and he slowly lowered his weapon. His face turned beet red, and he averted his eyes. "Sorry, Loy." He rushed back to the front of the house.

A chill came over Lombard, and she realized she was stark naked. She instantly put down the gun, snatched her robe off the hook of the closet door, and wrapped herself up. She said, "Hunter, it's all right. It's just Sam. Get up." She sat down on the edge of the bed.

Lyle wiggled out from under the bed and crawled back on top. She pulled the covers over her legs and reached out to Lombard. She stroked the back of Lombard's head and said, "You're shaking. What happened? I was scared witless."

"I almost blew his brains out. I very nearly did it." Lombard's voice broke. "Oh, my God, what if I had done it?" Her eyes moist and worried, she smiled at Lyle. "Just wait here for a few minutes."

Lyle pulled a sheet up over her bosom. "Okay. I think I need to lie down for a little while longer anyway."

McLean was sitting calmly on the sofa when Lombard entered the living room. "I'm sorry, Loy," he said. "I thought you were in trouble."

Lombard sat down. "You dumb son of a bitch," she cried, "I nearly killed you."

"I could have shot you too."

"You gave it the extra second because you thought you might see me. I didn't expect you. I could have panicked."

"You didn't. You wouldn't. I was never in danger, and you know it."

"What if it had gone off?" Lombard was weeping, so upset was she by what had very nearly gone wrong.

McLean looked very uncomfortable. "Loy, what's come over you?" he asked, patting her shoulder. "I've never seen you in such a state, all emotional."

Lombard swatted at him and sank into the couch. Nearly composed, she said, "Why did you think I was in trouble?"

"When I got here, I saw a strange car parked outside. Nobody comes here by accident, Loy, as far out as you live. Your front door looked like it was busted open, and there was furniture turned upside down…why, look around here!" He pointed to the overturned coffee table and magazines strewn about the floor, wreckage from last night's passion. "It made me nervous, seeing as what I came here to tell you. I should have called first, but I wasn't near a phone and I left my cell phone in my other car. I drove straight here."

"What's going on?"

McLean rubbed his face. He looked very tired. "I've been up all night with Mike Church. He called after I got home and told me to meet him at Wiley Faulks's building, or what's left of it. That fire we saw? That was the headquarters of the *Carolina Vigilante*. It's burned all to hell. Faulks's body was found crouched near a back door that had been blocked on the outside by an SUV, like somebody drove it up the alleyway, parked it tight next to the door, and ditched it. He couldn't open the door more than an inch if he tried, and it looks like he did. Mike got the call when they found the body, and he called me. Faulks was burned beyond recognition, but the medical examiner confirmed his identity an hour ago."

Lombard groaned, "Jesus. That's horrible news. I kind of liked that sad old loner. Why do you think Mike called you?"

McLean shrugged. "I think he's hoping Sig Mashburn will offer him some kind of post-retirement job. Mike's twenty years of service will be up next year. It'd be good money. And he says Sig likes you and brags about how he's gonna get you to work for him. I guess Mike wants to tighten up the bonds with us."

"He can have Mashburn."

"What I want to know is what happened here! Why did you have the door hanging wide open? And whose car is that outside?" He glanced at the hallway, where Lyle stood dressed in her emerald-green party gown. His mouth fell open. "Oh. Hello."

"Hi, Sam." She smiled affectionately at Lombard. "I have to go."

"Where?" Lombard asked, cocking an eyebrow. "It's Saturday."

"I work some Saturdays. The news never stops, you know." Lyle brushed back a stray strand of hair. "I need to get a shower and change. I've got a lot of work to do."

"Mmm-hmm. I bet you do." Lombard suspected she had been eavesdropping.

Lyle glanced around the room. "My bag, and my keys…oh, I must have left them in the car. I'll just be moving along."

"Don't be a stranger," Lombard yawned.

Lyle started for the door. She said, "I couldn't help overhearing a little bit of what you were saying, and…"

Lombard said impassively, "Wiley Faulks burned up in a fire. Could be murder. Go get it, girl."

"I got that part. While I was dressing, that is. I couldn't help overhearing, the way voices carry in these airy old houses." She eyed Lombard reproachfully. "Anyway, I was talking to Sam. Sam, did you say the medical examiner already has a report ready?"

"I don't know about a report, exactly. I'm going on what Church told me."

"Oh! Well, I suppose I'll check with the lieutenant, then," Lyle said brightly. "Well, you all have a good day." She looked a

Lombard a bit bashfully. "Loy, thank you for the, um, well, your hospitality in letting me stay here. It was very kind of you."

The screen door clapped shut, and after a few seconds Lyle's car engine started. McLean turned to Lombard. "Have you lost your mind?"

Lombard tapped the side of her head. "Gone. Nothing there."

"Loy, your private life is none of my business, but—"

Lombard pursed her lips. "You're right. It isn't your business."

"But this *is* business," McLean said, pointing in the direction of Lyle's car as it roared off in the distance. "This is not just about you."

"I'm not a fool, Sam," Lombard said defensively. "I know she's manipulative, vain, and conceited. She embodies all that I distrust about reporters." Her voice turned dreamy. "Mmm, but she's so pretty, and fresh as a little daisy." She coughed and straightened her shoulders. "Anyway, I know what I'm doing. Relax."

"Some things never change." McLean sighed. "Your only weakness, Loy: a pretty woman with cool manners and a fiery eye."

"You worry like an old woman." She got up stiffly and stretched. "Coffee?"

"Sure."

Lombard smiled. "Good. Let's mark a milestone."

"What milestone?"

"You being the first man ever laid eyes on my naked body since the day I popped out of my mama's womb." She laughed, and McLean turned scarlet.

———

They were in Raleigh before nightfall. They had planned to wait until Monday to make the trip, but Wiley Faulks's death made finding Ben Hartley too urgent to put off even one more day.

"I doubt the Pride office will be open tomorrow," Lombard said as they sat in her motel room dining on deli sandwiches and beer. "Tomorrow's Sunday. Even gay rights activists rest on Sunday, surely." She took a bite of her sandwich and scowled. "Where'd you get these? They're sloppy. They've got ugly lettuce too."

"This little mom-and-pop deli down the road," McLean replied through a mouthful. "You said to pick up some sandwiches."

"Good God. These tomatoes are heinous."

"Look, you said no fast food, so I didn't have much choice."

"I've gotta watch my weight, but that doesn't mean I want to eat this nasty stuff."

McLean reached for his beer. "Well, then you can go out cruising for meals and I'll sit here watching TV thinking of ways to criticize you when you get back." He belched. "By the way, I tried looking up Hartley in the city directory. He either lives outside of town or with somebody, because there's no address listed for a Ben or Benjamin Hartley. The only B. Hartley is a female. Brenda, I think was her name."

"See if you can find him tomorrow. I'll deal with McKenna in the meantime. He's expecting us Monday, but I'd just as soon get it over with. I've got his home number."

"And if I find Hartley?"

"Get him to talk to you."

"I don't know about that. He ran off in a hurry when I was at Tyler Rhodes's, and that was right after Slade's death. And if he knows anything about Faulks's death, my guess is he won't be eager to chat."

Lombard was vexed. "What do you think, Sam? There's got to be a connection between Faulks's death and all this Slade business. It's too close. Ben Hartley contributed information to Faulks's newsletter. Hartley knew Jay Hughes, who told him about his relationship with Slade. It makes me wonder if Hartley knew or met Slade somehow. Slade died, and Hartley took off before you had a chance to grill him at Tyler Rhodes's office. Now three men connected to Ben Hartley are dead. Here's the other thing that makes me wonder: McKenna pointed us straight at Hartley and Faulks. It's a tangled web, just like the old rhyme, and I think we'll find that it was woven by deceit."

———

Lombard called McKenna that night and told him to expect her the next morning. He sounded weak, and he gave her directions to his house with no qualms. When she arrived the next morning at his tidy Dutch colonial house in a wooded, upscale neighborhood, he was alone.

"My wife and children are at church," he explained. He looked troubled and very tired. He directed Lombard to follow him to a back patio, where he reclined in a chaise longue and offered Lombard a seat near him in a deck chair. "I haven't been feeling well, or I would offer you some coffee or juice."

"No bother," Lombard said. She noticed that he looked distractedly in the space behind her; his formerly sharp, icy blue eyes were dull.

"I've thought about sending them away," he said.

"Who?"

"My family. I've thought of sending them to the beach house of friends on the Outer Banks till all this blows over. I think I will. I must."

"Till what blows over?"

McKenna leaned forward and cupped his face in his hands. "The danger."

"What are you talking about? You worried somebody's after you?"

He leaned back and smiled in his flat, insincere way. "You'll be surprised to know that Wiley Faulks's death troubles me a great deal. Whatever diabolical mind is behind it frightens me."

"What makes you think there's a mind behind it? Surely it was an accident."

McKenna chuckled. "Oh, Loy Lombard. I told you how to find my house when there are so few people I invite here, let alone reveal the address. I don't like you, but I feel safe with you. How is that?"

"Maybe you've figured out that I don't believe in this bizarre conspiracy plot you're so convinced of. So I can't be a part of it."

"Still, you follow every lead to the letter. And that's what matters, because in the end you will discover that I was right. You're like the Doubting Thomas."

Lombard snorted. "Don't go painting me as a saint."

McKenna's head rolled heavily to one side and he closed his eyes. "I had it all figured out. I'm still certain Faulks knew something about that boy's death and Jasper's presence at that inn, if he wasn't behind it personally. It just doesn't fit, him dying the way he did. Maybe something's gone wrong on the inside..."

"What inside?" Lombard snapped. "McKenna, you're not making sense. I'm starting to get mad, the way you toy with me. I've got a job to do. Lay it on the line."

"I don't know!" he shouted. His fingers combed through his hair, and he looked paler than when Lombard first arrived. "Something's gone wrong, I know it. I'm in danger. I need to get my family out of town."

Lombard took a deep breath. "Mr. McKenna, I'm going to ask you one more time. What do you think is going on here? Because

I'm starting to wonder myself how much Faulks knew about Jay Hughes's death and Slade's involvement in it. I have a feeling what he knew got him killed. And I'm strongly suspicious a third party killed that boy and that maybe you were right about Slade not having a hand in it."

"I thought you said you don't believe me."

"I don't! I don't think Faulks could have killed a pigeon, nor even had one killed. He might have known something, but that doesn't mean there's a gay conspiracy or that anybody killed that young boy to get at Slade. The idea's preposterous. I wish you thought rational so my job could be easier. Isn't it enough that I might be able to clear Slade of murder?"

"No. You have to prove he wasn't *with* that boy…"

"He *was*! He was with Jay Hughes and he was fucking him! And he had been fucking him for a while! And a lot of people know that, people who don't give a damn about politics or religion or tobacco. People who just know the truth."

"Who told you that? They're lying. They're part of it!" McKenna spluttered wildly. "You're off this case, Lombard. You're not to be trusted, not if you're buying in to the claims of these hostile forces."

"Fine! But first, don't you want to know how I could clear Slade of murder?"

McKenna's gaunt face was tense, his features drawn together as though tied by string. "Yes, I want to know."

"I didn't get the chance to tell you this before Slade did himself in. But I found evidence of a break-in the day I looked at the room in the inn. There were fresh chip marks in the windowsill, like somebody had pried the window open from the outside. What I've run down—what Sam and I have run down—since then points to the possibility that Slade didn't kill Hughes, at least not alone. Now I'm close. I feel it. Real close. You tell me what you think. You want me out? I'm out. But there it is, only fair I tell you."

McKenna's brow tensed into hard creases. He began to weep inconsolably. "I can't figure it out, but I know I'm next," he wailed. "That much I can feel, Loy Lombard. I'm next."

———

A few hours later Lombard sat dejectedly in the car waiting for McLean to finish talking on his cell phone. He was happily informing his wife that he was on his way home and wouldn't have to stay another night. The trip, he smiled into the phone, had been a bust.

"You know something?" Lombard said after McLean clicked off his phone. "I never liked Raleigh, and this case has burned me on it for good. You would think that the epicenter of the nation's hottest criminal case would give us something, just one clue. This is our second trip, and we can't find a clue."

"Ben Hartley is one big dead end. He's vanished."

"There's one more lead. Jessamyn Frost, Hartley's boss."

"Well, let's go."

"No. I'll wait till her office opens up in the morning."

McLean frowned. "I just told Selena I was on my way home."

"Fine. Go home. Take my car and go home," she said sullenly. "I'll rent a car. I'm talking to Frost tomorrow. I'm gonna find Hartley."

"Loy, we're not even on the payroll, it sounds like. Not if McKenna fired us."

"I don't think he was serious about that. I don't care if he did. I'm on it."

"I say we go back to Asheville tonight and you call up Sig Mashburn and take him up on his offer."

Lombard said coolly, "I don't trust that goddamn lawyer as far as I can throw him. If McKenna fired me, then I'm solving this case on my own time. I still have plenty left from the money he gave us."

"It was a retainer, Loy. He might call back what we haven't spent."

"I'll cough it up if he does."

McLean pursed his lips and looked agitated. "I'll stay. I'll call Selena back."

"You don't have to do that, Sam. Go home to your family. There'll be plenty to do tomorrow. This case is ruining your days. Don't let it ruin your nights."

Lombard's cell phone rang. "It's probably McKenna," she said, hastily answering. "Yeah? Hello? Oh, it's Retta. Why you calling on a Sunday? What's going on?" She listened intently. "Is that a fact? Did he say anything else? Huh. No, that's okay. Good work. Thanks." She shut the phone and slapped McLean's knee. "Sounds like you have to go home after all."

"What for?"

"I call-forwarded the office calls to Retta's house over the weekend, just in case something came up with that Faulks business. Well, Tyler Rhodes called, and Retta says he was all to pieces."

"He and Faulks were close," McLean said.

"It's something else. He was frantic, she said. Wants to talk to you ASAP. So you get on home and talk to him first thing tomorrow. I'll stay here, and like I said, I'll rent a car. I've got to talk to Frost."

———

McLean was back at the office on Haywood Street in Asheville the next morning, where he found Rhodes waiting for him.

McLean immediately noticed a change in him. The gleam in his eye was gone; his taut lips seemed incapable of the charming smile McLean recalled from their first meeting.

"Sam McLean," Rhodes said. "I came on in without calling. I hope you don't mind."

"Not at all. Come on back."

He closed his office door behind Rhodes. "You all right, Tyler? I'm very sorry about Wiley Faulks. Loy met him one time, and she was genuinely saddened to hear about the tragedy. She's a tough one, that girl, so that tells me he was some kind of man."

"I admired Wiley Faulks very much. He was a great man, and he was my friend." Rhodes sniffed and ran his fingers through his thick black curls.

McLean sat in a chair next to Rhodes and said, "I understand you tried to reach me yesterday. What's on your mind?"

"You were in Raleigh, right? Your secretary told me."

"Yeah."

"Were you looking for Ben Hartley? I bet you were."

McLean nodded.

"Well, I can't help you find him. I wish I could."

"Why's that?"

"I misled you back at my office. I thought you were interrogating me, like you thought I had done something wrong. Maybe you do, I don't know."

"I don't regard you as a suspect, no. But I don't exactly rule you out either."

"I appreciate your honesty. And of course, I know you used to be a cop, and you have to stay objective. Then I was protecting myself. But the truth is, I have nothing to hide. And now, to protect myself, I feel like I have to tell you a few things."

"Protect yourself from what?"

Rhodes suddenly flashed his infectious grin. His eyes crinkled at the edges, and he seemed to regain his color. "You know what,

Sam? I don't know from what or from whom. All I know is, somebody murdered my friend, and I think it relates to Slade. I don't know how. Wiley had enemies, but he wasn't enough of a threat to warrant murder. Nobody felt that strongly about him. He wasn't a threat at all, just an agitator. Maybe it was a hate crime; some redneck wanted to kill a fag, who knows? Maybe it was a random arson. I doubt it was that simple, though. Somebody picked him out. But why pick on that meek old fuddy-duddy? I think it was personal. The only man with enough reason to want Wiley dead—Slade—is dead himself. And Ben has disappeared without a trace."

"How do you know?"

"I haven't heard from him since the day you met me last week. Jessamyn Frost called me looking for him. He hasn't been in touch with her since the day your partner visited her office."

"Sounds like he's in trouble."

"That's what I'm worried about. What kind of trouble? Think of how we'll look."

"How who will look?"

"If Ben had anything to do with this mess—Jay Hughes, Slade, Wiley—how will that look to the nation? A queer murder plot. Wiley Faulks's legacy tarnished."

"What makes you think Ben had something to do with it?"

"He knew all the dead men. He knew Wiley. I introduced them because of their shared interest in the press. He knew Jay, because of my relationship with him. And that's how Ben met Jasper Slade. Even I never met Slade. Neither did Wiley Faulks. And Ben was in town the night Jay died. I'm a lawyer, Sam. I've got sense enough to know that looks very strange. It worries the living hell out of me."

McLean could hardly conceal his excitement at hearing this news. He couldn't wait to tell Lombard. "I'm suspicious, sure," he said casually. "But what motive?"

"I don't know," Rhodes said abjectly. "All I know is, he knew all the dead men, and he's vanished. And, well, there's something else about Ben Hartley."

"What?"

"He's been in trouble before, years ago, when he was in college. He got arrested for stabbing a man in a barroom brawl. It probably doesn't matter."

McLean said, "You say Ben met Slade. What did he say about him? How many times did they meet? That kind of thing."

"I only know of one time. Ben told me Slade initiated the meeting. He wanted to confront him about the article Ben wrote. That meeting took place very shortly before Jay's death."

"Surely you were curious about what they discussed."

"I was dying to know. Ben told me Slade threatened him with a lawsuit. He tried bribing him to print a retraction. Ben refused. Next thing we know, Jay's dead, and it looks like Slade lost his mind and killed him. Made sense to me then. Now I'm not so sure."

———

Lombard employed the old "element of surprise" tactic that same morning when, not finding Jessamyn Frost at work, she called in a favor to a Raleigh police detective who used to work with her in Charlotte and found out Frost's unlisted home address from a city database. She drove there straight away, walked right up to the front door of a handsome town house and smiled victoriously when Frost answered the door.

Frost was livid. "How did you get my address?" she demanded.

"I asked around down at the local dyke bar last night," Lombard grinned.

"Very cute, Ms. Lombard. What do you want?"

"I came to tell you that Wiley Faulks is dead."

Frost closed her eyes and leaned against the doorjamb. "How?"

"In a fire, set by an arsonist, in all likelihood, at the headquarters of the *Carolina Vigilante*. I thought maybe you already knew, seeing as you didn't go in to work today. Figured you might be grieving."

Frost shuddered. "Please leave."

"I want to leave. But first I need your help."

"Why should I help you? What are you doing here anyway? Your employer died over a week ago, didn't he?"

"There are still a lot of unanswered questions, and Faulks's death has turned my investigation on its head."

"You're wasting your time bothering me with your petty detective game," Frost said with such condescension that Lombard took offense. "I don't know anything."

"Don't bullshit me, Ms. Frost," Lombard said. "And don't make the mistake of thinking I take any pleasure in inconveniencing you or your pride politics. Don't think I have all the time in the world to put up with your snotty attitude when I'd rather be back home pulling weeds out of my rose beds!" Lombard raised her voice. "I won't waste any more of your time as soon as you tell me where the hell I can find Ben Hartley. Unless, of course, you're helping him hide, in which case I might be all too happy to bring the full force of the Asheville and Raleigh and state police down on your ass and see if *they* can get any answers. The fact is, Ms. Frost, you are a material witness in this investigation as long as there's any chance you might know where he is, whether the hell you like it or not. Now, you can either tell me what you know and see the back of

133

me, or you can expect to hear from the police. How would *that* look for your civic reputation?"

Frost waited patiently for Lombard to spew it all out, as might a schoolteacher with a hyperactive child. She said, "I haven't seen Ben Hartley since the day you last spoke to me. I didn't think much of it for a few days, since he routinely canvasses the state on various projects we have running. He lives with his parents—well, he lives on their farm in a renovated carriage house—and this past Friday they called and told me he hadn't been home in over a week and hadn't called once. They sounded very worried, wanted to know if I'd heard from him. By now they've probably reported him missing."

"Who are his parents?" Lombard asked.

"Leonard and Matilda Hartley," she said coldly. "Is that enough?"

"Where do they live?"

"On a farm. Wait a minute." She left Lombard standing on the front stoop for a minute, and came back with a page torn from an address book. "This is the address I have." She handed the paper to Lombard. "And that is all I know. May I be excused?"

Lombard snatched the paper from Frost's hands. "You certainly may. With any luck, we'll never cross paths again."

"From your mouth to God's ear," said Frost, and she slammed the door in Lombard's face.

8

LOMBARD CALLED MCLEAN. HE ANSWERED AND SAID
without so much as hello, "The fire that killed Faulks was defi-
nitely arson, and Hartley met Slade at least once."

Lombard said, "How'd you know it was me calling?"

"Your cell number flashed across the caller ID screen. Where
are you?"

"I'm still in Raleigh, one more night at least. I got a lead on
Hartley's address, which is his parents'. He's been missing for over
a week. What did Tyler say?"

McLean gave Lombard the blow-by-blow of Tyler's visit to the
office, including Tyler's revelation about Hartley's violent past.

"Did you check up on that?"

"I ran an NCIC," an acronym for the National Criminal
Information Center, which provided law enforcement all over the
country with computerized data on anyone charged in the United
States with a criminal offense. "He was arrested for attempted murder but wound up with a misdemeanor conviction."

"When did he meet Slade?" Lombard asked. "Did Tyler
know?"

"He wasn't sure, but he thinks it wasn't long before the murder. He knows Ben Hartley was in town the night of the murder,
though. Tyler saw him early that evening. Anyway, the last time
Tyler saw him was that day I saw them together at his office, he
swears."

"And Frost hasn't seen him since shortly after Jay Hughes's
death. Let's get this straight. Hughes died on Friday, the ninth of

April. We first met Frost and Hartley early the next week. She never saw him after about the 13th. Thought he was out on business. Then you saw him the next Monday in Asheville, in Tyler's office, and he ran off before you could talk to him. That was the 19th. One week ago. By then his parents were already wondering what had happened to him. They told Frost this past Friday he'd been missing over a week."

"So he's deliberately hiding out," McLean concluded.

"Exactly. If he had come in harm's way, everyone would have missed him all at once. He's dodging the public eye on purpose. I'm gonna talk to his parents tomorrow."

"What do you want me to do?"

"I want you to go sweet-talk that old bag at the Rosemond Inn into showing you records of who was booked there the night of the murder," Lombard told him.

"That's all?"

"That's all. Then get a baby-sitter and take Selena out someplace nice."

"You're being generous. That means you've got hell in store for me."

"Things are about to start cooking, sure enough. Speaking of, what did the fire report say?"

"The fire started on the inside. Forensics suggests it was deliberately set in an area central to the first floor of the building…"

"Where all those papers were lying around," Lombard mused aloud.

"What's that?"

"There was this big table in the middle of the floor with all kinds of books and papers scattered about. They were even on the floor. Perfect kindling."

"Right. They think the area was doused with gasoline by a perp who entered through the front of the building. The fire started quickly and consumed the building in a matter of minutes. The whole building just ignited. Wiley's body was found downstairs near the back fire door. It was the closest door to the stairs leading down from his apartment."

"Didn't he have a fire escape?"

McLean gave a long sigh. "He had made the fire escape into a shade garden."

"Come again?"

"I said he had him a shade garden out on the fire escape. He would have had to move all kinds of heavy flowerpots and hanging ivy baskets to get down, plus he had rigged the trap so the stairs wouldn't descend. It looks like the perp knew that the first-floor fire door was the nearest possible exit, because a stolen SUV was parked up against the outside of it, trapping him inside while the front was already consumed in flames."

"If the perp knew that, then I'll bet he knew Wiley. Who owned the car?"

"The police report says it was a Land Rover, registered to a Dr. George Varner of Weaverville, who had reported it stolen three days earlier. I called him the minute I read the report, of course. He never saw who took it, but he sure would like to get his hands on whoever it was. Said the car insurance people won't cover the fishing tackle he had in back, and that'll set him back hundreds. He's fit to kill. I don't think he knows a thing."

"Was it stolen from his house?"

"No. He was out camping and fishing with some buddies of his on the French Broad River, near Hot Springs. It got stolen in the middle of the night, after he had packed up his fishing gear for the ride home the next morning."

"Exactly when?"

"Last Tuesday night or early Wednesday morning, in the wee hours. He doesn't remember if he locked the car, but he doubts it. They were in the middle of nowhere. He never locks up. I know how that is, the rugged outdoors, bunch of he-men, probably had guns with 'em for protection. Feel like a wimp locking up or even wearing a seat belt on the drive home."

"He didn't hear anybody driving it off?"

"Nope. I get the idea those boys were about passed out drunk, though he never admitted it. The perp probably rolled the car back a ways before hot-wiring it. Anyway, no alarm went off, and nobody heard a peep."

"Now, that was last Tuesday night. The day before that was when you first met Tyler, and that's the last *anybody* saw of Ben Hartley."

McLean yawned. "Well, I'm ready to head home. Now, I mean to take Selena out tomorrow night, like you said. So don't bother me with any earth-shattering break in this case till Wednesday. I mean it."

"Which case? Faulks's or Hughes's?"

McLean was silent for a few seconds. "Or Slade's, for that matter."

"Only one man knew all three dead men."

"Spoken like Tyler Rhodes," McLean said.

They spent a few minutes talking about regular business, which McLean reported was causing no end of frustration for Retta. Evidently the guards were slacking off in Lombard's increasing absence from the office, reporting late and leaving their shifts early. McLean said the guards were beginning to treat Lombard's involvement in her private investigation work as an occasion for a holiday. Lombard told McLean to call a meeting of the guards for 5 o'clock the next day, regardless of what shifts they were working unless their shifts called for them to be on duty at 5, and to "chew their asses off." Announce loudly, she told McLean, that Retta now had hiring and firing power and Lombard would back up any decision she made in that regard, and to plan on more hell when she got back.

———

Lombard arrived at the Hartleys' farm before noon the next day. She drove along the circular driveway to the main house, which looked more like a plantation manor than a farmhouse. Clearly, Leonard Hartley was what people in these parts called a gentleman farmer.

This was no surprise visit. The Hartleys had been expecting Lombard since their phone conversation with her the previous evening, Jessamyn Frost having provided their number to Lombard and even having interceded on Lombard's behalf, telling the Hartleys that Lombard might be able to help locate their son. They had simultaneously answered the phone when Lombard called, each one anxiously rattling out details of their last contact with Ben Hartley, who apparently told them little about himself.

A housekeeper showed Lombard inside, and soon she was sitting with the Hartleys on a screened veranda with a glass of peach-strained iced tea and a very nice Hartley-Craft cigar, fresh-cut and plucked out of Leonard Hartley's personal humidor.

"I like a woman who appreciates fine tobacco," Leonard Hartley said, chuckling in the tense manner of a man trying to mask a terrible anxiety. His face was red and round with small features and tight skin that looked ready to pop at the slightest strain.

"Tell her about the humidor, Len," Matilda Hartley said thinly. Her expression was so pale and crestfallen that the sight of her, paired with her husband, gave away their overpowering despair. She didn't give him time to respond. "Len makes cigars with his partner Dewey Craft, who has a farm hereabouts. We don't sell 'em."

"It's a hobby," Mr. Hartley added nervously. "My whole crop goes out to the big guns. I just trifle with a few fancy plants."

Lombard coughed. "I haven't had one of these in a long time. I quit smoking cigarettes a while back, but I don't suppose this is cheating."

"A cigar's not like smoking at all, not if you do it right. Cigars are all about taste and texture." Mr. Hartley smiled. "Smooth, ain't it?"

"Yes sir," Lombard replied, suppressing a gag and setting the cigar in an ashtray. "Thank you very much. Now, I'd like to talk about your son."

"Be glad to. I'm curious why you're interested."

"I'm a private investigator on a case for a client that Ben may be able to help. He's sort of a witness."

"Is he in trouble?" Mrs. Hartley asked.

"No, nothing like that. I just think he might have some information." Lombard very much wanted to avoid the revelation of murder being at issue. The very word, in view of their son's vanishing, could tip them both into despondency. "I used to be a police detective, you know. It's all perfectly legitimate."

"Can we see some kind of identification?"

Lombard produced a card. "You can check with the licensing board," she added.

"We haven't seen him for two weeks," Mrs. Hartley said. "He left here two weeks ago today, and this is Tuesday. We reported him missing last Friday. At first we didn't think much of it. Ben's business takes him all over. But he always calls, always. Never goes more than three days without letting us know where he is and he's okay. When we hadn't heard from him by the weekend, we got worried. We called Ms. Frost, and she said it was normal for him to be on the road like that, but he hadn't called in or anything after a week."

"Do you know a man named Tyler Rhodes?" Lombard asked.

The Hartleys looked imploringly at each other. "No," said Mrs. Hartley.

"Benny had a lot of friends," Mr. Hartley offered. "We didn't know most of them, on account of they're all over the state."

"Mr. Rhodes lives in Asheville," Lombard said. "My partner, Sam McLean, spoke to him a week ago, and Ben was in his office then."

Mrs. Hartley looked at once relieved and troubled. "Oh, Lord! Just last week! But surely he would have called us by then? What's gotten into him?" She glared at her husband. "Why hasn't he called us or come home? It's not like him!" She broke into tears, and Mr. Hartley patted her hand. "Who's this Rhodes?" she demanded.

"He's a lawyer in Asheville, very respectable."

"I wish we would have known that sooner," Mr. Hartley said. "I know you couldn't have known about our concern, Ms. Lombard. But if only we'd known a week ago that he was okay. Has anybody seen him since then?"

"No, I'm sorry to say. Have you spoken to anybody except the police and Ms. Frost about Ben's disappearance?"

"Just a few friends of the family," said Mr. Hartley. "People who would want to help us."

"Do you have an address book I can look at?"

"What for?" Mrs. Hartley snapped.

"I don't know what for. I sure would like a peek, though. You never know."

A few minutes later Mrs. Hartley produced the address book. You never know, indeed, Lombard thought the instant she turned to the D section of the address book and discovered a familiar name. "Drinnon, Mrs. A.C."

Lombard had always regarded casework as a puzzle, and most of the time—once she had located all the missing pieces—fitting them together had been simple. The trick then had been in finding them, but in the case at hand the discovery of each successive clue made the puzzle more confounding. No sooner had she begun to consider Wiley Faulks's possible role in Jay Hughes's death than she discovered a link between the missing gay rights activist Ben Hartley and the Drinnons. They were benefactors and allies of the AFFC and Ross McKenna's agenda to discredit all that Piedmont Pride stood for. Slade had died in their house. And they were friends of the Hartleys!

She turned it over in her mind all the way back to Asheville. It couldn't be a coincidence. The Hartleys had nodded when she pointed out the Drinnon address and asked, just out of curiosity, mind you, if they were well acquainted with such a famous North Carolina family. They had seemed pleased to inform her that Della Drinnon, wife of the late A.C., was a friend of all tobacco families and had been a guest in their house many times. Had she known their son? They doubted it, noting their son's lifestyle and professional associations had been something of an embarrassment to them, though they had never turned him out of their home and had always striven to maintain a loving relationship with him. "He's our son, and we love him no matter what," Mrs. Hartley had said in a trembling voice.

She got back to Asheville late. She had planned on driving over to McLean's house and telling him the news—so she could pick up her car and turn in the rental—but she remembered that he had taken her up on her invitation to take a night off with his wife. So she went home and poured a drink. She had to go into the office the next day and straighten out the guards, so she would just make it one or two stiff ones, and lights out. Then she checked her answering machine messages, and was soothed by Hunter Lyle's voice, asking her to call her at the TV station the minute she got in.

They didn't say much to each other when Lyle arrived later. They more or less melted into each other and kissed in a sensual slow-dance to the bedroom. Lombard let go of days' worth of frustration with her lover, though Lombard knew it wasn't love igniting every nerve ending in their bodies. By the time they loosened their embrace, Lombard lay quietly in the sudden, troubling realization that she was falling for Hunter Lyle.

Lyle lay on her side facing Lombard. A lock of red hair tumbled across her face as she reached out to rub Lombard's shoulder. "Are you tired?" she asked.

Lombard closed her eyes and feigned a snore.

"That sounds familiar," Lyle said, giggling.

Lombard's eyes opened wide and she swatted Lyle's backside. "I don't snore."

"Yes, you do," Lyle said beguilingly. "I had to turn you over twice when I was here last. But it's sweet. Not big and loud like a man's. A little wheezing sound."

"What do you know about men's snores?"

Lyle gave a sly look. "A lot."

"I knew it. I had you marked as a switch-hitter."

"That's an ugly word. Don't call me that."

"I don't mean it ugly. I'm teasing. I don't even care."

Lyle turned on her back and looked up at the ceiling. "I've mainly been with men. Just a few women. What do you think about that?"

Lombard pretended to be trying to sleep. "I don't think about it. It's your business."

"Does it bother you?"

"I said I don't care. Drop it."

Lyle rolled over toward Lombard again. "Have you ever been with a man?"

"No," said Lombard. "I'm a virgin." They both laughed.

"Never even thought about it?"

143

Lombard yawned. "No. Well, I've leered at a few of them nineteen-or twenty-year-old pretty boys, thinking at first they were girls."

"Jay Hughes was a pretty boy."

"Yeah." Lombard closed her eyes and drifted off.

"Retta told me you were in Raleigh all weekend. Are you about to close the case?" Lyle nudged Lombard.

"Huh?" Lombard snapped awake. "What'd you say?"

"I said are you about to close the case?"

"I don't know. Why?" Lombard looked alarmed.

"Well, you were gone for days. Must have been something going on."

"Honey, it's almost 4 in the morning. I have to get up at 7, well, 8 at the latest. If you want to talk about the case, fine. Come by the office tomorrow afternoon." Lombard turned off the bed-side lamp, and in a few seconds a whisper of a snore passed through her parted lips.

The moon hung low outside the window and bathed their bed in a bluish light. Lyle lay still for a few minutes and carefully slid out from under the sheet. She stepped lightly toward the bath-room, but on the way, she nearly tripped over Lombard's brief-case, leaning against an unpacked suitcase. She eyed Lombard, who lay still and serene, overcome by heavy sleep. Lyle carefully picked up the briefcase, tensing her shoulders in a breathless effort to stay perfectly quiet. She checked Lombard once more and tip-toed gingerly to the bathroom, briefcase in tow.

9

McLean informed Lombard that Room 204 of the Rosemond Inn had, on the night of Jay Hughes's murder, been reserved in the name of one Leonard Hartsell.

"Where is Room 204 in the house?" Lombard asked with keen interest.

"Room 204 is situated directly beneath the room where Jay Hughes died."

Lombard frowned. "So Ben Hartley signed in under his daddy's name, barely modified. Hartsell instead of Hartley. How stupid. What a transparent little effort. Why would he make it so easy?"

Retta bellowed from her desk that Mike Church had just arrived for his appointment with McLean. Lombard muttered something about getting an intercom installed in the phone lines. "Too much screaming around here. It's fraying my nerves," she said. "What's Church doing here?"

McLean yelled, "Come on back, Mike!"

"Why did you ask him here?" Lombard hissed.

"He's given me a slew of police reports, saved me a lot of time chasing papers. I told him to come over and we'd get a bite to eat. By the way, he's working on the sly for Sig Mashburn, for extra money. Now, be nice."

Lombard didn't trust Mike Church. She supposed it made sense that he'd snatch up an extra job working for Mashburn—she had worked second jobs when she had had to rely on a police officer's salary—but working for a defense lawyer was taboo for a cop. She didn't care what they paid; it was unethical, especially since Church was working Wiley Faulks's murder investigation. How would IAD like that? Their own homicide inspector, working on the sly for a lawyer whose associations connected him to the victim. It made her wonder if Church was working undercover.

The three of them ordered lunch in and talked around the subject of Church's underhanded work for Mashburn. Then Church brought it up himself. "Loy, I suppose Sam's mentioned that I took a side job working the Slade case for Mashburn. Sig wants to be the one to solve it." He averted his eyes when Lombard glared at him. "From a cop angle, it's a closed case. The man killed himself, it's over, so there's no conflict."

"Is that what you told your chief?" Lombard asked.

Church shook his head. "I haven't told him. I can't. Look, I need the money. I have a son going to college in the fall, and he wants to play in the band. It's expensive, even these state schools… Ah, hell, you don't understand."

"It's awful close to Wiley's case, Mike. You know that," McLean said.

"No, I don't know that!" Church said defensively. "I haven't found one lead that would put me in conflict with any official police investigation."

"We have," Lombard said dryly.

"I don't want to hear it," Church sighed. He wiped his mouth with a napkin and rose to his feet. "I'd best be moving along."

"Sit down, Mike," Lombard said. "I know how it is. I would've had a hard time passing up a job offer like that back in Charlotte. Go on, sit. Your kid needs college money. I understand that."

Church sat down. "Okay. This is how it is. If you can show me how the two cases connect, I'm gonna have to quit on Sig." He looked dejectedly at Lombard.

Lombard instantly realized that Church was using her. He was angling for a scoop, as Mashburn's agent. "Never mind. You don't need to know."

"Are you sure? Loy, if this could get me in trouble, I need to know."

"No, you don't." She eyed him. "Of course, maybe you know something that could help me. Then maybe I could help you."

Church grinned.

"You catch my meaning?" Lombard smiled.

Church shook in silent laughter. "You flatter me, Loy. You really think I'm on to something, don't you? Well, I don't know shit. Sig don't either. He's hit a brick wall. So all he's had me doing is running down personal information for him."

"Like what?" McLean asked.

"Oh, he's got a thing for that Hunter Lyle. She's brushed him off every time he's made a play for her, so he had me do some digging to find out what her story is. Now we know why she avoids Sig. You know who her husband is?"

Lombard's face turned ashen.

"Oscar Kelley, that big-shot promoter, books all the concerts and music festivals all over the region. You've heard of OK Entertainment? Well, those are her husband's initials. They have a big old Victorian mansion in Weaverville, but he's never there."

Lombard said, "He must travel a lot."

"Oh, yeah. He's in Nashville and New York and L.A. all the time and leaves honey at home. No kids, though. She's hell-bent on her career, that one. I found out about this agent Oscar got her. He's been paid to groom Hunter for a job at one of the big networks." Church sighed heavily. "So that's what I got for Sig so far. Now he can sleep nights knowing it wasn't his lack of charm that failed to win her." He glanced at his watch, then at Lombard. "Of course, that doesn't help you, does it?"

"Nope," Lombard said.

Church stood up and said, "I'm late for work. My real job, that is. We'll get together soon, all right, Loy? What's wrong?" He looked down at his feet. "Thought my fly might be open. You look embarrassed or something."

"I'm just tired," she said distractedly. "See you later, Mike."

After Church had gone, McLean sat quietly for a moment and said, "Loy, I'm very sorry about that. Mike didn't know."

Lombard looked at McLean as though through a fog. "Huh?"

"I said I'm sorry."

Lombard said, "She didn't wear a ring."

———

It was late in the evening, and McLean had worried all day about Lombard. He knew she had it bad for Hunter Lyle. He saw it in her face when Church bragged about finding Lyle out. Lombard had left the office early without saying goodbye to anybody and hadn't answered the phone when he called her at home.

He had to check on her. He told Selena he was worried about Lombard, but he didn't say why. When he arrived, Lombard's house was dark but for the TV's blue glow flickering in the living room window. He knocked twice. "Loy. It's Sam. Can I come in?"

He heard a dull thud of a voice. "It's open."

"You should lock up at night," McLean said on entering.

She was lying on the sofa with her arms folded below her chest. She had on her flannel robe and was rubbing her bare feet together slowly. She turned her head and smiled savagely at McLean. "What are you doing here? Thought I hanged myself?"

She was smashed and sounded like it. A fifth of bourbon sat on the edge of the coffee table. "I may need to take a vacation day tomorrow. I'm exhausted."

"I know better than to think you hanged yourself, you smart-ass," McLean grinned. "I just thought maybe you could use some—I don't know—company."

Lombard motioned for him to sit. "Hunter was supposed to come by the office today. Did she come by? Call, or anything?"

"I don't think so."

"Figures. She said she would come by for an interview, but I gather she got the information she needed last night and saved herself a trip."

"What do you mean?"

"She came over last night. I wanted her to. I thought she wanted to see me." Lombard drank from the bottle. "You want a shot, Sam?" He shook his head, and she went on. "My satchel. That briefcase I carry. I had a bad feeling when Mike spilled the truth about her husband, so I checked my satchel. She had rifled through it after I fell asleep last night. She must have been in a hurry, and I guess she figured I was such an idiot I wouldn't recognize things out of place. You know how I keep that thing organized."

"Like a file cabinet."

"It was all out of order. She even folded and wrinkled papers shoving them back inside the satchel." McLean could see her eyes well up in the light of the TV. "She must have gotten what she wanted. She didn't give a damn whether I found out."

McLean said, "You told me right here in this room not a week ago that you thought she was manipulative and conceited. Come on, you knew that."

"I had this stupid hope I was wrong. I liked her. And I was made a fool of."

McLean sensed Lombard was struggling not to become emotional. He said, "It's late. I'm going home. I hope I didn't embarrass you, coming here like this."

"Don't worry about it." She took a drink. "I'll be just fine in no time. Don't look for me at work tomorrow, but don't check on me either. I need time alone."

———

He was back at her house before 9 A.M. He pounded on the door until it cracked open and he stood before Lombard's incensed glower. "I told you I need time alone. I'm barely alive," she said miserably, leaning against the doorjamb, holding both hands fast to her forehead as though her brains might spill out between her fingers if she loosened her grip. "Jesus," she breathed, swooning, "I think I'm still drunk."

"You're gonna have to sober up fast," McLean said. He grabbed her by the arms and shuttled her through the living room to the hallway and into the bathroom. He sat her down on the toilet seat and turned on the shower spigot, and held his hand under the hard spray until it was ice cold. "This shower will fix you right up. Get in while I make a pot of coffee."

"What the hell's got into you?" she snarled.

"Ross McKenna was on the line the minute I got into work. He wants you in Raleigh, and today. Says we're fired if you don't get moving."

"Who does that son of a bitch think he is?" She slumped over her knees.

"Just look at the shape you're in," McLean muttered, pulling her upright. "This'll straighten you out." He stood her up and shoved her into the shower, pajamas and all.

The frigid spray made Lombard gasp and hoot like a wild chimpanzee. "Get out of here!" she screamed. "This is private."

A quarter of an hour later she sat across from McLean at her kitchen table. She was wrapped in a dry terry-cloth robe whose collar she clutched with her left hand as she sipped coffee from her right. Her eyes were heavy and sullen, her wet hair sticking out in every direction. "I look like shit, don't I?" she asked.

"Yeah," McLean said. He glanced at his watch. "We'll have to stop by the house for me to pack some things."

"No point in your going," Lombard said. "I want you to stick by the office, keep after those guards. And find out what Sig and Mike are up to."

McLean shook his head. "I think you'll need backup on this trip."

"Why? McKenna just wants to see me, right?"

"Right, but I have a bad feeling. He sounds unstable."

"Unstable? He's a crazy son of a bitch, is what he is."

"All the more reason I should go with you."

Lombard slid her cup across the table. "Pour me some more coffee. Why the bad feeling?"

"He just didn't sound right. I didn't like his tone."

"In other words there's no danger, and no reason for more than one of us to waste a day kissing his ass. You stay here and keep an eye on Sig and Mike."

"They won't be in town," McLean said.

"Where will they be?"

"Oh," McLean shrugged. "Just gone for the weekend."

"Business or sport?"

"They say sport." He got up and poured her coffee.

"Sam, what's on your mind? You got that hangdog look."

"Well, it ain't nothing. It's dumb. Too dumb to mention, really."

"Sam, I'm getting my strength back. Don't make me swat you."

"Oh. Old Mike Church called me up this morning before I talked to McKenna. Asked me if I'd go on a weekend hunting trip with him and Sig."

Lombard narrowed her eyes and bellowed, "Aw! You want to go!"

"I don't know. They kind of get on my nerves."

"So what? You could get something out of this, for our case. You ought to go."

"Loy, here you are doing all the work, running back and forth to Raleigh. No." He shook his head rapidly. "I'm going with you. Or at least staying here where you can get a hold of me. Like I said, I'm worried about you making this trip."

"Stop treating me like an old lady. I want to go by myself. It'll keep me occupied. And sober too." She rubbed her forehead.

"You okay to drive?"

"Yeah. I'm down to about a .04 by now. You go on that trip. When are they heading out?"

"They want to set up camp tonight," he said with an air of indifference.

"Go. Consider it part of the job. It's important you stay close to those boys, more so than me chasing after McKenna."

"What if something comes up here in town? What about the guards?"

"Retta has everything under control. We ought to make her a partner."

"All they're gonna do is pump me for information," McLean said.

"So? You'll do the same to them, and get more for it. Sig's ego's so brittle he's got Mike chasing after women for him. He'll never catch on to us. You, on the other hand, can find out what he talked to Slade about. He's bound to have a transcript of that interview. I'm sure McKenna has it too, but for some curious reason he won't let us have it. You work on Sig, now. We can up our advantage by your going on this little jaunt."

———

Lombard checked into her usual motel in Raleigh—a dive called the Fairland Court that advertised adult cable—and waited for McKenna to call. She flipped the switch on her cell phone from vibrate to ring and set it on the bedside table. Her head still ached; despite several bottles of water consumed on the road, she was so dehydrated she hadn't needed to stop once for a pee and barely produced a trickle once she arrived in her room. She lay down on the bed for a nap. It was evening when her phone finally rang.

Their conversation was brief, McKenna telling her where to meet him and at what time. She noticed there was no fear in his voice; he had regained that ring of arrogance she recalled from their first meeting, that air of control. It wouldn't have bothered her much if it weren't for the fact that he didn't want to meet her at his home. He wanted her to meet him at the Drinnon house on Stonebridge Farm.

She showered and dressed, fidgeting as she got ready, as though to delay the meeting. For no reason she could pinpoint, she felt strongly ill at ease. She didn't know whether to blame her own intuition or McLean's. All of a sudden she wished McLean had accompanied her. She threw on a jacket to conceal the revolver strapped to her side. It was damp and windy outside anyway.

Dusk settled over the countryside as she drove through the gate to Stonebridge Farm, its name affixed in wrought-iron letters to a rail connecting two stone pillars. Lombard surmised the name itself was attributable to an old stone viaduct she had just crossed. The house was barely visible through old oaks rising snobbishly about the property, its several windows and gables dark save for the pale gold glimmer of three windows near the door.

Della Drinnon was not at home, Cora the housekeeper announced when Lombard introduced herself at the door. Mrs. Drinnon had left a few days earlier for her summer house in Maine. She explained that Mr. McKenna was a guest of the house for as long as he wished while Mrs. Drinnon was away. No one else was there except for Cora, who then excused herself for the night after she had led Lombard into a quiet study where McKenna was waiting.

The sight of him startled Lombard. His hair looked as if it hadn't been trimmed or brushed, and a rough beard had begun to sprout in random patches about his face. He was just as pale as last she had seen him, and thinner. His soft robe and pajamas hung loosely on him, and his body looked too small for the wing-back chair in which he sat with crossed legs and erect shoulders. His faint blue eyes had glacial severity, with no fear in them. McKenna now looked like a conceited mad man.

"How are you, Miss Lombard?" he said with his reptile smile.

"Very tired," she said, sitting down. "How are you?"

His brow rolled up over suddenly bulging eyes. "Oh, I'm very well. I feel so much better since our talk on Sunday. What a difference a few days can make."

She couldn't have said it better, she thought. She felt an unease that made her want to laugh in apprehension. "How's your family?" she asked uncertainly.

"They left me." He turned a cheek to her, staring out the corner of one wide eye. "It seems I make them nervous. At least, I make my wife nervous. It's for the best, though. They're safer without me around. So Della's been letting me stay here. Della's very patient, but on the other hand, she isn't here, so I suppose I can't be much of a test to her patience. And that's good, because I feel safe here. Well, as long as I stay away from ropes and no one goes around kicking chairs out from underneath my feet."

Lombard asked sternly, "Why did you call me back here?"

"Because you're looking for Ben Hartley and so am I."

"How did you know that?"

"Well, I am your employer, am I not? I should know about what you're doing. For all I knew you had quit the case and stowed my payments away. You should keep in better contact."

"I just saw you this past Sunday. Things happen fast. What do you know about Hartley?"

"When I arrived here, there were messages for Della from Leonard Hartley, to whom you spoke, correct? Good work, Miss Lombard. He wanted her to know that you had asked about his precious little faggot son's connection to the Drinnons. So that's how I found out. And I thought it would be a good idea to get you back here in a hurry and find the little faggot, because he's bound to know something about the whole sordid mess we're in."

"What mess?" Lombard asked flatly.

"Oh, we're in a pickle. A big mess of pickles."

"What does Hartley have to do with it?"

"First, you tell me why you want to find Benny Boy. Then I'll tell you why *I* want you to find him."

A few silent seconds passed, and Lombard said, "He evidently knew all of the deceased."

"All?"

"Hughes, Slade, and Wiley Faulks."

McKenna smiled exuberantly. "Very good, Miss Lombard. See? And you thought I was crazy. What do you think happened at the Rosemond Inn the night little Jay poof-boy got slashed to pieces? Of course, your first clue must have been the manner of death. Poof-boys like to slash. They use knives when they kill."

"That wasn't my first clue." Lombard began to explain why she believed a third party might have committed the murder. She described the possible break-in through the bathroom window. "The killer might have climbed that old elm but more likely came up from the balcony below the room where Hughes was killed. Ben Hartley seems to have rented the room below Slade's that same night."

"Well, there you have it."

"I'm close. The other thing that helps your theory is the missing weapon. If Slade used it and pitched it out the window, either the police or Sam would have found it. A bystander coming by and picking it up is a long shot, though anything could happen in the night. It was hours before daylight. Still, I think it would be in evidence by now."

"So you've established that Slade didn't kill anybody!" McKenna exulted.

"I wouldn't go that far. I think it's possible he didn't," Lombard said. "But I don't know anything for a fact yet."

McKenna rolled his eyes. "Well, what about Hartley? He knew all three dead men. And he lodged in the room below Jasper's."

"That bothers me. It also bothers me that Hartley has disappeared. Guilty men flee; they run and hide. I guess it's just possible that this case could turn out the way you want it to, McKenna, but don't think that pleases me one little bit."

"Aw, you feel bad about how things look. Think of how disappointed all those queers will be when you get to the bottom of this one. How untidy for gay rights." He squeaked, "Look, Toto, we're not victims anymore."

Lombard shouted, "What do you want, Ross? You can taunt me long-distance by phone, goddamn it. I'm tired of running back and forth just to hear you rant!"

"I want you to tell me when you find Hartley. I want to talk to him before you do. Grendel will be looking for him too, so watch out."

"Grendel?"

"Grendel Roper. You've met him."

"Yes, at Sig Mashburn's. What does he have to do with Hartley?"

"Mmm-hmm. He knows a lot about you, Miss Lombard. And about Mashburn and about Sam McLean...and let's see...yes, about one Miss Hunter Lyle too. Or is that Mrs. Oscar Kelley?"

Lombard got hot. "So you've been keeping me in your sights, is that it? Spied on and followed? Is that what you use Grendel for? I should have figured that out by now."

"Oh, don't be fretful. Nobody's followed you here. It's just you and me and Miss Cora, up in her neat little spinster's attic apartment. Grendel is nowhere near here, and that's just fine with me. Because, you see, I believe he wants to kill me."

Lombard stood up, mindful of the gun strapped to her side. "That's why you were so terrified when Wiley Faulks died. Grendel killed him."

"No, Ben Hartley killed him. Grendel was with you, at dinner at Sig's."

"Why did you hire me, McKenna? What am I helping you cover up?"

"You're not covering anything up. You're working to help clear Jasper's name and expose Ben Hartley and Wiley Faulks as partners in a vicious crime. You're doing a good job."

"Then why have me tailed? Who is this Grendel character?"

"Grendel is sort of like an operations manager. Don't take it personally. He makes sure I get what I pay for."

"So why does he want you dead?"

McKenna eyes filled with tears. "Because I no longer control the situation. He's taken it over, and he's very, very angry with me about something."

"Where is he?"

"Grendel? He's gone camping. Boy, is Sig in for it! Grendel's mad at him too."

Lombard thought of McLean. "Grendel told you that?"

"Yes. Then he said he's coming back here, to deal with me."

"Where's their camp?" Lombard demanded.

"You're good at finding people. Find out where Hartley is first, and I'll deal with him. Then you can find Grendel. You're on my payroll, don't forget."

"There isn't time. Tell me where Grendel has taken Sig."

"No. Now, be a good girl and do as you're told."

Lombard pulled the revolver from her jacket and pushed her free hand against McKenna's frail neck, shoving him back against his chair. She tightened her grip on his throat and held the gun to his head. "I quit," she said. "I've had it with your games, McKenna. But before I leave here, you're gonna tell me where Grendel is."

"You wouldn't dare shoot me," McKenna croaked.

"I've done it before," she reminded him, recalling his review of her IAD dossier. "That suspect back in Charlotte raised his weapon on me, and look what happened. Got the carotid artery. Messy."

"Yet you felt remorse about it. You've got a conscience…"

"I didn't know him. I know you. And I don't like you."

He broke into a sweat. "I don't know exactly where the camp is. Some forest near the Tennessee border, west of Asheville."

"That's got to be the Pisgah Forest. Which part?"

"I swear to God I don't know. He didn't say. He never tells me specifics, and he always threatens me when I ask. It's how I know he wants me dead."

"What's the real reason he wants you dead? I'm not buying this control shit. He's got it in for you some other how. He's got some connection to Ben Hartley, hasn't he? That's why you want me to find Ben first. Come on, tell me."

"I don't want to die, but I'll take a bullet in the brain before I tell you that."

Lombard pressed the muzzle of the gun against his temple. "This weapon here operates kind of like a polygraph. You know what a polygraph is, McKenna?"

"A lie detector?"

"That's right. When somebody tells me the truth, I relax. When they lie, I get nervous, and this thing has a hair trigger. Don't make me start shaking."

"I can't tell you what you want to know."

She twisted the muzzle against his scalp. "Talk, McKenna. When did you last speak to Grendel?"

"Yesterday."

"Good boy. Now, have you spoken directly with Ben Hartley?"

"Not since before…" He closed his mouth tight.

She pressed her thumb into his Adam's apple. "I don't know whether to choke you to death or just blow your goddamn brains out. Not since before when?"

"Since before Jay Hughes's murder."

"Grendel and Ben Hartley! They killed him together, didn't they?"

"Please let go of my throat," he gagged. She relaxed her grip, and he took a deep breath and said, "You might as well shoot me. I'm not telling you any more."

Lombard dragged McKenna out of his chair and pushed him facedown onto the floor. Holding the gun to the back of his neck, she pulled the silk sash from his robe and ordered him to hold his hands together behind his back. She bound his wrists in a tight knot. He huffed, "I'm surprised you aren't cuffing me, what with all those other cop shenanigans. Ow! That's very tight."

"It's an anchor hitch. Cuffs are easier to wiggle out of than this knot. Just tell old Cora she'll need a razor to undo this tangle, and mind the veins." She bolted for the door.

"You didn't quit, Loy Lombard!" he shouted. "You're fired!"

10

MASHBURN GAVE A GREAT SIGH AS HE REACHED THE climax of his story. "So anyway. The Indian guide moored that rickety old boat in this lagoon about twenty miles upstream of where we'd last camped. I don't think I could point it out on a map, I just know it was some godforsaken Amazon pit of hell hundreds of miles from civilization, if you take Brazil for civilization. I was weak and hungry, and the biggest, meanest insects you've ever seen taking chunks out of me, and I mean constantly." He pointed to his chest, his back, his crotch, and his rear end. "I was plum eat *up*. And the sun beat down mercilessly upon us, and the air was so thick and humid you could drown from breathing. And the noise, my God, the sounds of the jungle were deafening. Animals and insects of every species hollering all at once. I begged the Indian to take me in for a bath, but he said the water in those parts was full of these little maggot-like things that swim up in your butt hole and suck your blood, and—"

"Damn, Sig," Church muttered. "We don't want to hear that." The men were leaning against their bedrolls around a campfire, drinking beer and trying to one-up each other with tales of wilderness survival. McLean had begun with a story about being snowed in at Mount LeConte, in the Tennessee Smokies, during the great blizzard of 1993. It had been his one brush with the tyranny of nature. Church had followed up with a tale about his close call with an alligator in the Everglades.

By his own account, Mashburn had been on safaris, had hiked

in the Himalayas, had proved himself a worthy outdoorsman in points all over the globe. But he knew Grendel Roper, a Vietnam veteran, would be hard to beat. So he droned on and on about his agonizing three-week journey up the Amazon Basin with a group of ornithologists. "I'm sorry to disgust you, Mike, but it's a true story. You don't just *not drink* the water down there, you can't even get *in* the fucking water without something trying to kill you. I don't see how the Indians could survive all that and not be fit to whoop the conquistadors."

It was Roper's turn. He seemed not to be listening, and he gazed pensively into the fire, whose crackling and popping echoed in the night air as the men grew silent. An owl warned the forest of its impending hunt, and Roper looked up at the tree-tops. He set his unfinished bottle of beer next to the fire and picked up his sleeping bag.

"What about you, Gren?" Mashburn cajoled. "I bet you've got some tall tales."

"I do at that," Roper said softly. "Morning comes early, though." He picked up his bedroll and walked off to a spot sever-al yards away from the others.

"He's an odd one," Church said quietly when Roper was out of earshot. "No personality."

"He's taciturn," Mashburn said.

"What does that mean?"

"He doesn't talk much. He's a loner."

"He's a wet blanket, if you ask me," said Church. "Takes all the fun out of the outdoors. He didn't drink two beers. Even Sam over here is on his fourth."

"Well, he might be a wet blanket, but this spot was his idea, and it's fine hunting."

"With him asleep," McLean said in a low voice, "it's easier to talk shop."

"Who wants to talk shop?" Church frowned. "I'm here to relax."

"It's always a good time to talk shop," Mashburn said.

"Mike, that arson case you've been working, who did the paperwork on that stolen SUV?" McLean asked.

"I don't recall. Some cop."

"But you didn't follow up on it?"

"No. The arson inspectors would have that detail."

McLean opted not to embarrass him by revealing what he had found in his own investigation. It hadn't been much more than a week since the fire; but Church should have interviewed the SUV owner, whether the arson inspectors had done so or not. He must really be burned out, McLean thought. "Sig, Hot Springs isn't far from here, is it?"

"Just a few miles north."

"Is there good fishing around here?"

"There's fishing just a couple miles from here, down along the French Broad."

McLean took a swig from his bottle. "So what's the hunting like around here?"

Mashburn grinned, "We aren't supposed to be hunting here period, so keep your head low. It was Grendel's idea. He knows these woods backward and forward. Don't ask why. I couldn't tell you. Anyway, he knows where we can find game where the rangers won't be snooping around."

McLean asked, "Is Grendel Roper still working for McKenna?"

Mashburn gave McLean a suspicious look. "I don't know. Are you?"

McLean smiled and leaned back on his bedroll.

"I don't know what Grendel's deal is lately," Mashburn said. "I hadn't talked to him since y'all were at my house for supper, then he called about this hunting trip. So, Sammy old boy, you're barking up the wrong info tree. Have you another beer and loosen up. This ain't work."

———

The instant she hit the interstate, Lombard phoned Retta, rousting the weary woman out of her sleep to find out what she knew of McLean's whereabouts. "How should I know?" Retta said. "All he told me was he was going camping, when he ought to be helping you get this aggravating case solved so I can have some help around the office."

"You mean to tell me he didn't let you know where you could find him?"

"No, and for that matter, neither did you." Retta sounded resentful.

"Well, I need to find him."

"Why don't you call Selena? Surely he told his wife where he was going."

"You call her. Never mind why I won't. Listen, Retta, it's important that you don't let on like there's anything wrong. Act like I'm calling him back to Raleigh on some big lead. I don't want Selena all sick with worry. She's got bad nerves as it is."

"There ain't anything wrong, is there?"

"There might be. Retta, I think Sam's in danger."

Retta's tone softened. "What if Selena doesn't know where he is?"

"Then call up all the guards. See if Sam let any of them in on where he was going. But I think Selena will know. She always knows where and what Sam is up to."

"So what if she tells me where he is? What then?"

"Leave me a message with the night dispatcher. I'm on my way back now."

"To the office?"

"Yes. Maybe Sam wrote down where he was going. I'll look around his office."

Lombard sailed at ninety miles per hour along I-40, pitch-dark and desolate in the small hours. She had run-ins with two highway patrol cruisers. The first trooper threatened to arrest her for reckless driving but gave her a speeding ticket when she told him she was a former cop; the second let her go with a warning. She screeched to a halt in front of the office door past midnight.

She found Jeb, the night dispatcher, at his post, typing a new detective story. "Did Retta call you?" she asked.

"Yep. She told me Sam had gone on a hunting trip with Sig Mashburn and Mike Church." Jeb didn't stop typing while he spoke to Lombard. "I know Mike Church, from back when I was in law enforcement. He's an asshole."

"I know that. Did she say where they went? That's what I asked her to find out."

"Pisgah."

Lombard bobbed her head impatiently. "Which part of Pisgah? It's a forest, Jeb. A great big enormous forest."

"Sam evidently didn't know which trail they were going to, only that they were going to visit a nearby sporting goods store called Delaney's." Jeb looked at Lombard. "I already checked on it. The Internet, you know. Delaney's is near a campground called Mosier Creek. There's a ranger station nearby."

"Good work, Jeb," Lombard said gratefully. "I need all the help I can get."

"Evidently," he said.

Lombard glared at Jeb, who had a way of casting light barbs that didn't quite get past her. "I'm gonna look around Sam's desk just in case he wrote down the specific location somewhere," she said. She walked into McLean's office and began rifling through papers on his desk and in the drawers.

"I certainly hope they're not hunting," Jeb called out. "It's off season."

"I didn't think about that," Lombard snapped loudly.

"Why should you?" he sang back.

Finding nothing, she stomped back into the lobby. "Because I suggested that he go with them. I should have known better."

"Oh, that's right," Jeb said, looking at his manuscript. "Retta told me it was your idea." He pulled a sheet of paper out of a tray on his desk. "I printed out a little map here." Jeb also had a way of spelling things out for her that suggested low confidence in her ability to grasp basic concepts of police work. "I've color-coded it with highlight ink so you know the difference between the state highways and the county routes."

She snatched the map from his hands. "Thanks, Jeb. Nice work."

"One more thing Retta told me," Jeb added.

Lombard was pouring a mug full of coffee. "What is it, Jeb?"

"Selena wants to go with you."

"Why?"

"Apparently, when Retta called her at an ungodly hour with the urgent request to know Sam's whereabouts and news of your dire need of said knowledge, Selena got the funny feeling something was awry. Retta tried to head her off, but Selena kept on her, and, push coming to shove, Retta will be safeguarding Sam's offspring while you escort Selena to the wilds of the Pisgah forest."

———

Lombard hoped the company would at least keep her awake. She drove to the McLean residence and found Selena waiting on the front porch steps. She was wearing sweatpants, a T-shirt, and sneakers. Her long black hair hung in a thick braid over her shoulder. She picked up a very large paper shopping bag and brought it to the car, placing it in the backseat. She sat down next to the bag behind Lombard and fastened her seat belt.

So this was how it would be, Lombard thought as she put the gear in reverse and backed out onto the street. She spotted a thermos sticking up out of the shopping bag and said, "I'm tired, Selena. I hope you won't mind sharing some of that coffee."

"Fine," Selena snipped, "though I brought it for when we find Sam."

"Well, we're not gonna find him if I fall asleep at the wheel and drive this car into a guardrail."

Selena carefully turned the thermos lid and poured coffee into a Styrofoam cup she pulled from the shopping bag. She handed the cup to Lombard and asked, "What's happened, Loy? Why are we looking for Sam?"

"I just need Sam to come with me to Raleigh. I—"

Selena blew out in disgust. "Please don't lie to me. I'm not stupid. What's happened to Sam? Is he missing? Retta wouldn't give me a straight answer."

"He's not missing. He shouldn't have gone on this trip, but he's not missing."

"Then why did you let him? He said you wanted him to go."

Lombard, who already blamed herself for the peril in which McLean now found himself, decided to come clean. She said, "Okay, Selena. I'm going to tell you everything about what Sam and I have been doing for the past month. You've taken enough shit off of this case, so it's only fair that you know what it's all about. Anyway, it will help me stay awake."

By the time they reached the Pisgah forest just before dawn, Selena was fully informed about everything Lombard knew or suspected about the deaths of Jay Hughes, Jasper Slade, and Wiley

Faulks. She knew that Ben Hartley was missing, that Tyler Rhodes was afraid of him for reasons he would not or could not disclose, and that Hartley's family was connected to the Drinnon family, close allies of Jasper Slade and the AFFC. She even knew that Ross McKenna's employment of Lombard and McLean had effectively ended the night before, when Lombard had threatened him at gunpoint. Even her husband was not yet aware of that.

"God, I'm tired," Lombard said as they pulled into a parking lot near the Mosier Creek picnic grounds. She stepped out into the early morning mist and felt refreshed by the brisk damp air and burgeoning light of the morning sky.

"You drank half the thermos," Selena said. "You should be wide awake."

Lombard pulled a folded piece of paper from her hip pocket. "According to this map Jeb printed off the Internet, there's supposed to be a ranger outpost up the trail about a quarter of a mile."

"What are all those colors?"

"Jeb thinks I'm an idiot," Lombard explained. "The brown highlight is the trail. He used a blue marker to color in the creek. This orange circle up here, with stars and exclamation marks drawn around it, is the outpost."

"Jeb did that?"

"Yes. He's an arrogant little shit, but he's efficient and smart."

They started up the trail together. "Let me carry that bag for you," Lombard said.

"It's not heavy. I can manage it," Selena huffed.

"Honey, you're barely five feet tall. The bottom of it is dragging the ground. Pretty soon it's gonna tear open. Hand it here."

Selena frowned and handed Lombard the bag. "Don't drop it," she warned.

Once at the outpost, they met two park rangers, a man and a woman. They listened intently as Lombard introduced herself and explained that she had reason to believe her partner and two other men were in danger, and that one of the men in his camping party was a suspect in a crime.

The man, who introduced himself as Josh Silvey, asked, "So you're a cop?"

"I'm a private investigator. I used to be a police detective."

"Your friends didn't check in here," said the woman. "We prefer it when back country campers check in. They rarely do, but it helps us avoid situations like this. We don't even know what trail they started on."

Lombard shook her head. "I don't know either."

"There's one way of pinpointing where they might possibly be," Silvey said in a dubious tone. "That is, if they happen to be hunting out of season."

Lombard pursed her lips and averted her eyes. "Sam isn't hunting," she said. "I can't speak for the others."

"That's right!" Selena said. "I'm his wife, and I know Sam doesn't hunt. He never has, and he knows I don't like it. It's cruel."

The woman ranger said, "It's not hunting this time of year. It's called poaching." She eyed Silvey. "They're probably up at Six Mile Ridge or in that vicinity."

"Hunters think we haven't figured out that's where they hide off season," Silvey explained. "It's not exactly beyond our reach. It's just a pain in the ass to chase them back in there. We're understaffed, as you can see. But I'll go look for them." He stood up and snatched a set of keys off a hook on the wall. "I bet I know exactly where they are."

"How far is that ridge?" Lombard asked.

"It's actually not close," he said in a faintly resentful tone. "I'll have to go back down to the creek, grab my jeep, drive around the loop to Gordon's Bend trailhead, hike four miles up to Six Mile Ridge, and hope they haven't ventured too deep in the woods beyond that. If they left late yesterday, they couldn't have gone very far to set up camp."

"Sounds like a cinch," Lombard said.

"It won't be if they have another day to traverse the area around the ridge. They'll be needles in a haystack." Silvey motioned Lombard to stay seated when she started to get up. "You stay here. I don't hike with women. Nothing personal, just a policy I have. Ask her," he added, pointing to his partner.

"He got accused of sexually inappropriate behavior with a female hiker," the woman ranger said. "It was bullshit, but you can't be too safe with these new laws."

———

"Wake up, boy."

McLean ignored the voice and rolled over in his sleeping bag. He was half awake and feeling amorous. The voice annoyed him.

"Come on, Sam. They took off without us."

McLean cuddled up to his pillow and gave it a little kiss. "Mmm. Selena. Come on, sugar. The kids are still asleep," he murmured.

"What the hell are you doing? Get up before you rip the pillowcase off and try to make love to your sleeping bag."

"Huh?" McLean awoke abruptly. Mike Church was sitting a few feet away with a cigarette and a cup of coffee. "What time is it?" McLean asked groggily.

"Eight. You gonna sleep all day?"

"Where is everybody?" McLean sat up and rubbed his eyes.

"I said they took off without us. Must have been before dawn. I woke up and Sig and Grendel were both gone." Church shook his head and looked off into the woods.

"What did they do that for?"

Church rolled his shoulders. "I don't know. We're in the way, I guess."

"In the way of what?"

A distant blast of gunfire could be heard echoing off the ridge. Church set his jaw and stood up. McLean asked quietly, "You figure they got a deer?"

"I hope so."

"Mike, what's going on here? You didn't come here to hunt, did you?"

"No. I don't hunt. They know that. Sig just brought me along for the ride."

"I think you asked me out here as backup, and you're here to protect Sig."

Church said, "I'm here to conduct an investigation, Sam." He tossed his cigarette on the ground, then raised his coffee mug to his lips and stared out into the wilderness. "I'm gonna let you in on a secret, as a last resort. The fact is, I'm working right now, as we sit here, without authorization. My chief would bust my ass if he knew what I was up to. I'm working for Sig Mashburn on the sly, only Sig doesn't realize it's because of his connection to Jasper Slade. I gave up on the Hughes case when Slade died, but Wiley Faulks's death made me wonder. I don't have anything concrete to give my chief, but I have a hunch Sig knows something. I can tell that you share that feeling. Loy too."

"What do you want from me?"

"Your help. There's no obvious connection between Hughes's and Faulks's deaths to justify an official reopening of Hughes's case. When Slade died, everybody at work, me included, breathed a sigh of relief and brushed that nasty investigation off the table. Nobody at headquarters would understand why I want to keep my eye on Sig. There's no tangible connection between him and Faulks. I just have a hunch."

"Surely you haven't decided Slade is innocent," McLean said.

"Of course I think he did it. But the cases are pretty close, don't you think?"

"Oh, sure. Yeah. I don't suppose Sig has told you much of anything."

"Sigmund Mashburn only talks about Sigmund Mashburn. For him, Jasper Slade, the case of a lifetime, has become an obsession, and he's not letting a little thing like his client's death put an end to it. There's still publicity to be milked out of it, spots on CNN and the like. He talks like he believes he's really on a crusade to find out the truth behind what happened." Church threw down his cigarette and looked in the direction of the gun blast they had just heard. "But all anybody gets out of his talk is a look at Mashburn. Meanwhile, Sig gets interviews in magazines, and pretty soon he's about to sign a book deal. He doesn't really give a shit what happened to Hughes or Slade. It's better for him the poor bastards died. That way at least he can brag about how he was going to win the case and speculate on why. That's why he likes to have Grendel Roper around. He thinks he can tap Roper for facts about Slade. He can't see that Roper is using *him*!"

"What makes you think Roper's using him?" McLean asked.

"Roper works for the AFFC. He's keeping tabs on Mashburn, whose inflated ego can't let him believe for one second that he's being tailed. You see, I believe Sig Mashburn really knows something about the Hughes murder, and when I saw Wiley Faulks's burned-up body, I got this cold feeling that a witness had just been disposed of. I think Roper is connected to it, but I can't think of how."

"I can," McLean offered. "I talked to the old boy that owned that stolen SUV parked outside the burned building. It was stolen from around here, while the owner was camping near the river."

"So?"

"So here we are. Roper knows these woods. He suggested the locale. A car stolen from here last week was used in the fire."

Church said, "Right. Sig said last week at that dinner party that Roper had been out camping the night before."

"Now tell me," McLean asked, "why do you think Sig knows more about the Hughes murder than he's telling?"

"Because he interviewed Slade. You know that."

"Well, if he says he wants you to help him work the Slade case, hasn't he shown you the dadgum transcript of that interview?"

"No. I don't think he has it. I think it's in Raleigh."

Another gun blast split the silence of the forest, and Church went for his holster. "They ain't found *two* deer this quick. I take it you brought a sidearm, Sam."

"Yeah, and Mike, I sure appreciate you warning me what I was getting myself into beforehand," McLean said angrily.

Church fastened his holster. "I didn't have time to explain, with Loy around that day, looking at me like I was a traitor."

"What makes you think you can trust us now?" McLean asked.

Church looked into the woods. "We'll never find them in there. Damn it, I wish Sig had woke us up before he left! My plan was to play sick and stay behind, and get the park rangers out here to bust them both for hunting out of season. That would at least keep Roper locked up long enough for questioning about the fire."

"And Ben Hartley's disappearance," McLean added. "It's never too late to call in the rangers. Let's head back down the trail. I spotted the outpost on the way up here."

———

"I'm Christine Campbell," the woman park ranger said. "Want some coffee?"

Lombard patted the thermos Selena had brought. "We got some. Thanks."

"That's for Sam," Selena snapped.

"Then I guess ranger coffee will do," Lombard said. Campbell poured a mug full and handed it to her. Lombard sipped apprehensively. "Not bad. Not terrible, anyway." She winked. "Just kidding. It's good. Much of this as I've been drinking lately, it's a wonder I don't pee black."

Campbell gave a startled laugh. "Nice," she said.

Lombard covered her mouth. "Good God, I don't know why I said that. I'm just so damn tired. I say things out of line when I lose sleep."

"Think nothing of it," Campbell smiled. "Drink up. You need it."

Lombard settled back in her chair and savored her coffee, as well as a look at Campbell's tanned, athletic body. She had on the typical ranger khaki shirt and shorts. She looked to be in her early thirties, lean and muscular, with curly sandy-blond hair pulled back in a ponytail, and freckles. Something about Campbell's demeanor made Lombard study her, out of curiosity. No sooner had Lombard begun to speculate on Campbell's likely sexual orientation than she got a glance from the ranger, quick and coquettish. Campbell blushed, a little smirk curling the corners of her lips.

"So you go by Christine?" Lombard asked.

"Chris. Well, my folks call me Christy. But I never liked it much. Sounds sissy."

"Where you from?"

"Cherokee."

"The town? Or the reservation?"

Campbell laughed. "The town. Surely you didn't take me for an Indian."

Selena whirled around. "What's wrong with Indians?"

"Nothing," Campbell said. "It's just...well, look at me. I'm pure Scotch, a real Appalachian girl. Wish I was part Indian."

"I'm three quarters Cherokee," Selena said boastfully.

"I didn't know that," Lombard smiled.

"My great-granddaddy was a chief. I'm very proud of my heritage."

Lombard narrowed her eyes and pointed at Selena. "That's why your kids are so cute. They got that dark look."

Selena beamed. "They do take after my side. Of course, they're sweet like Sam."

"He's a sweet one, all right," Lombard said.

Campbell stood up. "I have to make some rounds. Y'all help yourself to the coffeepot and whatever else you need. I'll be back in a few minutes."

Lombard and Selena sat in silence for a while, both of them staring out the broad window at the forest. "Do you think Sam's okay?" Selena asked.

"Yes," Lombard said.

Selena looked at Lombard, and it occurred to Lombard that Selena had never directly looked at her, never met her eyes until now. "Loy, I want to talk to you."

"About what?"

"I'm really a nice person."

"I know."

"No. You don't. I've never been nice to you."

Lombard averted her eyes and sipped coffee.

"I've never liked you much," Selena said. "Surely you've noticed that."

Despite her air of indifference, Lombard's feelings were hurt. She shrugged. "I gathered you weren't altogether comfortable with me."

"You must think me awfully ungrateful."

"What for?"

Selena's eyes welled up. "I know how you helped Sam in

Charlotte. You were a true friend to him. I think your loyalty saved him. For a while I was afraid he might break down, the pressure was so hard on him. He was humiliated; none of our friends would talk to us. He was a good man being made a scapegoat, and I thought it would kill him. You stood by him. I was grateful to you, but I was glad when you left."

"Why?"

"Because we owed you."

"Oh, come on, Selena. You did *not* owe me."

"Yes, we did, but not just on account of Charlotte. When you offered Sam the job in Asheville, we were desperate. He had to take it. But more than that, he wanted to. And that's when I realized that you two have a bond."

"Oh, hell, Selena—"

"I'm an Indian. I can spot these things. I knew it from the start, and I was so jealous. You're really special to him."

"Selena, I'm about to get mad. Now, there has never, and I mean *never,* been the slightest degree of any such kind of feeling as I think you're talking about—"

"I don't mean sexual. I mean spiritual, like real family, blood kin. I resented having to share him with you. I resented his dedication to you. But now I know I was wrong to be like that." Selena began weeping.

Lombard patted Selena's thigh, felt a little out of line, and then patted her back. "Cut it out. I mean, hush, sugar. You're just a nervous wreck."

"God's taking him away from me because I was jealous and unjust," Selena cried through choking sobs. "Loy, will you pray with me?"

Lombard drew a deep breath. "Sure. You lead."

Selena prayed emphatically to God for the safe deliverance of her husband from evil. Lombard listened quietly and threw in a silent Hail Mary, because you never know.

———————

Silvey had not been hiking toward Six Mile Ridge for very long before Church and McLean rounded a curve of the path several yards ahead. He stopped and waited for the two men to reach him, holding up his hand and waving at them as they descended the hill. "Park Service," Silvey said as they approached him. "Are you Church and McLean?"

"Yes," Church said. "How did you know?"

"A couple of worried ladies are waiting for you back at my station." Silvey radioed Campbell immediately with the news that two of the missing men were safe. Silvey began questioning McLean and Church about their roles in the hunting expedition, but both men vehemently denied any part in hunting. Silvey spent half an hour demanding every detail of their campout and scribbling notes on a notepad, while Church insisted they were both investigating a homicide and that it was just possible another one was taking place while he wasted time fooling with paperwork.

A guttural cry in the woods stopped their bickering. They were quiet for few seconds, and another cry followed, closer. "What was that?" Church wondered.

A third cry followed. McLean said, "Sounds like Sig, calling your name, Mike."

"Mike!" a booming voice clearly called out. "Sam!"

Mashburn appeared at the bend up the trail, carrying a rifle on his shoulders. When he spotted the men gathered at the foot of the hill, he shouted, "That goddamn son of a bitch tried to kill me! Where the hell were you?"

————

Roper was still on the loose, but everybody else was cramped in the rangers' outpost, where tempers were flaring. Mashburn was officially in custody for poaching, and he spared no lady present his obscenity-laden outrage, which he directed alternately at Church and Ranger Silvey. "You yellow-bellied traitor, Mike Church! Goddamn you to hell!" And to Silvey: "You prissy little tree-huggin' worm, you're gonna be sorry you fucked with Sig Mashburn. By the time I get done with your skinny ass they'll be calling this place Sig Mashburn State Park and you'll be wiping shit off the stalls down at Mosier Creek picnic grounds."

Silvey ignored the abuse and questioned Church and McLean about Grendel Roper. "I'll need a description."

"Description, my ass!" Mashburn thundered. "I've got a picture of the bloodthirsty bastard! I want him hunted down and shot on sight. You got that?"

"Where's the picture?"

"At my office. He's got a Web site on munitions and survival tactics. I downloaded his picture."

"Well, we can get that right now," Silvey said, rolling his swivel chair over to a desk, on top of which sat an outdated Mac monitor. "What's the Web address?"

Mashburn recalled the address and added, "I want government-issue black helicopters on his sorry ass by nightfall. And I want him dead."

"We'll certainly search for him, and when we find him we'll charge him with attempted murder, Mr. Mashburn."

"None of this state shit either. This is a national park. Get the feds on his ass."

Church asked, "Say he tried to shoot you, Sig?"

"Fuck you! Getting me arrested, you damn Judas. I ain't talking to you."

McLean spoke up from his seat on a small sofa, where Selena lay with her head in his lap, her long braid draped over his knees. "Tell us about it, Sig."

Mashburn scowled at McLean. "Grendel got me out yonder, and after a few minutes he stopped me dead in my tracks, like he spied something in the wood. He held his arm out, bidding me to stay quiet. I thought he'd spotted a buck, by the look in his eye. He wasn't ten feet ahead of me. Then he turns around, and if it hadn't been for the savage glint in his eye I'd be dead right now. It was that quick. But I spotted that look, and in an instant I fell to the ground, him turning on me and firing right at where my belly would have been. I stuck my rifle up and aimed for his face. I fired once, and he was gone. I tell you, I ran like hell out of those woods." Mashburn eyed McLean maliciously. "But you two yellow lizards were gone! And on top of that, you reported me for hunting off season." He jerked his head away and seethed.

Lombard was peering through a telescope while Ranger Campbell stood close behind her. "Just look at that," Lombard said. "Did you say that's a mile away? I can see that red bird like she's inches in front of me."

Campbell said, "Never a dull moment around here. What's really fun is when you catch a couple making out. They think they're isolated in the wilderness, and sometimes they really let themselves go." She grinned wickedly. "It's pretty cool."

"Now, this is what I call a fun job," Lombard said.

Campbell leaned in and whispered, "Female couples, seventy-five percent of the time. Swear to God."

Lombard's eyes widened. "Do you watch everything?"

"Oh, yeah," Campbell said enthusiastically. "It can be hysterically funny."

McLean whistled. "Hey, Loy. You ready?"

Lombard heard him but didn't answer. She withdrew a business card from her wallet and gave it to Christine Campbell. "It would be a big help to me if you would call and let me know what happens, whether Grendel Roper is found or not."

"Okay. Should Josh get a card too?"

"Naw, I don't want anything to do with that sexual harasser."

McLean tore Lombard away from Christine Campbell, and everyone but Mashburn was allowed to leave. Church sat at the wheel of Lombard's car. "We rode with Mashburn," he explained. "Hope you don't mind. You look like you could use a driver."

Lombard was nearly demented from exhaustion. "Thank God," she said, sliding into the passenger seat next to Church. The McLeans were in the rear. "Sam," she said, "Pretty soon every agency in the state will be on the lookout for Grendel Roper. We're going to have to go back to Raleigh, to meet with the police there, after I rest a little."

"Why don't you just call them?" Selena asked.

"Because Roper will be in Raleigh soon enough, and we have to be there."

"How in the world will he get there? He's lost in those woods, and there's all those police after him…"

"He's a survivalist," McLean said. "A militia type. The forest isn't much of a challenge for him. He's dead familiar with the landscape, if my facts serve me."

Lombard added, "He'll find his way out and head straight to Raleigh. He's got a reason to go there, and he isn't afraid of anybody. The authorities don't know what they're dealing with."

11

"WE NEED TO COLLECT OUR THOUGHTS BEFORE WE LEAVE,"
Lombard said. She was sitting on her living room sofa looking
refreshed. She had slept hard for a few hours, showered, and
dressed in pressed cotton pants and shirt. Her legs were crossed,
and her arms stretched out along the top of the sofa. She looked
at McLean, who was standing in the doorway ready to leave. "Sit
down," she said.

McLean sat. "We're losing time. Make it fast."

"I know Roper is working with Ben Hartley. I think we have
to assume that Ben is in danger. I have a hunch his association
with Grendel Roper is anything but voluntary. He may be a
hostage."

"How did they come into contact to start with?" McLean
asked.

"Roper works for McKenna. McKenna must have come
across Ben Hartley through Hartley's parents, who know Della
Drinnon very well. I now believe that Jasper Slade was innocent of murdering Jay Hughes. I think Roper did it, but I think
Hartley was involved. I'm certain Ben Hartley planted
Demerol in Wiley Faulks's house as part of McKenna's plot to
throw suspicion on Faulks. He knew an autopsy would show
Demerol in Hughes's body, and he counted on my finding it at
Wiley's. I think Ben Hartley most certainly set the fire that
killed Faulks, and that either he or Roper stole the SUV used to
block the fire door. I also suspect that Slade's death was not a
suicide and that the transcript or tape of Mashburn's interview

will explain why Slade was later killed and why Mashburn very nearly got killed. I hope it will explain why McKenna set this whole thing up."

McLean smiled crookedly. "Wait, Loy. Set what up?"

"Set up Ben Hartley to look like a murderer, with Ben Hartley's own help, and Wiley Faulks to look like a conspirator, and set us up to validate the clues he laid out."

She got up and picked up her suitcase. "Let's go. Two things, though. One, I think Roper has Hartley, but I think we should focus the attention of the police on finding Roper. It's the only way of getting to Hartley."

"And two?"

"I will not leave Raleigh this time until I have heard a tape or seen a transcript of Slade's interview with Sig Mashburn."

———

By nightfall Roper was the subject of a statewide manhunt. He had tried to kill Sigmund Mashburn, a prominent lawyer, and he was suspected in the arson murder of Wiley Faulks, according to the affidavit of Lt. Mike Church. Lombard and McLean briefed Church on their theory and asked him to follow them to Raleigh, where they met with Raleigh police. A search warrant for his residence was obtained, and Church agreed to accompany the authorities in the execution of it. Lombard and McLean were disqualified from assisting, owing to their status as mere private citizens, and would have to stay behind.

They had expected to be left out, but it stung, and their moods blackened. They walked doggedly to Lombard's car and sat quietly for a few moments before McLean spoke up. "Do you think they'll find Hartley?"

"I don't know. Depends on whether they find Roper," Lombard replied flatly.

"Where do you think Roper is?"

"Do I look like a psychic?" Lombard snapped.

"You don't have to be so blasted hateful."

"Well, how the hell should I know where he is? Why do I have to come up with all the answers? You've got a brain. Use it."

McLean opened his passenger-side door. "It's a damn good thing they left you behind. All you're good for is bitching and cussing. I've had it." He started out the door.

"Go on! I'm better off on my own. Run along and dig up some records now."

McLean glared hideously at her, got out and slammed the door, muttering something with the word "bitch" in it.

Lombard sat numbly for a few moments, watching him stomp off, her eyes wounded at first, then narrowing to wrathful black slits. When he disappeared into the police building, she scowled and pressed her foot to the gas pedal. "Fine. The hell with you and all you arrogant bastards. I'll solve this case by myself."

―――――

A narrow, bumpy gravel driveway twisted through thick, isolated woods for nearly a mile off the county route where Grendel Roper's mailbox stood. Treetops obscured the dim moonlight, darkness pouring over the officers' path like pitch as their vehicles crept slowly toward Roper's cabin. It was impossible to see a foot forward without headlights, though Lieutenant Church worried that if Roper was about, the lights would give fair warning.

Church didn't expect to find Roper, who surely wouldn't venture home when he was being hunted. What Church thought he might find was evidence that would connect Roper to the deaths of Jay Hughes and Wiley Faulks. A state police investigator named Captain Williams was driving Church to the cabin. "So this fella tried to kill a man and hiked clear out of the Pisgah forest and made it across the state in a day?" Williams asked.

"We think he's on his way back to Raleigh. He's pretty handy with stealing vehicles, I suspect. He got one easy enough a few days before he killed the last man."

"And you think he's got somebody hostage?"

"Yeah."

"How many you say he's killed?"

"Two, at least. He's got one alive, we think, and he's liable to kill a couple more before it's all over with, unless we catch him first. He's a mean son of a bitch."

Headlights illuminated a moss-covered cedar cabin, its dark front windows staring back at the officers like dead eyes. There were four patrol vehicles in all. Church got out of the lead car brandishing a flashlight.

Four men remained outside, securing all sides of the house, while Church and Williams approached the door. "It's locked, though it's easy to bust in, but be careful," Church warned Williams as he prepared to kick the door open. "I wouldn't put it past him to have a shotgun rigged to that door."

Williams said, "In that case, you do the honors." He stepped aside, and Church stepped up to the door. He stared at it for a few seconds, then peered in the windows on either side. He rubbed his jaw and studied the door again. "Hell with it," he mumbled, and in one movement threw all his force through the heel of his boot against the door, splinters flying as it cracked open and smacked against the wall inside.

Church rolled to one side, half anticipating a gun blast. Still black silence greeted the men after the last splinter fell on the threshold. Church stepped inside, readied his weapon, and flipped on a light switch. An enormous figure loomed from a corner of the front room, nearly stopping his heart. He gave a low gasp and nearly shot it before realizing it was a stuffed black bear.

The house was cluttered with dozens of bankers' boxes, crammed to capacity with file folders which in turn were stuffed with reams of papers. Some of the papers bore AFFC insignia, some NRA, others various survivalist and militia organizations. Most of them appeared to be the personal musings of Grendel Roper himself, each bearing the header "Memorandum: Private and Confidential."

"There's a mobile crime lab on the way," said Williams, "but we may need another van if we're going to haul off this load of boxes."

Church suggested looking at all the file folder headings for any reference to Ross McKenna or Jasper Slade. Within an hour of poring over box after box, three file folders bearing Slade's name had been pulled. None of them yielded anything useful. "Nothing but his goddamn stupid speeches," Church muttered. "A man like Roper usually keeps a journal, at least." He tore into another box. "There's got to be something."

"There's nobody and nothing here," said Williams. He told the other men to start loading the boxes into a waiting van.

After the boxes had been removed and everyone but Williams had left the house, Church sat down in a plaid-upholstered reclining chair and pulled out the footrest.

Williams came out of Grendel Roper's bedroom carrying a laptop computer. "This might have a journal in it," he said. He frowned at Church. "Hey, what are you doing? We're done. Let's get out of here."

"I'm staying behind," said Church.

"No, you're not. As soon as I get back, I'm gonna ask for a SWAT team to stake out this house till we catch him. So come on."

"That'll take too long," said Church. "I have a feeling Grendel Roper is on his way back here now."

"Of course he isn't," said Williams. "If he's been the least bit aware of the news, he knows he's a hunted man. Anyway, like I said, I'll have the area under surveillance."

Church laid his gun across his lap. "Roper thinks he can out-smart us. He told me he was once in law enforcement. If that's true, he'll know that his place has been searched by now, and he'll know he has a limited time frame to come back here and check on the damage. But he'll want to do just that, being the way he is. For all we know he's out in those woods right now, watching us with high-powered binoculars."

Williams sighed. "You sound paranoid. Listen, I'm the lead inves-tigator here, and I'm commanding you to get up and leave with me."

"Captain, somebody has to hold him if he shows up. Call in a backup unit to assist me right now, and I probably won't have any-thing to worry about." Church patted his gun and said, "I'll be fine."

A thin beam of early-morning sunlight trickled over a hilltop and splashed across Lombard's windshield. Her eyes rolled around under tightly shut lids, and she sat up abruptly and squinted at the quiet roadside where her car rested. A few hours before, she had stopped to call Jeb and ask if McLean had called the office. Then she had lain down across the front seat for a brief rest that turned into hours of sleep.

She pouted and thought how unjust all these swaggering, egotistical men were, not giving her credit where it was due. And McLean had a lot of nerve running off on her like that, come to think of it. He ought to be used to her moods by now. Why, if it weren't for her, where would he be? How dare he take off and leave her alone to cruise these dangerous roads, left out cold from what by all rights was *her* investigation, *her* case, while he groveled for attention back in the Raleigh state police headquarters?

That's where she was headed, by God, she thought as she started the ignition. She was going back to headquarters to reclaim her case. Those fools weren't going to find Grendel Roper at his *house*, where they had all headed after ditching her and McLean last night. If they were going to find him anywhere, it would be at Ross McKenna's throat.

In that instant it occurred to Lombard that headquarters was the last place she needed to be. Instead, she sped off deeper into the country. Of course, McKenna would by now be aware of the bounty on Roper's head and would be lying in dreadful wait at the Drinnon house at Stonebridge Farm.

Lombard wished for dark as she sped toward Stonebridge, and she got it. The sun disappeared behind a mass of black thunderclouds, and dull grays fell over the landscape. It was early morning, but it could have passed for dusk. As she approached Stonebridge, she thought of trying McLean on her cell phone but suspected her calls might be picked up on a scanner inside the Drinnon home. She pulled off the main driveway and parked her car behind some trees. As she made her way across the lawn on foot, there was rumbling overhead, and a cold wind gust rushed over the trees and nearly pushed her over. She had no coat or umbrella. She had on only the windbreaker that concealed her holster. It began to rain hard. Lombard was afraid of lightning, and the first flash nearly stopped her heart. She got away from the trees and loped across the lawn, rain beating against her body, nearly blinding her as it descended in draping cascades from low clouds. She thanked God the wind was on her back, and before she was out of breath, she had reached the north wing of the house.

"What am I doing?" she muttered to herself. She had no back-up. Nobody knew she was here. "Loy, you crazy fool," she mumbled. "What if there's more than two of them? What if Hartley really is in on it? Why didn't you think of that? What if that Drinnon lady is here too? What the hell were you thinking?" Wind howled around the corner of the house, and thunder crashed over the sky. Lombard was leaning against the wall in back of the house, nearly drowning in the downpour. She looked to her left, where steps led to a basement door.

Lombard had learned at a young age how to trip locks, back before Aunt Anna Mae had got hold of her. Even in grand houses like this one—or especially in these houses, it seemed—basement doors were unusually easy to manage. She got in and made her way through the basement to an air-duct vent. She leaned near it and listened for voices, to figure out how many were there and who they were.

She heard a familiar woman's voice, not Della Drinnon's. She strained her ears to make out the words, but they were interrupted by a man's voice. His voice was clear enough: Ross McKenna. The woman giggled, and Lombard instantly recognized Hunter Lyle's voice. "It's a fake laugh," she grumbled. "Don't fall for it."

She had been listening for nearly an hour before she decided that Lyle and McKenna must be alone. She had also picked up on their conversation and suspended her initial thought that Lyle was involved in McKenna's plot. It was apparent that Lyle had followed a lead to interview McKenna for her blasted coverage of the Slade case and had snatched that lead—and the hideaway at Stonebridge—right out of Lombard's briefcase.

Lombard was still damp. She reached inside her jacket, pulled her cell phone out of the inside pocket, and dialed Retta. When

Retta answered, Loy said, "It's me. Don't speak. Just answer yes or no. Have you heard from my partner?"

"Yes."

"Will he be calling back?"

"Yes. He's worried sick…"

"Shh. Just yes or no. When he calls back tell him I'm at the farm. Tell him I need him right away. Tell him to bring friends. Looks like a party. You got that?"

"Yes."

"Word for word?"

"You're at the farm. Bring friends right away. Looks like a party."

———

McKenna was sitting in the study where Lombard had held a gun to his head. He sipped coffee and smiled at Hunter Lyle. "Don't worry about dropping by unannounced. I do it all the time to other people. I am curious about how you found me."

Lyle was caught off guard, and looked it. "Well, I…I think it's common knowledge that you and Della Drinnon work closely together in the AFFC." McKenna stared at her in a way that demanded more information. "I just followed a few leads and surmised that you were here." She swallowed and felt like her throat was closing in. "Is Mrs. Drinnon home?"

"No. She's in Maine, I think. We're all alone. Even the housekeeper has the day off. Tell me, how do you plan to use the information I've given you about the AFFC?"

"Oh, well, as I said, I'm covering the story of Senator Slade's final days. I wanted a full perspective on the case, including the insights of members of the AFFC."

"I know. You told me. I just wonder if what I've said is helpful."

"Of course it is." Lyle smiled uncertainly. She had had no idea that coming here might be a mistake. She had hoped for some of McKenna's thoughts on the murder, but she had noticed early in the interview McKenna's deliberate avoidance of that topic. He had interrupted her the instant she suggested a future televised interview in such a way that she had felt ill at ease ever since. She wished she hadn't come alone.

"I wonder," McKenna began slowly, narrowing his eyes at her, "if you are still in cahoots with Miss Loy Lombard."

Lyle lost her smile. "Who?"

"Loy Lombard, PI. You slept with her. Surely you remember that."

Lyle began to tremble. "I, um, don't know where you got that."

"Well, I didn't get it from Loy."

Lyle cleared her throat. "I feel that this interview is…that I've wasted enough of your time." She stood up.

"Sit down, Miss Lyle. Or Mrs. Kelly. Or Mrs. Lombard. You tell me."

Lyle picked up her bag and backed away.

"I said sit down. You're not going anywhere."

She slowly went back to her seat and eyed him fearfully. "What's wrong?"

He stood up and withdrew a pistol from a desk drawer. "After what Loy did to me the last time we met, I learned to keep this old boy handy. Oh, I know Loy Lombard couldn't have sent you here. Loy Lesbo couldn't possibly send anyone she cares about in my direction." He grinned. "You're in a pickle, young lady. You should have asked your good gay friend about me before visiting. I'll bet you would have stayed home. The fact that you're here tells me you've pinched a lead or two out from under Superdyke's nose and that you probably know more than you need to know."

He was facing Lyle, his back to the doorway leading to the main hall. Suddenly Lyle spotted a shadow in the hall. She steeled herself for what might come next. "Are we alone?" she asked. "You said we were alone."

"Hmm?" He glared at her, then whirled around to the door. "Do you see a ghost?" He turned to face her again. "Get up. I think I know what's going on here." He walked behind her and held her fast around the waist with one arm while pressing the muzzle of the pistol to her temple. He whispered in her ear, "Walk forward, just like we're dancing in an odd way, my toes to your pretty heels." They approached the door. "Did somebody tail you? I mean, in the following sense of the word, dear."

"No," Lyle said sharply. "I thought somebody else was here. Why would I say anything if I were followed…"

Lombard stepped in front of them by about ten feet with her revolver raised. "Hunter, shut up."

"Oh, God," Lyle wailed. "I didn't know. I was afraid…"

"Shut up," Lombard repeated. "Drop the gun, McKenna."

"I'm afraid that's a negatory, Marshall Lombard. Tell you what, let's do it my way. You drop your weapon, and I won't blow Miss Kitty's brains out. Deal?"

Lombard stood firm, her revolver steady. Lyle eyed her imploringly and whimpered.

"Eek!" McKenna mimicked. "Eek! Did you hear that, Marshall? Miss Hunter's in distress. She's gonna be pushin' up daisies if'n ye don't drop it. What d'ya say, pardner?"

Lombard's eyes met Lyle's. "I'm thinking it over."

"Please, Loy," Lyle sobbed. "Do as he says. I'm sorry. I'm sorry, I swear it."

Lombard said, "I'll let it down slowly. If you don't follow just on the mark, I'll kill you."

"You're bluffing," he sneered. "Why not just kill me now?"

"Because I want something."

"What?"

"Slade's statement to Mashburn."

McKenna rolled his eyes. "Well, why didn't you just *say* so? I'll let you have a listen. Just drop the gun."

"No. You drop yours, and I'll holster mine. It's like this, Ross. I don't want to kill you. Like I said, I want to see the transcript or hear the tape. Roper is on his way. If you've watched the news, you know that by now. I'm probably all the hope you have against him."

"I don't trust you."

"You're gonna have to."

Minutes later Lombard stood next to the door of the study with her arms folded in front of her while McKenna unlocked a cabinet and pulled out a tape recorder. Lyle was handcuffed to a chair. "You okay, Hunter?" Lombard asked.

Lyle replied sullenly, "I can't believe you cuffed me like this."

"It was part of the deal. It beats the alternative."

McKenna brought the tape recorder to a desk and plugged it in. "I feel for you Miss Lyle, having such a vixen for a girlfriend. My own wife left me days ago and went only the Lord knows where with our children."

"Play the tape, Ross," Lombard said.

"Patience! My, my." He pushed play. The beginning of Mashburn's interview was routine, with Mashburn asking for details of Slade's whereabouts in the hours before the murder. Slade gave sluggish responses. He said he had come to Asheville to meet with Ben Hartley, who had been blackmailing him. He said Hartley had threatened to write more exposés portraying him as a homosexual unless Slade gave him money. Slade had meant to confront him and threaten a lawsuit or criminal prosecution if the lies didn't stop. He agreed to accompany Hartley to the Rosemond Inn, where they would agree on a final payment of $25,000 in exchange for an end to the blackmail. Hartley had said it was a neutral location, and they could meet in the privacy of one of the rooms. After following Hartley into one of the rooms, Slade lost all memory of what followed.

McKenna started to press the stop button. Lombard said, "Not so fast, Ross. It isn't over." McKenna scowled at her and stood back.

The tape recorder was silent for a few seconds, and Mashburn's voice resumed questioning. "You say you never met Jay Hughes at all that night, is that right, Senator?"

"No, no," Slade's voice moaned. "I never loved that boy like I loved A.C. Never, never." The tape stopped.

McKenna turned the recorder off. "He was sedated during that interview. That last bit was just talking out of his head. A.C. Drinnon had committed suicide years before, and I guess all that death got to Jasper's Demerol-dazed brain. He missed old A.C."

"Sounds like it," Lombard droned. "He did a pretty good job following your orders on what to say up to that bit about A.C. Drinnon."

McKenna pursed his lips. "That is ridiculous. He told the truth."

"No doubt by that point he thought it was the truth. How long had y'all been hammering him on what to say before Mashburn showed up to talk to him?"

McKenna looked contemptuously at her, but then his complexion waned. He looked over her shoulder with a terrified gaze. Lombard turned abruptly to where Grendel Roper stood behind her.

"Foul weather for a journey," Roper said softly. He held an assault rifle to his side. "I'll have to ask you to go yonder alongside Mr. McKenna, ma'am."

"I stopped by my house earlier," Roper said a few minutes later, after he had bound Lombard and McKenna and sat them on the floor next to the chair to which Lyle was still handcuffed. "I met up with Mr. Church. He's not too quick on the draw." Lombard's face turned scarlet, and she looked at Lyle, who averted her eyes. Roper held Lombard's weapon and examined it. "Heavy piece for a lady," he mused aloud. "Use it much?"

Lombard said nothing. She wondered if she was about to die. McKenna broke the silence. "Grendel, I wonder if I could ask a question."

Roper sat in a wingback chair and laid his rifle across his lap. "Shoot."

McKenna chuckled. "Good one. You are so very clever. I suppose the question of the hour is, do you plan to release me?"

"No, sir."

"Why not? I'm not a sodomite, as these two women are and as those others were. I'm one of the righteous. And I am your employer, I should remind you."

"I ain't killed anybody for being a sodomite. You know that, sir. And you know why you have to stay put. I do what's necessary. I bear no grudge against these two ladies. They're just in the wrong place at the wrong time."

"Well, that's a bit disingenuous, I must say," McKenna said. "You know good and well you've never trusted Loy Lombard."

"I thought it was a mistake to get her involved, yes, sir."

McKenna looked at Lombard. "You'll be flattered to hear that Grendel thought you were too smart to work the case. I said we needed somebody smart, the best." He turned to Roper. "Well, Grendel, you were right. She's so smart she came straight here, knowing you would show up, and now look at her."

"Quiet, sir," Roper said. "At least she don't talk so much."

Lombard followed their banter closely, hoping McKenna might spit out where Hartley was.

McKenna pleaded with Roper. "Why don't you just let me go? What are you going to do next? Answer me! I don't know what I've done wrong."

Roper glowered at McKenna. "You're weak. You should have been up front with me on what this was all about, sir. I wouldn't have signed on if I'd known. You deceived me."

"Don't go into that," McKenna interjected. "You don't want Loy Lombard to hear any of *that*. The thing is, you're mistaken, if I understand your meaning. Let me go, and kill them. I'll explain everything and pay you handsomely."

"I don't care about money, sir. That's all you think about, isn't it? I stand for a strong conservative nation, which is what I thought you stood for."

"I do! Shh!" McKenna implored, jerking his head in Lombard's direction.

Roper sat calmly with his rifle. "I believed in your story about Senator Slade. But the deeper I dug, the more I realized he was a sick man. Queer. You knew it too."

"Shh! Grendel, our *guests*."

"They won't live any longer than you will. Everybody here has to die." He looked at Lombard. "I'm sorry, ma'am. You shouldn't have been here. Senator Slade's secret must be forever sealed. You know too much."

Lombard broke her silence. "I don't expect mercy from you, Grendel Roper."

He set his rifle beside his chair and stood up. "It has to be quiet. Don't move, any of you, if you want a clean death. I can make it messy." He left the room.

"Oh, my God," McKenna whispered. "He's going to get the knife."

"The knife?" Lombard repeated.

"Yes, the knife! The one he used to kill Jay Hughes. It's in a safe in the library."

"So that's where it was," Lombard mumbled. She felt queasy

and fought to stay calm. She had always hoped that when the day came, she would die with dignity and without fear, but the idea of being stabbed to death or having her throat cut brought her close to panic. She took deep breaths to stop from shaking and looked out the window. She prayed silently for strength.

Lyle shrieked, "He's going to cut us up! He's going to cut us up! No!" She kicked furiously in her chair, screaming like a madwoman.

"Hunter, quiet!" Lombard yelled. "Keep your cool now of all times!"

Lyle gave out, as though spent of will. She wept quietly, whimpering alternately about God saving her and forgiving her. Suddenly Lombard noticed a figure appear in a window. The air outside was dark gray, and the window was fogged over and streaked in rain. The figure raised up a hand. Lombard wanted to believe it was McLean and hoped the room's light made it clear enough for him to see what was going on.

Roper reentered the room, the knife at his side. Lombard screamed, "He's going to kill us, Sam! Do it now!" Roper raised the knife and lunged at Lombard. In that instant, glass exploded in a blast of gunfire, Roper's chest blew open, and he crashed heavily down on the floor.

Hunter Lyle lurched furiously in her chains, screaming and writhing until she brought her chair down on top of her. The front door burst open, and McLean rushed inside, followed by a squadron of police. McLean bent over Roper's body. "Anybody else loose?" he asked.

"No!" McKenna said, then looked at Lombard. "I knew all along Sam would save us. I just threw in that bit about Grendel killing you to delay things. Peace?"

"Fuck you."

McLean pulled Lyle up off the floor. "Who cuffed her?"

"I did," Lombard said.

"What for?"

"Never mind. The key's on my key chain. Now turn me loose!"

Lyle was sobbing as McLean released her. "Who was scream-ing?" he asked.

"I was," Lyle sniffed.

"Well, it's a good thing. That's what got us scrambling over on this side of the house."

Ross McKenna was soon in custody for the kidnapping and felonious assault of Hunter Lyle and for questioning about his role in the deaths of Jay Hughes and Wiley Faulks. Lombard was talking to McLean outside the Drinnon house, which was sur-rounded by police cruisers and ambulances. "Roper said he shot Mike Church back at the cabin. You need to get people out there right away," Lombard said.

"We know," McLean said. "Mike's in the hospital, though with less of a shoulder. Police arrived not long after Roper left him for dead. He's lucky to be alive."

"They won't be able to hold McKenna," Lombard said. "He'll post bail before nightfall. He'll never talk now. We have to find Ben Hartley as soon as possible."

"Where's Mrs. Drinnon?"

"Maine." Lombard suddenly looked wide-eyed. "Or maybe not. Sam, if she's still alive and in the state of North Carolina, I bet we can find her within the hour."

They started for Lombard's silver Pathfinder, hidden in the woods near the front drive. Along the way, they passed Hunter Lyle, smoking a slender brown cigarette inside her black Jaguar with the driver's side door open. She threw down her cigarette, smiled at Lombard, and started to speak. Lombard pushed the door shut and kept walking.

12

LOMBARD AND MCLEAN WERE ON THE FARM OF LEONARD and Matilda Hartley just as the sky began to clear. Lombard knocked on the door to no avail. There were three other cars and a truck parked near the garage, including a white Lincoln with an old bumper sticker that read SLADE '92. Lombard pounded on the door again. She said, "If somebody doesn't open this door in the next sixty seconds, I'll open it any way I can."

"Maybe nobody's home," McLean said.

"There's a truck and three cars sitting there. What did they take? A tractor?"

"What if you're wrong? What if Della Drinnon isn't here?"

"I have a feeling she is. I don't see a woman like her leaving her estate in the hands of a lunatic in the middle of a scandal. And the Hartleys called for her at home just a few days ago, McKenna said. I think they'll at least know where she is." Lombard gave the door one last blow. "That's it. Sam, shoot it open."

"That a girl, Loy. Get us arrested for home invasion and shooting in an occupied dwelling. Remember, we're not the police anymore."

"Police!" Lombard screamed. "Open up! You have one minute."

"All right!" someone cried on the other side of the door. After a pop and a slide, the door opened slightly, and Mrs. Hartley stared at them silently through the crack.

Lombard said, "I want Della Drinnon. She's here, isn't she?"

"You're trespassing," Mrs. Hartley said wearily. "You're not the police."

"That's right. I'm trespassing. You should call the police. I'll wait here."

Mrs. Hartley looked puzzled. "Please go away. We don't want to involve the police."

Lombard looked past Mrs. Hartley. "Who's in there telling you what to say? You tell them I'm not going anywhere until I speak to Mrs. Drinnon."

Mrs. Hartley abruptly stepped back and tried to slam the door, but not before McLean rushed forward and blocked the doorjamb. The door caught his arm, and he cried out in pain. "Push, Loy!" he gasped. "God*damn* it, that hurts! A-a-ah! My shoulder!"

Lombard threw the weight of her body against the door, and the two of them stumbled into the foyer of the house. Mrs. Hartley ran toward the staircase, shouting, "Stay upstairs! Go back to bed, dear!"

A young man stood at the top of the stairs. Lombard asked, "Who are you?"

McLean, clutching his wounded shoulder, looked up and said, "Pleased to see you again. Loy, meet Ben Hartley."

The Hartleys, by now less like family than an assembly of broken spirits, sat in their living room and gave quiet, terse answers to Lombard's questions. McLean leaned back along a sofa, taking steady breaths to control the pain shooting through his shoulder. Only Ben Hartley remained utterly quiet, and seemed barely present in the room as he stared off into space. "What's wrong with him?" Lombard asked, pointing at him.

"He hasn't said a word since we got him home," Mrs. Hartley said.

"When was that?"

Leonard Hartley said, "Let me do the talking, Mattie." He asked Lombard, "How do I know we can trust you? How do I know you aren't part of all this? You work for McKenna, and Della says…" He stopped himself.

"Della says what?" Lombard asked. "Where is she?"

Leonard Hartley looked softly at his wife and said, "Mattie, go on upstairs and get her. It's all right." He turned back to Lombard when Mrs. Hartley was gone. "He came home the very night after you left, last Tuesday."

"I just missed him then, huh?"

"It was no coincidence. Frankly, Ms. Lombard, if it hadn't been for your nosy questions about our address book, he might not be here. Neither would Della."

Lombard glanced at Ben Hartley, who was suddenly looking at her. "You got something to say?" she asked, but he looked away.

Leonard Hartley went on. "Mattie and I called Della after you left."

"At her house? You spoke to her?"

"Yes."

"Ah. So she *was* at home on Tuesday. When did she come here?"

"Well, Ross McKenna is her guest lately, and he apparently picked up the phone when she did and overheard our conversation."

"So if McKenna claims you only left a message on an answering machine, he's lying, right?" Lombard asked.

"Yes, he is," said a woman standing in the doorway, and all eyes fell on Della Drinnon. "But first you have to hear me out and know this: I did not know what was going on right under my own nose. That shouldn't surprise anybody. Self-deception has been the constant of my life." She frowned at Lombard and McLean and sat down.

Lombard said, "Tell me why you left Stonebridge Farm, Mrs. Drinnon. And how and where you found Ben Hartley."

"Leonard has already explained how Ross eavesdropped on our conversation. Leonard told me on the phone that night that you had asked about Ben's disappearance, wanted to know how well acquainted I was with him and Mattie, and Ben. I was astonished when they told me Ben was missing. I didn't know anything about it. I assumed it had something to do with his association with that gay rights outfit he works for. I knew all about his writings about Jasper Slade. Figured he must be in trouble on account of all that evil he's mixed up with." Della glanced at the Hartleys. "Sorry to put it like that, but you all know how I feel." She turned back to Lombard. "Of course, I didn't say that to Leonard and Mattie at the time. Their dear son was missing, and my judgment would do them no good. I wished them the Lord's blessing and hung up.

"Then Ross came charging up to my room. I knew he'd been acting strangely of late, but I figured the pressure of Jasper's troubles, the suicide, and Mrs. McKenna leaving him had thrown him off a bit. I didn't realize how paranoid he was—how downright batty—until he confronted me about that phone call." Mrs. Drinnon stood up and went to a sideboard arrayed with several glasses and three liquor decanters. She poured herself a glass of what looked like scotch. "He told me I'd better pack my things and get out that night if I knew what was good for me. Get on to Maine, he said, though I had delayed my season there until all this hoopla died down." She sat down again and took a drink. "I told him I'd do no such thing. He told me he had listened to my talk with the Hartleys and was convinced we were all in cahoots to destroy him. We were part of Ben's 'plot.' He practically frothed at the mouth. I was so shocked I decided I'd get out that night and call the police. Then he told me that Grendel Roper was after us all, that Grendel would string me up like cut tobacco, just like he had done Ben Hartley."

Lombard was leaning forward with her elbows resting on her knees. "Did you have any idea where Ben was at that time?"

"No, at least not before Ross made that last remark. Grendel Roper had lived at Stonebridge and worked as a groundskeeper up until A.C.'s death. He became interested in the AFFC. I knew he had once been with the state police, so I thought he might be of use to us. Of course, at the time I didn't realize what I found out later, which is that he was fired from the state police for excessive force and brutality." She shrugged. "Not that it would have bothered me so much. I introduced him to Jasper and Ross. He left Stonebridge to work for them, but I knew the minute Ross made that chilling remark about Ben's being strung up like tobacco that there was only one place Grendel could have done it and got away with it."

"Don't tell me it was…"

"An abandoned barn, an old relic from the early 1900s, before we got more modern, you know, but I never wished to tear it down because it added a bucolic charm to the grounds. I told Ross I would leave. I packed my things and told Cora I was going to New York to attend the funeral of a friend who had died unexpectedly and that I would go on to Maine and would send for the rest of my things later. I drove down the main drive and took an old country route to a back entrance to the farm. There's no road, just grass down there, but I knew the path to that old barn like the back of my hand."

Mrs. Drinnon killed her scotch, and Lombard asked, "Why didn't you call the police?"

"I wasn't sure I would find Ben. I wasn't sure Ross wasn't just blathering on and that I wouldn't look like a fool. I also knew that if Ben was dead—as I thought he was at that point—and 'strung up' on my land, I would have a headache with the police." Mrs. Drinnon shuddered and asked Leonard Hartley to refill her glass. She waited until he had poured it and belted back two swigs before continuing. "All right. I went inside the barn with a flashlight and found Ben alive. He was asleep on the floor with his feet shackled. He flinched when the light hit him. He didn't look like himself. I had known him since he was a boy. He was a bright, smart, happy person. But not when I found him. He just stared at me and didn't move. I began crying." Della drew her lips tight together and held back emotion. "I thought nobody deserved to be treated like that. I wondered what kind of person... Well, I just got terrified. I didn't know what to think. I pulled him up and rushed him outside as fast as he could shuffle with his legs chained like that, thinking the whole time that Ross or Grendel, one might turn up and kill us both. I've never been so frightened in my life. The sight of my dead husband's brains and bone scattered about the floor hadn't unnerved me as much, because at the time I had no fear for myself."

Mrs. Drinnon drank the last of her scotch. "Then I brought him here, to home."

Lombard drew a deep breath. "A tobacco barn. How gothic."

"It's the truth," Mrs. Drinnon scowled.

"I believe you. You're a tough lady, Mrs. Drinnon. I'll give you that in spades. But I wonder. Did it enter anybody's mind to get this poor boy to a hospital these past few days? Or call the police? Christ almighty, what did you plan on doing? Hide out here for all eternity, just ignore the situation?"

"We weren't ignoring anything. I told you," Della hissed, "that I was terrified. I only knew that as crazy as Ross was, he could be right, and Grendel could be after me. After seeing Ben like that, I didn't know what to do. I know you'll do the right thing and call the authorities now. I know the truth will out, and I'll have some peace again. I just want to go home as soon as it's safe."

"It is now," Lombard said. She glanced at McLean. "How's your arm, sugar?"

"Busted. Feels like it's gonna fall off," McLean mumbled.

Lombard announced, "We just came back from Stonebridge Farm. Grendel's dead, and Ross McKenna is under arrest."

"For what?" asked Mrs. Drinnon.

"For now, just the kidnapping and assault of an Asheville reporter who came to your house this morning to interview him. It's a long story." She smiled at Mrs. Drinnon. "If I was you, I'd hire a lawyer."

"I've done nothing wrong," said Mrs. Drinnon.

"All the more reason. If I knew a lawyer who wasn't under indictment, I'd refer you to one."

"What about our son? What about Benny?" Matilda Hartley cried.

Lombard looked gravely at Ben, sitting motionless with downcast eyes. "Call the police and report his kidnapping. Get him to a doctor as soon as possible. And let me know when he's fit to talk. I promise you this, Mrs. Hartley: I want to help your son. I may be able to help him avoid possible charges."

"He didn't do anything!"

"That won't stop the police from charging him and sorting the truth out later. He may have started a fire and could be charged with arson. He may know something about two murders back in Asheville. They'll take a serious look at him, but I can help Ben." Lombard wrote down her cell number and handed it to Mrs. Hartley. "Promise?"

"Yes," Mrs. Hartley said. She looked at Mrs. Drinnon and said, "My God, Della! How is all this going to make us look?"

Lombard picked McLean up at the hospital emergency room where she had dropped him off earlier. While McLean's shoulder was being treated, Lombard had visited the Raleigh police and informed them of Della Drinnon's story. Investigators were on their way to interview Mrs. Drinnon, and more serious charges awaited Ross McKenna. McLean's shoulder and upper arm were bandaged, and his arm rested in a sling. "I can't believe it wasn't broken," he muttered. "The doctor said I just had some bruised tendons. I think we ought to get a second opinion."

Lombard asked, "Do you think Della knows more than she's telling?"

"Probably."

"She said self-deception is the constant of her life. Wonder if that has anything to do with what Slade said on that tape, about A.C. being the only man he ever loved. I bet all that ties in, along with A.C.'s suicide. I've always thought it odd how casually Della mentions finding A.C. dead. The two times I've heard her discuss it, she's sneered about it, like it was dog piss or something vile, and not her husband's dead body."

"But she really did save Ben's life," McLean pointed out. "She might know more than she's telling, but I don't think she had anything to do with the murders."

"I've figured out why Ross McKenna wanted me to find Ben," Lombard said. "He must have looked after him down in that barn. After McKenna chased Della off, he noticed Ben Hartley was missing. That's why he wanted me to find him, why it was so urgent that I get him back."

"Before Grendel Roper found out?"

"Partly. But I think he was already in trouble with Grendel Roper."

"Why the falling-out between Roper and McKenna?"

"Grendel Roper mentioned it before you got to Stonebridge, before he went for that knife to kill us all. He said something about McKenna being weak, about McKenna deceiving him, about McKenna only caring about money."

McLean yawned. "Well, it's in the hands of the police now."

"They don't know what they're doing. This is our case."

"Really?" said McLean. "Just how are we gonna fund further investigation of *our* case, Inspector Lombard?"

"It won't cost anything, just a little more time. I know how Ross McKenna and Grendel Roper devised their plot and used Ben Hartley. I just don't know why yet."

"Convince me," McLean said. "And I'll keep working the case with you."

"McKenna had suspected all along that Slade was homosexual. Not that Slade was indiscreet. People can know somebody for years and never suspect they're gay, never imagine it. But I believe McKenna had suspicions about Slade's sexuality from way back."

"What brought you to that conclusion?" McLean interrupted.

"This morning at Stonebridge, before Grendel Roper came sneaking inside, I finally heard Slade's voice in the tape recording of Mashburn's interview of him, and in it he said A.C. was the only man he ever loved. Now, you can read all the Christian meaning of the word 'love' you want into that, but that doped-up son of a bitch was talking about romantic love. A.C. Drinnon had been a founding member of the AFFC. He and his wife, Della, were friendly with Leonard and Matilda Hartley. But A.C. was a lot friendlier with the AFFC's other founding member, Jasper Slade. Now that's in the past. A.C. died years ago, and for years Ross McKenna let any misgivings he had about A.C.'s relationship with Jasper Slade die with A.C."

Lombard pulled the Pathfinder into the parking lot of the Fairland Court Motel. "This good enough?" she asked.

"It's all we can afford at this point," McLean said abjectly. "Go on with your story."

As Lombard parked the car, she went on with her theory.

"Then the Hartleys' gay son, Ben, decided to become an activist, got into all that gay rights, green earth, save-the-world shit. He got work at the Pride office, and he wrote articles for Wiley Faulks's Green newsletter. He still lived on his parents' land, though his life was everyplace but there. The Hartleys loved their son but were conservatives and moved in right-wing circles. Their association with the Drinnons is proof enough of that. Ross McKenna found out about Ben Hartley, probably through Della Drinnon. She might have whispered something about the Hartleys' shame to McKenna, who would have been curious about that. He would have checked into Ben Hartley's activities, would have eventually read those scandalous articles about Jasper Slade."

Lombard turned off the ignition and unhooked her seat belt. "Imagine how McKenna felt when he read them. Disgusted by the attacks on Slade and the AFFC, and outraged by Ben Hartley's hand in them. He must have viewed Ben as a traitor. He had a powerful ax to grind with him and with Wiley Faulks." Lombard paused during her speculation on McKenna's motives. "Are you convinced yet?" she asked McLean.

"I think I need another pain pill," he said.

"Wait," she said. "I'm almost through. Now, McKenna read the allegations about Slade and he was disgusted by them. But he wondered about whether there really was a young male lover with a flashy new jacket. Brought back all those nagging thoughts about Slade and poor old dead A.C. So he had Grendel Roper tail Slade and discovered that the *Vigilante* rumors were true. Right then, Ross McKenna began devising a scheme. He would frame Slade for the murder of his own lover, but he would create an out for the AFFC, a way for Slade's followers to maintain belief in him and his organization. They would say Slade had been framed. Before it was all said and done, you and I and Sig Mashburn and Grendel Roper would have devised a solid case casting doubt on

Slade's guilt. No weapon. Evidence of a forced entry from outside. Ben Hartley's shallow alias registered in the room below. Slade kills himself, then Wiley Faulks dies trapped in a fire arson inspectors believe was started by somebody who knew the layout of the place. The only man left alive who links all three dead men is on the run, and it's Ben Hartley."

Lombard paused, and McLean asked, "Why did Hartley go along with all that?"

"He was forced to. Ever see that movie *The Manchurian Candidate*?"

"Yeah. The old fifties movie with Laurence Harvey. He's in the war overseas, gets kidnapped and brainwashed and tortured, and they set him loose in America. He acts normal, but he's really operating as a subversive. His mind ain't his own." McLean grimaced. "Gimme a break, Loy. Do you think that's what Grendel Roper did to Ben Hartley?"

"Nah. I just wondered if you ever saw the movie. I think it went something like that, but I don't believe Ben Hartley was brainwashed. I think Roper tortured him, though, and threatened him into submission. He might have threatened his family. He probably kept him in that barn for days before the killing started. He would have killed him sooner or later too, but he let Ben Hartley think he could survive by doing what he was told. Anyway, Ben was transformed by terror into some other being, and he did as he was told. He met Slade and Hughes. He probably drugged them; there are pill forms of Demerol. That would account for the toxins mentioned in Hughes's autopsy report. And Hartley later planted the vials of liquid Demerol in Faulks's bathroom, where McKenna counted on my finding it."

"I could use some of it right now," McLean groaned.

"So Hartley registered at the Rosemond Inn when he was told to, and he left the room for Grendel Roper. Ben Hartley did all that without even knowing what Roper was up to. He was too

tormented to realize he was framing himself for murder."
Thunder rolled outside, and a soft rain fell on the windshield.
"Now, here's the evil part," said Lombard. "Grendel Roper came
to the inn and launched himself up to Hughes's room from the
balcony below. He killed Hughes and left Slade naked, high and
dry. Afterward he kept Ben Hartley at arm's length. By the time
Ben realized what he had assisted in doing, it was too late. He now
depended on Grendel Roper. But he reached out to Tyler Rhodes.
You saw him in Rhodes's office after Slade's death."

"Let's say Hartley was framed as Hughes's killer," said McLean.
"Then why wouldn't Roper kill Slade too? It would only make
sense for him to kill them both."

"It's a frame within a frame, Sam. A made-up one inside a real
one. McKenna would have us believe Ben Hartley had a motive to
kill Hughes and *frame* Slade for it, and sooner or later you would
have dug it up that the motive had to do with Tyler Rhodes."

McLean's brow arched, and his mouth fell open. "Oh, no.
Rhodes and Hartley?"

"Were lovers," she said. "Tyler Rhodes fucked Jay Hughes and
broke Ben's heart. Sam, we have established a motive and an opportunity for Ben Hartley to murder Jay Hughes, and also to frame
Jasper Slade for it. Ross McKenna would have the world believe that
Ben Hartley killed his lover's new piece of ass and threw the blame
on a man he had dogged in the radical press. The motive for ruining Slade could be found in Wiley Faulks's editorials. Faulks had to
die because he knew too much. Diabolical scheme indeed, all of it
contrived by Ross McKenna and executed by Grendel Roper. Now
we just have to find out why McKenna hated Slade that much."

Matilda Hartley phoned Lombard the next day and asked her to come to the Durham hospital where Ben Hartley had been admitted. He wasn't talking yet, but Mrs. Hartley had heard from the police already, and she wanted Lombard there. She told Lombard she trusted her to help her son.

When they entered the lobby of Ben Hartley's hospital floor, Lombard and McLean found Tyler Rhodes waiting. Before Rhodes could spot them, McLean dashed to a corner just off the elevator, pulling Lombard alongside him. He told Lombard he'd just spotted Tyler Rhodes and would take him to the cafeteria while she talked to Hartley.

Lombard went to Ben Hartley's room. His mother was sitting in a chair by his bedside, holding his hand and murmuring something to him as he looked into her eyes, listening with childlike attention. Mrs. Hartley smiled when she spotted Lombard standing in the doorway. "Benny's talking," she said brightly. "Benny, do you remember meeting Miss Lombard yesterday at the house?"

He turned his head slowly toward Lombard, and narrowed his eyes as though bringing her into focus. Lombard stepped forward and smiled tentatively. "No," he said. "You were at my house?"

"Yes, back at your parents' house, yesterday," Lombard said.

"I don't remember. Who are you?"

"My name is Loy Lombard. I'm a private investigator."

He closed his eyes and sighed. "I should have guessed."

"She's not with the police," Mrs. Hartley said reassuringly. "She's working for…um, well, she's a private detective, honey."

"Can I talk to you alone, Ben?" Lombard asked.

"What about?"

"I want to talk to you about what you've been through. I want to help you. I know you don't feel like it, but the police will be standing right here soon enough, and I'm not so sure they'll understand your situation as well as I think I do."

He asked his mother to help him rise up a bit, and Mrs. Hartley arranged his pillows so that he could scoot up and rest half-sitting in his bed. He looked warily at Lombard. "What are you talking about?"

"I believe you're innocent."

Hartley looked confused. "Of what?"

Lombard looked at his mother. "Please, Mrs. Hartley. Just a minute?"

Mrs. Hartley kissed her son's head with a whispered promise that she would be right outside in the lobby if he needed her and excused herself. Lombard sat in the chair, still warm from the constant presence of Mrs. Hartley's backside. Lombard asked, "What is the last thing you remember before waking up in here?"

He tensed his brow and stared straight ahead. "I don't know."

"Aw, come on," she said gently. "I can't give you a good enough reason to believe that I'm here to help you, Ben. But I am." She paused, deliberating for a few seconds on how to bring up Grendel Roper's name. "Grendel's dead. My partner, Sam, split his chest wide open with a .35 caliber hollow-point while Grendel came at me with a knife. So there's nobody gonna hurt you now."

"Grendel," he repeated, as though placing the name. "I haven't seen him in days."

"What did he do to you?"

"I honestly don't recall. I don't recall much at all…what's your name again?"

"Loy Lombard. Loy."

"Loy. You know my parents?"

"Not well. I know your boss, Jessamyn Frost."

He smiled. "How is she? Is Jess okay?"

"I suppose so. Was the last time I saw her, a few days ago."

"Good. Oh, I wonder when I saw her last? You know, I don't recall that either."

Lombard leaned back and crossed her legs. "Take your time."

He turned and caught her easygoing smile. It made him smile back, and his eyes welled up. "It's too much, Loy. I can't talk about it."

She picked up a rag soaking in a pan of cool water on the bedside table and wrung it out. She leaned forward and stroked his brow with the rag. "You just tell me what you can talk about, sugar. The more you tell me, the more I can do to help."

"But what are you going to do?"

"I'm going to see Ross McKenna get sent up for life, is what I'm going to do."

Ben Hartley chuckled softly. "That would be sweet." His expression fell back into sadness, and he began. "Grendel came to my bungalow one night to drive me out to Stonebridge Farm, where Della Drinnon lives."

"Your bungalow? Where's that?"

"At my parents' farm."

"You mean the carriage house?"

Ben rolled his eyes and chuckled softly. "It was never a carriage house. Christ. Mother and Daddy, always wanting to be gentry. It used to be a shack, and I renovated it myself. Whatever."

Lombard impatiently tapped the armrests. "So Grendel stopped by…"

"I was expecting him, sort of. I'd been invited to a dinner party at Della Drinnon's house. I thought that was no big deal, since my parents had always known Della. I thought I'd use the opportunity to dig up dirt about the AFFC and Slade. I'd been writing about him for Wiley Faulks…" His voice trailed off on the sound of Faulks's name, and he gave a look of pure pain.

"I'm listening," Lombard said hastily.

"Where was I?"

"At the bungalow."

"No, I mean…"

"Oh, uh, uh, it was Grendel came to get you. I mean, drive you out to Della's."

"Right. I was expecting a car. I was surprised to see Grendel, though. He used to be some kind of farmhand on her property. But I thought nothing of it. Figured maybe he was like her driver now. I got in the car, only I never went to dinner. Never saw Della at all. I passed out along the way. I guess he knocked me out. I woke up in some dark place."

"It was the barn," Lombard offered.

"What?"

"Some old barn on Stonebridge Farm, is my guess."

"I don't know." He took several sharp breaths. "I was hanging from a beam or something. My wrists hurt, horribly." He paused and turned away. "Loy, it's all blank after that. I swear to God. It's all dark and cold and split with flashes of, like, water."

"Water?"

"God, I can't breathe!"

"What?"

"I can't breathe!" Ben screamed. He began grunting and heaving wildly, as though his throat was closing in.

In an instant, the door swung open and Matilda Hartley stormed into the room with two nurses. "What are you doing to him?" she shrieked at Lombard.

"Nothing!" Lombard said defensively.

"He can't breathe!" Mrs. Hartley cried.

"I don't know what happened," Lombard spluttered. "He was just talking one minute, and the next he was choking like that."

One of the nurses stuck a needle in his arm, and Ben began to relax as a clear substance disappeared from the syringe into his body. His breathing grew steady, and his eyes closed. "He needs to rest," the nurse said.

"I'm sorry, Mrs. Hartley," Lombard said. "I didn't mean any harm."

"Surely you've helped him enough for one day," Mrs. Hartley snapped.

"Surely," Lombard said.

———

Tyler Rhodes had followed McLean to the hospital cafeteria without so much as asking what he wanted to talk about. He had seemed almost relieved to see McLean. While Lombard tried her hand at the sensitive interrogation of a traumatized witness, McLean and Rhodes chatted over coffee and muffins as though they were old friends. At first they avoided the ugly events that had brought them together and talked briefly about the weather and highway traffic until McLean got to the point.

"I was surprised to see you here, Tyler," he said.

"You shouldn't be," Rhodes said. "I heard about Ross McKenna's arrest on the news, and I called Jessamyn Frost to find out any news about Ben. Well, I called your office first and learned that you and your partner were in Raleigh. Jess told me Ben's mother had called telling her about Ben being found. She wanted to make sure he still had his job. I came here right away."

"Why so urgent?"

"I felt bad for Ben. Jess told me Ben was in the hospital but didn't know why. I thought maybe he had been injured. I wanted to tell him how sorry I am."

"About what?"

Rhodes looked troubled. "I was shocked when I heard news

accounts of what McKenna did to Hunter Lyle, the television reporter. Hearing about it made me realize Ben had, in all likelihood, been victimized by McKenna all along."

"Is there any other reason you have for feeling sorry for Ben Hartley?"

Rhodes said, "Very skillful, Sam. Have you thought about law school?"

McLean smirked. "I'm too honest a man."

"I'm an honest man," Rhodes said solemnly. "Have you already talked to Ben?"

"No. Loy's in his room right now, though. Tell me what Ben was doing at your office that day I came to interview you. He disappeared after that, and you know it. That was two days after Slade hanged himself."

"Oh, now you're playing the intimidating cop bit, is that it? You were so nice just a minute ago."

"This isn't a game, Tyler," McLean said. "What was he doing there?"

"He was begging me to help him."

"Well, that's just great," McLean said disgustedly. "Why didn't you mention that the day you turned up at the office all white-knuckled with worry about where he was?"

"Because I thought he had gone off the deep end. That's why." Rhodes sounded angry. "What was I supposed to do? Tell you about how he came to my office with this insane story about being kidnapped by a big blond ogre?"

"He was. The ogre was Grendel Roper."

"I know that now! But then it sounded insane. Almost like some freakish S/M fantasy. Ben was a hothead, always has been. I told you about his arrest history. The more he talked, the more I wondered if he hadn't killed Jay himself."

"What did he say?"

"He said Grendel had picked him up at his house on the pretext of a dinner party A.C. Drinnon's widow was giving. You've heard of A.C. Drinnon?"

"Yes."

"Well, the Drinnons knew Ben's parents. So Ben thought he could get a story Wiley could use. He said the next thing he knew, he was hanging from handcuffs in a warehouse or barn or something. Grendel beat him. He let him down and told him he was going to work for him. Ben resisted. Grendel dragged him to some kind of trough full of water and held his head under until Ben passed out. He brought him to and repeated the process, damn near drowning him until Ben listened. He showed him pictures of people he had killed in the past—Ben said they were like souvenir snapshots of mutilated corpses. Grendel said he would do that to Ben's parents if Ben strayed off course an inch."

"But you didn't believe him."

"I didn't believe or disbelieve. I just wanted him out of my life."

"You said you wondered if he had killed Jay himself at that point. Why?"

Rhodes rubbed his face. "Christ, I'm tired."

"We all are."

"Look, when you came to my office, I was in shock. I know I seemed normal, but I was determined not to believe what I'd just heard. I wanted to believe that Jasper Slade had killed Jay Hughes. It made sense. It looked obvious."

"You seemed convinced when I talked to you."

"I had to be! I didn't let what Ben told me sink in until after Wiley died." His voice cracked, and his eyes became teary. "I miss Wiley, you know. He was a good man. I'll damn myself forever for not listening to Ben that day. I might have been able to prevent Wiley's death."

"How?"

"I should have believed Ben's story. He ran off that day, and I never saw him again. I was afraid of him. If I hadn't been, if I had believed in him, I could have saved him, and Wiley would still be alive."

"Why were you afraid of him?" McLean asked, watching Rhodes intently.

"I thought maybe…" Rhodes's brow creased, and he averted his eyes.

"What? Tell me, Tyler."

"I thought he had killed Jay, by that point. That's all."

"He didn't like him?"

Rhodes looked sharply at McLean, then smiled vaguely. "No. He didn't. You've already figured that out, haven't you?"

"Why didn't you tell me about your relationship with Ben?"

"Because it was over, and I didn't want whatever he was into to affect me. It's that simple."

"He didn't kill Jay," McLean said.

"Hindsight's twenty-twenty." Rhodes took a drink of coffee and said, "If you'd heard his story about meeting Slade, you'd have found it hard to believe too."

"What story?"

"You'll be very upset with me when I tell you, but fuck it. I have nothing to hide yet everything to be sorry about. You walked into my office while he was pleading with me to help him. God, I was glad when you arrived. Do you remember how happy I was to see you? And I didn't even know you. He told me he'd met with Slade on the afternoon before the murder. Slade was furious about the articles, and Ben promised to stop. He gave Slade a box of his favorite chocolates as a peace offering, saying they were from his parents, who were friends of Slade. They were laced with narcotics, he said. He checked into the Rosemond Inn using his father's name. He didn't know why he was being made to do these things. The next day, he knew."

McLean shook his head. "I guess drugging them made Roper's job easier."

"When Ben told me these things, I told him he needed thera-py. I told him that a life growing up among conspiracy theorists had warped him. He looked so despondent, now I think about it. When Wiley died and Ben went missing, I thought Ben had killed Jay. I thought perhaps he killed Wiley because Wiley knew too much. I blamed myself. I worried about my own safety. That's why I met you at your office. I hoped you would find him, because I thought he was a murderer."

"And now?"

Rhodes said, "Now I want him to forgive me."

13

MIKE CHURCH MET LOMBARD AND MCLEAN AT A BAR called the Alibi in Raleigh. His left shoulder and arm were bandaged and strapped in a sling, and when Lombard spotted him, she laughed and smacked McLean's sling, causing him to wince.

"Easy!" McLean shouted.

"Oh, I barely tapped you, tough stuff. Look at you two," she grinned. "You're like blood brothers now."

"What happened to you?" Church asked McLean. "You get shot too?"

"Some old lady slammed the door on his arm," Lombard cackled.

"Mrs. Hartley is not old. She ain't much older than you," said McLean.

"I'm only forty-one. She's got at least ten years on me." Lombard smiled at Church. "Have a drink, Lieutenant. You earned it."

"I'll pass. I'm on pain medication," Church said.

"I can hook you up with some Demerol," Lombard said, winking.

"I only came here to deliver some news. The good news is, Ross McKenna can't post bail. The magistrate ordered him held, pending a mental health evaluation. That could take weeks."

"I take it you have bad news," Lombard said dryly, sipping a glass of bourbon.

"Della Drinnon was questioned by police and released. The captain who interviewed her called me in as a courtesy. She won't talk to me. That's bad."

"What did she tell the police?"

"She convinced them she knew nothing about Ben Hartley's abduction and imprisonment on her property. Even if she did, they don't want to believe it. The Drinnons have a lot of sway in the Raleigh-Durham area. Still, she's afraid, even though McKenna is a long way from getting out." He eyed the mug of beer McLean was drinking. "All right. One beer. I have to get home. I still haven't told my wife I got shot."

"How bad did you get hit? Sam said you were missing a shoulder."

Church rolled his eyes. "My colleagues in the Raleigh police have a flair for drama. Grendel got me with a .22. It was all he had on him. He shot four times in the chest, but I was wearing a vest. He got me in the shoulder, where I wasn't protected. I hit my head falling down and got knocked out." Church sniffed. "Otherwise I would have killed him."

"Sam took care of that," Lombard snidely reminded him. "So Della's back at home. Good. I'll pay her a visit tomorrow."

"You don't have to. The last part of my news is, she's sitting out in my car."

Lombard and McLean traded glances. "In your car?" she asked. "Why?"

"She wants to talk to you." Church asked the bartender for a draft. "But she won't come in here. A bar, you know."

"Oh, give me a break," Lombard said. "I saw those fancy crystal bottles full of booze in her parlor…what did she call it, Sam? That room we were in when we met her."

"Library," said McLean.

"Right. And she was guzzling it at the Hartleys' too. Get her ass in here."

"She won't be seen in a public bar," Church said. "She was firm on it. She's waiting out in the car. She wants to talk to you, and then she's heading straight to the airport and her house up in Maine." Church glanced at his watch. "You'd better hurry. Her flight's in two hours." He pushed McLean gently back on his barstool when McLean rose with Lombard. "Just Loy. Lady's orders."

Lombard sauntered through the bar and out onto the street, where Church's Buick was parked curbside. She tapped on the window and smiled at the severe-looking woman seated in the back. Della Drinnon opened her door. "Get in, Miss Lombard. I don't have much time." Lombard scooted inside under Drinnon's disapproving glare.

"What's the look for?" Lombard asked.

"What look?"

"The dagger eyes."

"You've been drinking," Drinnon said haughtily.

"So have you. What's your pleasure, Mrs. Drinnon? Bourbon? No, I think that potion I saw in your parlor had the color of a good scotch." She leaned into the corner of the rear seat. "Anyway, at the moment I'm sober as a preacher's wife."

"I have a question for you, Miss Lombard," said Mrs. Drinnon. "I was at Stonebridge, gathering my things for the trip north, and I noticed something missing. You know what I mean, no doubt."

Lombard shrugged. "I only took the cassette tape of Slade's interview."

"Don't be coy with me, Lombard. That tape is my property. You are not the police. You have no authority to take what belongs to me. Give it back this minute or I'll report you to the real police, who, by the way, were right pleased to see things my way when I explained how I had nothing to do with Ben Hartley's abduction."

"So far, so good."

"Give it back!" Drinnon shouted, tears pooling in her eyes. "I've had enough." She jerked forward and raised one shaking gloved hand to her forehead.

"Shh, calm down, Mrs. Drinnon," Lombard said casually.

"This is the thing. That tape doesn't belong to you, and you know it. It belongs to Ross McKenna. If the police ask me how I got it, I'll tell them that my employer, McKenna, handed it over as he had meant to do for a long time, as he had hired me to find out the perpetrators of a frame-up of Jasper Slade." She paused and watched Mrs. Drinnon, who had begun weeping, grab a tissue from her purse and snort into it. "Another thing is, you don't want the police to think that tape belonged to you. Oh, I figure you've heard it. I'll bet you were thereabouts when Sig Mashburn took Jasper Slade's statement. But I doubt you would want the police to know that. Would you, Mrs. Drinnon?"

Lombard stared at the sobbing woman like a cat studying a wounded mouse. She had no sympathy for Della Drinnon, whom Lombard now suspected knew a lot about Ben Hartley's abduction and even more about why Jasper Slade was set up to look like Jay Hughes's killer. She knew even more clearly why Della Drinnon would never complain to anybody about the missing tape. She waited until Mrs. Drinnon had stopped crying, had let go one last gasp of sorrow, and sat upright gazing miserably out the window of her door. Then Lombard said, "You don't really want *anybody* to hear that tape, do you, Mrs. Drinnon?"

"No," Drinnon said softly, like a child might whisper after a paddling.

"When did you find out about A.C. and Jasper? Right before A.C. died?"

Mrs. Drinnon's brow creased, and she stared at the floorboard of the backseat as though scrutinizing every fiber in the floor pads. "They had been carrying on for years," she said. "Years and years. But they stopped," she said firmly, nodding her head once. "Stopped sudden, that day in the library."

"The day you say you found A.C. dead of a gunshot to the head."

Drinnon turned an icy glare on Lombard. "Yes. That's right. *Found* him."

Lombard checked her watch. "I'll get Mike. I guess he's driving you to the airport." She opened the door and glanced out at the dimming May sky. "Nice in Carolina this time of year. I've heard the summers are best in New England. I'll bet Maine is just picture-perfect in summertime." She hopped out onto the street, and leaned back inside before closing the door. "Of course, New Brunswick's next door to Maine, and Canada doesn't extradite. Not if the defendant could be facing the death penalty."

———

"She practically confessed," Lombard told McLean later, as they watched a televised baseball game in her motel room. She was sitting up against the headboard of her made bed, while McLean sat in a chair near the TV.

"She said she found him, is what you told me," he reminded her, yawning.

"It was in her eyes. She killed A.C. That's why she's so cold every time she's brought up finding his body. She figures he deserved it. What's more, she was right on about why she did it. He was cheating on her with Slade. She knew it all along."

"How did she get away with it? Not easy making a shotgun death look like a suicide."

"I don't know. It doesn't even matter how. She's Della Drinnon, unimpeachable and highly regarded in these parts. She's smart too, and mean. She probably could have talked him into doing himself in. Either way, she's glad it happened."

McLean stood up and stretched. "Sleep on it," he said. "I'm going to my room. Time to check in with Selena."

"Does she know about your arm?" Lombard smirked.

"Shut up," he muttered, rubbing his shoulder.

Lombard chuckled as he left her room and closed the door behind him. She turned up the volume on the TV, when suddenly the phone rang. She picked up the receiver and quipped, "That was quick. Need some quarters for the magic fingers?"

"This is Hunter," said a soft voice. "Loy, please don't hang up."

Lombard immediately hung up. A few seconds later the phone rang again. After the seventh ring Lombard reached for the phone, listened to a couple more rings, and unplugged it.

———

The next morning, at 9 o'clock on the dot, Lombard and McLean stood at the counter of the probate clerk's office of the Raleigh courthouse. A tiny old woman in soft flannel pants, moccasins, a cranberry cardigan, and matching lipstick stood on the other side of the counter, her bespectacled, white-powdered face screwed up in incomprehension. "What are you asking me to do?" she demanded in a shrill piedmont accent. "I don't understand. Say you want to see a probated will? What for?"

"We want to see the last will and testament of Alexander Clayton Drinnon," Lombard said. "The one and only. You know who I'm talking about."

"When did he die?" the old woman shouted.

Lombard said, "Six years ago, ma'am. Now, surely you remember old A.C. Drinnon shooting himself to death. It was all the talk."

"Oh, I remember that," the old woman said irritably. "We've archived that by now. You'll have to order your copy and come back next week."

"Next week?" Lombard said, nearly gasping. "We don't have till next week, ma'am. We've got to get a hold of that thing right now!"

"You're not authorized to gather archived materials without notice unless you got a warrant," the woman said coolly, folding her arms on the counter.

Lombard gave her a dead stare and reached inside the breast pocket of her jacket.

"Loy, no," McLean murmured. "You're pushing it."

Lombard pulled the black-encased badge from her jacket and flashed it once. "Do I have to go get a warrant, ma'am? Because if I do, it'll take me all day, and by the time I get back you're liable to have to stay past 5 to help me fetch it out of archives."

An hour and a half later the three of them were cramped inside the old woman's cubicle behind the counter, where Lombard sat in a chair studying a thick dossier that contained A.C. Drinnon's will. "Damn, he was particular," Lombard muttered, scanning each page through her reading glasses. "He named Slade as his executor," she noted with interest. "Left the bulk of his estate to his wife, then split up the remainder among a bargeload of little charities and whatnots. This is wearing me out." She leaned back and flipped through the will. Suddenly her tense expression relaxed, and her lips parted in a dubious smile.

"What is it?" McLean asked, leaning over her shoulder.

"Read this. Things are coming together, Sam," she said.

McLean snatched the paper from Lombard's hands and read aloud the portion to which Lombard had pointed. "One and a half million dollars of my estate I bequeath to my loyal friend Jasper Thomas Slade, in the event that I precede him in death, for the establishment of a conservative foundation."

———

"What are we doing?" McLean asked as they left the courthouse.

"We're following Della Drinnon's lead. I got the idea to look at the will when I figured out she might have killed A.C."

"We'll never prove that."

"We're not trying to prove it."

"Then what are we trying to prove?"

"A.C.'s death is related to our case, I'm sure of it," Lombard said. "I thought his will might give us something." She sat down on a park bench outside the courthouse and patted a spot next to her. "Sit down, Sam. Let's talk."

McLean gave a labored sigh and sat. "Talk," he said.

"A.C. Drinnon and Slade were lovers. The complexities of that are obvious but more than I can delve into right now. But the fact is, they loved each other, and whatever morbid shame might have haunted them, they managed to suppress, though they were not able to suppress the suspicion of others. Della Drinnon and Ross McKenna in particular suspected. They were closest to them."

"Did McKenna know Slade before the AFFC was started?"

"He did. He was Slade's press secretary while Slade was in office. That's been on the news. I didn't think much of it until I began piecing things together. Like I figured before, he had the odd, nagging thought every now and then about Slade and A.C., but he let it go until the rumors about a young lover, presumably Jay Hughes, emerged in the *Vigilante*. Della had known about her husband and Slade long before. If she didn't kill A.C., I'd be surprised. Why would a man of A.C.'s wealth and prominence kill himself?"

"Over shame, maybe?" McLean offered.

Lombard shook her head. "I don't think so. These rich people, they do whatever they want with impunity. They don't think about their own morality unless it threatens to bite them in the ass publicly."

"So what about the will?"

"I need to have a lawyer take a look at it."

"You have the copy, right?"

Lombard patted her breast. "Right in here, next to my trusty faux badge."

"Who's gonna look at it?"

Lombard stood up. "Come on. It's time to go home."

"Now you're talking sense," McLean said merrily, hopping on his feet. "But who's gonna look at the will?"

"Sig Mashburn," she said.

"You think he'll talk to us after what happened to him?"

"He won't talk to *you*," she said. "He'll certainly talk to me."

———

Early the next morning Lombard was waiting in Sigmund Mashburn's office on Patton Street in downtown Asheville. Mashburn stepped into the lobby and said, "Professional courtesy dictates you call first before barging in. What do you want?"

"I want you to take a look at a will."

"Ha! Not unless I'm in it. I don't do estates."

"It's A.C. Drinnon's." She waited patiently while he looked at her with eyes full of distrust. "I bet you never thought to check his will," she added. "It's hot. Wanna see?"

"Come on back," he said.

Mashburn showed her into his office and sat her in a chair in front of his desk. He sank into his chair and sighed heavily, his face a mask of fatigue and ill temper. He held the will in front of him and began perusing it without the faintest trace of enthusiasm.

"You mad at me, Sig?" Lombard asked.

"That goddamn poaching case is gonna eat me alive," he said. "I hired Denning Stewart to get me out of it."

"Denning Stewart," Lombard said. "Well, well. Who's he?"

"He's the kind of lawyer people just give way to. Judges, prosecutors, even politicians. He walks into court and cases just go his way. Of course, at a hefty price," he said, scowling at her. "Costing me $20,000 for a piece-of-shit hunting-out-of-season case. So you tell Sam McLean and Mike Church they can kiss my ass."

"You already told them to, and more."

"I probably should tell you to kiss my ass as well. What makes you think I owe you even the courtesy of this visit, let alone a review of this irrelevant, probated will?"

"Because you know it's relevant, Sig. It doesn't tell much, but it says a lot about Slade and A.C. Drinnon. And I heard the tape of your interview with Slade. So read on."

His brow furrowed when she reminded him of the tape, but he said nothing and brushed the tip of his index finger along his tongue and flipped to the next page. He read as though he found the whole exercise distasteful or boring, but soon he pulled himself forward in his chair and drew his eyes nearer the document. "Didn't Della Drinnon contest this will?" he asked.

"It passed probate uncontested."

Mashburn threw the document down on his desk. "She should have contested it. Might have kept that 1.5 mil for herself, along with everything else that went to charity. Not easily, but she could have."

"She got twenty times that," Lombard said. "What makes

you think she could have kept the money A.C. left Slade?"

"The clause bequeathing that sum to Slade contains a restriction on property. You can leave your property to whoever you want, but you can't tell them what to do with it unless you set up a trust. She should have contested it. If she'd had me for a lawyer, I would've argued the entire will was void. Then everything would have gone to her, minus my share." He grinned. "Might have won. Might not have."

"I bet she didn't even try. I don't think she would have wanted people to know Slade was in the will."

"I suppose not," he said, pushing the dossier across his desk. "Take it. I'm not interested in it. He left Slade a bundle of money, and Slade got it, and that's that."

"But why did he leave it to him?" Lombard asked. "That's what I want to know."

"They were friends."

"Sig, I heard the tape. It got cut off right after Slade moaned about how much he loved A.C. Drinnon. What did he say after the tape got cut off? And who cut it off?"

"McKenna cut it off. And Slade didn't say another damn thing. McKenna cut off my interview right along with the tape." He glanced out the window behind his desk. "And I got cut out of the case not long after that."

"And Slade died… Sig, when did you take his statement? What day? Slade died on the second Saturday after the murder, or early Sunday morning, more likely."

"Oh, it was the Monday or Tuesday before he died."

"I need to know for sure."

"Why?"

"Timing. Come on. Think. What day?"

He screwed his face up as though trying to recollect, but looked like an insolent, overgrown child. "When did we meet, out at the crime scene? What day was that?"

Lombard pulled her appointment book out of her handbag and flipped through the April dates. "Thursday, just two or three days before Slade's suicide, and less than a week after Hughes's murder."

"Then I talked to him on the Wednesday. I know it was the day before I met you."

Lombard threw her hands up in the air and let them fall slapping onto her thighs. "He admitted his homosexual affair to you on Wednesday and was dead before daylight on Sunday," she said. She pointed at Mashburn. "You as much as told me you didn't think it was suicide."

"I most certainly did not tell you that."

"Yes, you did. I've got a memory like an elephant. Crisp and clear. I mentioned Slade's suicide that night at your dinner party, when you took me back to show off your sport room, remember? Then you got high-handed with me." She grinned when he let a smile cross his face. "Yeah, you remember. I called you an arrogant son of a bitch."

"The truth's a defense."

"You said, 'I wish I could be sure of that,' when I brought up the suicide. Said 'bastards were coming at him from every direction.' You had your doubts then. Why?"

Mashburn looked down at his lap, and brushed some invisible substance off of his belly with the flick of his right hand. "I want you to leave, Loy," he said.

"Not till you tell me what you meant by that comment you made that night."

"You'll leave now," he said firmly. "I have nothing more to say to you."

"You either suspected or knew it wasn't suicide," she said hotly. "Your refusal to discuss this makes me wonder if you're hiding something from me now, like you were then. Where does that put you, Sig? On the wrong side, is where!"

"I never knew. I suspected. He talked that crazy talk about A.C. being the only man he ever loved, and next thing I know, he's dead. Even a fool would have his doubts. I just don't trust you, Loy. You're angling me. Now you can leave." He stood up, all burly six foot four of him, and glowered. "You heard me. Fuck off."

———

Jasper Slade had died intestate. Lombard learned this after McLean checked with the Department of Revenue, whose record of his estate inventory reflected that he had not recorded a will nor possessed anything of consequence beyond his house and household personalty, all of which had been auctioned to satisfy tax debts. No stocks, savings, investments of any kind had he left to his estate. He had died virtually penniless.

"That's impossible," Lombard said as she sat at her desk rifling through copies McLean had obtained from the revenue office in Raleigh. "He traveled all over. Took Hughes places. Dressed like a millionaire, flew around on a Lear jet. He was a former senator. He was rich, Sam. Where did the money go?"

McLean said, "I don't know."

"He had to have had a will."

"He didn't have one, Loy. There was an inventory—"

"I don't care. A man like him has a will, somewhere."

"He had no family. His wife was dead, no kids, no close relations. Maybe it wasn't a huge concern since he was still healthy and not old."

"He had the AFFC," she said. "He would have at least left it all to the foundation he and A.C. started, or barring that, given it to them somehow…" Lombard's mouth froze open. She stared at McLean as though she were looking straight through him.

"What is it, Loy?" he said. "You look like you seen a ghost."

"I have," she said quietly. "I mean, the next best thing. Something tells me Slade had a will and changed it."

"What tells you?"

She bit her lower lip and shrugged. "A hunch."

————

The next day McLean went into the office and nodded quietly at Retta, who was stationed at her desk, radioing the guards. He poured a cup of coffee and sat glumly on the lobby sofa until Retta had finished her first round of calls. These calls she made every hour on the hour to make sure the guards were alert and on duty at the various warehouses, factories, and housing projects with which Secure Services had contracts. In the nearly five weeks since Lombard had taken on the Slade case and all its ensuing odd turns and pitfalls, Retta had relied on herself to make the kinds of judgments and calculations that had normally called for the direct management of Lombard or McLean.

Retta hung the radio receiver on the hook and caught McLean watching her. "What are you looking at?" she said.

"Been busy?" he asked.

"Busy? Funny you should ask. It has been busy, almost more than one woman can manage alone for over a month." She got up and moved to a filing cabinet near where McLean sat across from her desk.

"Loy and I appreciate all you've done for the business since this mess started."

Retta harrumphed. She pulled a file folder out of the cabinet and slammed the drawer shut. "Where is Loy today? Back in Raleigh?" she asked, her voice edged with resentment. She walked back to her desk and plopped heavily into her swivel chair.

"She's going to Tennessee, actually," he sighed.

"What for?" Retta asked rather mechanically, not even feigning interest.

McLean shook his head slowly. "I don't even know. Well, I know. I just don't understand." He sipped his coffee and thought for a moment whether he should say what was on his mind, feeling a slight pain of disloyalty in even thinking it. Still, he was worried and knew he could talk to Retta. "Retta, I think this case is wrecking Loy's nerves. I think she's chasing after shadows, and I fear for what might happen to her when she finds out it's all been for nothing."

Retta whipped out a few reams of thin paper that appeared to be some sort of invoice and began marking on the top page. "She'll find the business is doing all right. She can take comfort in that."

"No, she won't." His voice was grave, and Retta looked sharply at him over the top of her reading glasses. "This case has opened up something in her that she let die back in Charlotte. It's gotten a hold of her. She's counting on solving a case that's already been solved for her. We were pawns, and she can't let herself believe it. Well, she believes we were pawns, maybe, but she can't accept that we got licked." He set his mug down on the coffee table and leaned back in the sofa. "See, she thinks there's something deeper to all this that nobody has figured out, and she has a weird hunch that this 'something' is just under her nose."

"Well, maybe she's right," Retta said.

"I hope so. Otherwise she'll be crushed for good."

Retta smirked. "Aw, Lord, Sam! Loy Lombard? That hellion can't be crushed. She's having the time of her life. I heard her say not three weeks ago she was in this thing for the fun of it, and the big paycheck was just a ticket for a chance to play the cop role all over again."

"That's how it started out, all right. But the deeper we sunk into it, the more it began to turn into the opposite of what we both expected, and she got excited, Retta. She got that hard focus I hadn't seen since we worked in homicide together. You know, she never left a case cold back then. Not before me, not after. Her job was the most important thing—well, it *was* her life. When it went..." McLean's voice faltered. "When it went, and she was humiliated on top of it, I thought I'd never forgive myself. And when she hired me on here, when I didn't know where else to turn—you know, I was working store detective jobs to make ends meet right before I came here. And Selena had to put the girls in day care and work in a dress shop full-time." He paused. "I swore I would never let her down and I would never see her humiliated again, not under my watch."

Retta's eyes were suddenly soft. "Do you think Loy's smart?"

He blew a chuckle. "Smart? Smartest woman, *person*, I ever met."

"Then what makes you think she's wrong about this case?"

"I'm not sure she's wrong. I just worry. She's got so much of her heart in it, and she's fighting powers that can't be beat down."

Retta removed her glasses and rubbed them with a handkerchief. "Well, she needs to put her heart in something heart is meant *for*, like love or something."

"She has even worse luck there, I suspect."

Retta stared cautiously at McLean for a second. "Sam," she began, "I'm curious about something. I know about Loy's, you know, woman thing. It's none of my business, but she's a fine-looking lady, got a good business, a good heart, plenty of brains, and..."

"You wonder why she doesn't want a man." McLean arched his brow and said with a tone of authority, "That's just how she is, and to be honest, I can't imagine her any other way. Once you get to know her well, you'll understand what I mean."

"I was going to *say,*" Retta bellowed, "that I wonder why she chases after trash like that TV woman. Must be a nice lady somewhere would like a fine woman like Loy."

McLean was startled. "How did you know about the TV woman?" He reflected for a moment. "For that matter, how did you know Loy's a lesbian? She's not been with a woman other than Hunter Lyle since she came to Asheville, as far as I know."

"Loy told me she was a lesbian almost as soon as I started working for her, back when I cleaned houses and before you moved to town."

"She told you? She talked about it?"

"I knew she was single, and this man that painted her house—he was a friend of my oldest son's—asked me if I thought she'd be interested in him. I told her, and she told me that when she was ready for romance, she'd find herself a woman." Retta smiled. "So I know her well, and I understood a long time ago."

McLean said, "I just heard talk around the department, but she never said anything to me about it. Never talked about her private life."

"Weren't none of our business, is how she probably sees it. Still, she'll lay it flat out on the floor if you try to fix her up."

"I never tried that," he said. "Now, I saw a couple of her girl-friends back then. They were both nice-looking, very feminine. I think Loy goes for that."

"She goes for trash, is what she goes for," Retta said sourly.

"Now, Retta. That's not true. Those girls I saw were classy. So is Hunter Lyle, at least on the surface. Anyway, how did you find out about her?"

"I'm no fool, Sam. I saw Loy's eyes light up like Christmas

bulbs that day Hunter come into the office. And I saw the shame on Loy when she walked out of the office, that day Mike Church ran his loud mouth about Hunter being married. Poor thing called me when she got home, telling me she felt ill and wouldn't be in the next day." Retta abruptly swept a pink slip of paper up off her desk. "And this here's the fourth message Hunter Lyle has called in this week, every day for three days in a row, wanting to talk to Loy. Now, you tell me what's going on between those two."

"Nothing," McLean said. "Or at least I hope not. I can't be sure, though. Loy's pretty weak right now. I'm not sure how she holds up against women."

"Anything to do with why she's going to Tennessee, then?"

"Oh, that's nothing to do with Hunter Lyle. She's heading for Ramp Hollow."

"Where? What for?"

"That's what I can't figure out, exactly."

14

THERE WAS NO HIGH SCHOOL IN RAMP HOLLOW,
Tennessee, but there was a nearby county school called
Rhododendron Regional High. Lombard drove into the sprawl-
ing parking lot of the high school, which looked to have been
built in the past twenty years, judging by the soft corners of its
architecture. The Tennessee Valley Authority had brought elec-
tricity and industry to this region more than fifty years ago,
bringing its people into the twentieth century as well as jobs and
a connection to the outside world. On the strength of this
progress the local population had later been able to afford to
replace the few dilapidated holler high schools with a centralized
complex of secondary education.

Lombard walked into the school with only a vague idea of
how she was going to talk Tracy Hughes into confirming what she
was certain the girl had to know: that Jasper Slade had made a
will and that Jay Hughes was at least one of its stated heirs. She
had turned the whole idea over in her head a hundred times on
the drive from Asheville. She had no evidence from which to
deduce that Slade had made a will, that Hughes had been an
heir—or even if he had been, that he knew it, and even if he had
known himself to be an heir, that he would have told his sister.
However, Lombard had a theory about Slade's death, about why
he had been made to look like Hughes's killer, and about how it
all tied to the AFFC. The tie that would bind it all was the discovery of a will that had in fact existed and been destroyed and
that Jay Hughes had been a part of. Outside the AFFC, the only

person alive who might know about it would have to be Jay Hughes's closest friend, his sister.

Lombard flashed her fake police badge to the school secretary, swearing to herself it would be the last time. She had to pull Tracy Hughes out of school immediately, she explained, order of the juvenile court of, um, Knoxville. Yeah, that was it, Knoxville, in Knox County, Tennessee, about fifty miles due northwest, Lombard recalled from her familiarity with Southern geography.

As the secretary checked Tracy's file to determine which classroom she would be in, Lombard wondered whether her clearly criminal conduct constituted a felony or a misdemeanor in the state of Tennessee. Impersonating a police officer was probably a misdemeanor, but she whiled away the minutes with a private game of cataloguing all the offenses with which she believed she could be charged. Abetting truancy, obviously, she thought. Contributing to the delinquency of a minor, maybe even kidnapping, depending on how Tennessee defined it. She considered how perfectly—in view of her sexuality, the girl's age, and the circumstances under which she was spiriting Tracy out of here—the whole scheme could destroy her if she were caught. She grinned, thinking if worse came to worst, she could always get into the gardening business like she had dreamed of in the past, as soon as she got out of jail.

Lombard heard the secretary call over an intercom to the classroom in which Tracy was assigned that hour. "Now I'll just call her mother," the secretary told Lombard when she had summoned Tracy, "for her permission for Tracy to leave."

Lombard bit her lower lip. "Oh, let's just wait till Tracy gets here," she said. "It may not be necessary for me to take her off campus, if I can just speak to her privately outside. Police business, you understand. Wouldn't want her mother to worry."

"Is she in trouble?" the secretary asked with an attitude that suggested she wouldn't be surprised to hear an affirmative.

"No, ma'am. She may be an important witness, however. An innocent bystander."

"Innocent? Tracy?"

Tracy walked into the office. She was wearing baggy jeans, an army surplus jacket, and combat boots. Her long hair was brushed, at least, Lombard observed, and draped in gauzy golden layers over her shoulders. She looked sullenly at Lombard, who noticed she had pinned her left eyebrow with one of those hideous facial studs that were so common nowadays. "What's up this time?" Tracy asked. "Somebody else die?"

The secretary sprang from her chair, shock written all over her face. "Are you sure there's been no trouble, Lieutenant Lombard?"

Tracy eyed Lombard. "Lieutenant?"

"No trouble," Lombard said hastily. "Tracy, we need to talk."

"All right!" Tracy beamed. "We going for another ride? I hope you got a better rod than that dorky SUV you took me out in the last time."

Lombard glared at her. "Let's go, Tracy."

"Fine," Tracy said indifferently, and walked ahead of Lombard to the front doors.

As they opened one of the doors, the secretary could be heard in the background, insisting to some unknown listener on her phone line, "She's in trouble, I'm sure of it. What did I tell you about those Hughes people? You've *heard* about the boy by now."

"I hate this fucking place," Tracy said as they walked to an empty stair stoop leading up to a gymnasium. "I thought you were taking me for a ride."

"I brought the dorky SUV," Lombard said. "So we might as well walk. It's better we talk here, anyway, out in the open."

Tracy sat down on the stoop and pulled a pack of cigarettes out of one of the zipper pockets of her oversize jacket. She withdrew a cigarette and, creasing her brow as she lit her smoke in about as calculated an effort to look cool as Lombard had ever seen, said, "What about?"

"About your brother and Senator Slade."

"I already told you about them."

"Did you know that Slade planned on leaving some money to your brother?" said Lombard, sitting down a few steps below Tracy.

"Some? Try 1.5 million. That's how much he was leaving Jay."

Lombard couldn't believe how easily Tracy had forgotten to mention that the last time they spoke. It made her suspicious. "How long have you known that?"

"You look pissed off, Lombard," Tracy said.

"I'm not pissed off. I had a feeling you knew about the will. I just wonder why you left that important fact out of our last chat."

"Oh, like I'm gonna tell some gypsy-looking rent-a-cop from North Carolina all about the will Jasper Slade put my dead brother in. When you so much as told me you were working for the fuckers at the AFFC."

"Why tell me now?"

"Because since then I've found out we're not getting shit out of the will. At the time we thought there might be some money in it for us. Look, we're not greedy. But how did we know you weren't checking up on us to try to get at that money?"

Lombard was silent for a moment, studying Tracy's bland expression. She shook her head and said, "You're a smart girl, Tracy. How *could* you have known? Why trust a gypsy-looking rent-a-cop?"

"You talk funny."

"I know. Tell me this: Do you have a copy of the will? Or is it Jay's word?"

"I think I have the original."

Lombard was astonished. "What?"

"I didn't know anything about this until a few days before you showed up in Ramp Hollow, Lombard. I doubt Jay even knew he was in the will. It was after he died, a week after he died, that we got this little package in the mail. It had Slade's will in it."

"Who sent it to you?"

"I don't know," Tracy said, rolling her eyes and crushing her cigarette under her boot. "Somebody. I guess Slade."

"He couldn't have. He was under lock and key at a house near Raleigh, doped up. He didn't have the presence of mind to lick an envelope, let alone mail his last will and testament to the family of his recently murdered lover, a man he was accused of killing."

"Now you sound like a complete nerd."

"I am a complete nerd." Lombard looked away in disbelief. "Mailed it. Why? And who? Who could do it?"

"I really think Slade sent it, Lombard. Maybe he felt bad about killing Jay and wanted us to have it."

"When did you say he sent it? A week after Jay's death?"

"We got it in the mail the Friday after Jay died. We didn't know what to make of it. Thought of calling the cops, until the dick killed himself the next night. We weren't about to call anybody after that."

Lombard stood up. "Where is the will now?"

"At home."

"I don't suppose your mother would appreciate another visit from me."

"You have no chance of getting the will out of her. I'll send you a copy."

"You will?" Lombard beamed. "Promise? Here's the postage." She dug in her handbag for a few seconds and handed Tracy a twenty.

"I can't break this," said Tracy.

"It's all I have. Take it. Spend it. I don't care. Just get me that copy."

"Thanks," Tracy said softly. She stood up erect and, apparently catching herself in accidentally correct posture, abruptly assumed a slouching pose. "Have you always been such a dork?" she asked.

"No. When I was about your age I had neon-blue spiky hair and a dog collar around my neck. I looked like a goddamn fool, but at least I looked like I took a shower once in a while."

Tracy broke into hilarious laughter. She had a beautiful smile and bright happy eyes when she let herself go. "I take a bath every night, Lombard."

"You're a pretty girl. Why do you young kids try so hard to look like shit?"

Tracy looked at Lombard as she might look at a hopeless imbecile. "Because looking like shit is cool, Lombard."

———

McLean seemed relieved to see Lombard the next morning. "We were worried about you," he said when he spotted her at the coffee machine.

"Who was worried?" she asked.

"Me and Retta." He glanced at Retta, who was running envelopes through a stamp machine and not paying evident attention to anything they were saying. McLean cleared his throat. "You should have called in, Loy."

Lombard shrugged and started toward her office. "I don't see why. It's a short trip. I was back by supper time." She called to Retta, "Did you put those contract renewals on my desk?"

"Yup," Retta said.

"Is that the only pressing thing I have to do today? Anything else on the front burner, contracts-wise?"

"Nope." Retta pursed her lips and threw the envelopes she had just stamped into a large postal bag. "I'll take these out and check on the P.O. box," she said, and walked breezily out of the office to her car.

Lombard frowned as the front door swung shut. "Huh. She usually waits till lunchtime for the mail run. What's eating her? She acts like she's mad at me."

"She's worried about you," McLean said.

"What's all this worry talk?"

"Loy, maybe you ought to slow down the pace on this case."

"Hey, just because you dropped out doesn't mean it's over," she snapped. "Not by a long shot."

"You asked me to drop out," he said, looking wounded. "You said you could handle it fine from here on out and that even you thought it was more important I spend the extra time with my family."

"I meant it," she said. "I just don't need the nagging."

"I'm not nagging!" he nearly shouted.

"Don't get snappy, Sam."

"You're letting this thing go to your head." His expression was resolute and stern.

She stopped at her doorway and turned around. "What did you say?" she asked.

"You just—you need to take a deep breath. Focus on business for a while. Let this Slade thing set on the back burner."

"No," she said, and walked into her office, shutting the door.

McLean opened it and followed her inside. "What are you gonna do after you sign those contracts?"

"I'm gonna gas up the car and head back to Raleigh. I'm gonna talk to McKenna."

"He's in a psychiatric hospital."

"I know. I called ahead and got permission to visit."

"You're liable to end up in an institution yourself. Just what are you gonna get from McKenna, Loy? How can he help you now?"

"How? Well, he might be able to tell me who sent Slade's will to Jay Hughes's family, just a few days before Slade strung himself up, or got strung up." McLean's complexion turned ashen. "And he might be able to explain why Slade intended for Jay Hughes to have $1.5 million, same as A.C. Drinnon left to Slade." She sat down and whipped the first contract out of the pile in her desk tray. "And he might just be able to explain what happened to all that money and all of Jasper Slade's other assets."

McLean sat in a client chair and said softly, "I'm sorry, Loy. I was just worried."

"You worry too much," she said, furiously signing one contract after the other. "I need support from the people around here, not their goddamn talk behind my back."

McLean smiled bashfully. "You see a lot."

She signed the last contract. "I didn't even glance over these. I'm sure Retta did, but you read through them anyway. Just be sure she gets them and tell her I'll be back at work on Monday, and for good. No more trips to Raleigh."

"Why so sure?"

"I'm going to close the case this weekend. I'm right on top of the truth. I mean I'm standing right dead still on top of it. I just have to dig it up."

She stood up, grabbed her keys, and hurried out to the lobby, pausing at Retta's desk to pick up her message slips, which she stuffed into her shoulder bag before breezing out the door to Raleigh.

———

The Oaks of Saint Anselm Hospital rested in a leafy country-side estate outside the Raleigh city limits. Lombard was sitting in her car with her window rolled down, staring at the facade of the hospital. A soft breeze rustled over treetops nearby, marking the solitude and quiet of the place. She turned on the radio and then turned it off again. She started to turn the key in the ignition and then stopped, pulling the key out and dropping the key ring in her lap. She didn't want to leave, despite having just been informed by the nurse in charge of Ross McKenna's ward that he was unable to speak.

Lombard had insisted on seeing him, reminding the nurse that she had been cleared for a visit twenty-four hours in advance, had driven more than 200 miles, and done so on urgent legal business. She had then been allowed to see him, see him as pale and vacant and dead-eyed as any corpse she had ever beheld, only with life still in him and blood still coursing through his veins. The nurses had explained that he had become catatonic. They didn't know why or how, only that it had happened a few days before. Nobody had told Lombard about his condition because she hadn't asked.

Now, as she drew her thoughts together on what to do next, something the nurses told her replayed over and over in her mind. It was one nurse's response when Lombard had asked how long his condition might last. "A few hours, a few days, months, years, forever. Who knows?" the nurse had said.

Thunder rumbled overhead, and Lombard bitterly recalled the angry weather she had encountered at Stonebridge Farm the Saturday before and the showdown with McKenna that it had antic-ipated. She rolled her window up as the first stray drops of rain sprinkled the pavement. The sky darkened, just as it had last week, and a loud crack split the sky open, sending a torrent down upon her car. She withdrew her cell phone and started to dial the office, then realized it was after 6. McLean would be at home. She called there.

A child answered. "Who is this?" Lombard asked. "Is this little Hannah?"

"No," the little girl's voice said flatly. "I'm not little."

"Well, go get your daddy, whichever one you are."

When McLean picked up the phone and spoke, Lombard said, "I'm leaving Raleigh. You were right. McKenna can't help me."

"Why not?"

"He's shut down. Catatonic, they say. A veggie. Son of a bitch will do anything to avoid telling the truth."

"You called to tell me that?"

"Sure I did," she said, pausing as thunder crashed overhead. The raindrops beating against her windshield had merged into watery curtains cascading out of the dark gray murk of sky. "I had to tell you before I leave so you won't be surprised when I come back a failure. And you'll know better than to say you told me so, won't you?"

"Loy."

"I lost the case, but I still got my head on straight."

"Good," McLean said. "Because you can't leave Raleigh just yet."

"Why not?" she said dully.

"Somebody's waiting to hear from you. I left you a message earlier on your voice mail. You haven't checked it, I take it?"

"No."

"I counted on that. So I left a message at the front desk of the Fairland Court Motel too."

"How did you know I was staying there?"

"You're a creature of habit. We've stayed there every time we go to Raleigh so far. They know you by your first name yet?"

Lombard grinned. "Yeah. Who's waiting for me? Is she good-looking?"

There was a dim chuckle on McLean's end. "No. He is. Tyler Rhodes."

"He's still in town?"

"I thought he might be, and he is. He's waiting to see how things play out for Ben Hartley. Ben's in trouble, you know."

"Arrested?"

"Not yet. There's a grand jury convening in Asheville, according to Tyler."

"How did you find him? Why?"

"I got his cell number from his office. For some reason he gave them permission to give it to me in case I called. He wants to talk to you, Loy. He might have some answers. I don't know."

Lombard felt her heart lift a little on realizing McLean still had some spark of faith in her. "Thanks, Sam."

"All I did was make a phone call."

"You did more than that. My mind is so crammed full and tired, I doubt I would have thought to call Tyler Rhodes. Well, I might have," she said on a second thought. "In fact, I'm sure I would have, after getting some rest." Minutes before, she had decided to leave Raleigh behind and lick her wounds. Now she had nearly convinced herself she would have checked that last angle, Tyler Rhodes, without any reminders. Nearly, but not quite. "Well, I hope I would have," she said wearily. "Thanks."

"He'll meet you at the Alibi, that bar where Mike met us."

"I remember. Della Drinnon was out in the car. Old cow."

───────

Lombard and McLean had chosen the Alibi at random the night they had met Mike Church there, because it was only a few blocks from the Fairland Court Motel, there was a parking spot right in front, and they liked the name. It had been dead the night they'd traipsed in off the street, but now it was Saturday night and the place was packed. Lombard had arranged to meet Tyler Rhodes at 9 o'clock, but she'd arrived a half an hour early, in what was probably an unconscious habit of establishing her territory before meeting a stranger. This evening would be the first time she met the inscrutable Mr. Rhodes.

She sat on a bar stool and glanced at everyone who walked through the door. She had only caught a glimpse of Rhodes in the hospital before her interview with Ben Hartley, but she had noticed he was unusually good-looking, a characteristic largely absent in most of the men and women here. It appeared to be the kind of decades-old tavern that had changed its tone and clientele with each successive new manager. There was enough oak, copper, and glass to give it the feel of an amiable neighborhood pub, but the present proprietors apparently had decided to create a sports bar, and the clientele were the perfect picture of down-to-earth white folk. The men wore golf shirts and khakis, and the women were dressed to attract them in denim jackets and short skirts with lots of makeup and gold jewelry.

Then a man who looked like he didn't belong breezed through the door, paused, and put his hands in his pockets. He was wearing a black cotton shirt of some Italian design, blue jeans, black Doc Martens, and a sparking platinum watchband. With his tousled black hair and black eyes that danced around the room, he caught the eye of every woman in the place. Lombard stood up and waved him to a booth near the bar.

"You Tyler Rhodes?" she shouted.

"Yes!" he said, smiling, and followed her to a booth.

"You'd better duck," she said as they scooted into the booth, "before the girls in here burn holes in your shirt with the way they're eyeballing you."

"How did you know it was me?" he asked. "We haven't met, have we?"

"No. I just knew. You want a drink?"

"I'll wait for the server."

"What do you drink?" Lombard asked.

"I'd love a scotch and soda."

Lombard called a server over and ordered for both of them. When she turned her attention back to Rhodes, he had lit a cigarette. "You smoke?" he asked.

"I used to smoke nearly a pack a day," she said. "I quit two years ago."

"That's admirable."

"What's an anti-tobacco lobbyist like you doing smoking?" she asked.

"This is a British brand."

"Made with North Carolina tobacco," Lombard guessed.

"Good point." He stared at her a bit curiously. "So. Sam tells me you're still dicking around the state, searching for clues in the Jay Hughes's murder case."

"That's right."

"Is it all right if we talk small for a while, before getting into the nitty-gritty?"

"I suppose so. Why? Are you nervous?"

"No. I just feel like having a little fun," he said, folding his arms on the table and leaning in. "I love to people-watch." He glanced outside the booth at a gaggle of women two tables away. "How old would you guess the women at that table are?" he asked.

Lombard gave them a look. "Mid twenties," she said.

"Do you think they're attractive?"

"In a common way."

"Ouch. You don't like blonds?"

"Sure I do. I just don't like peroxide jobs, fake tits, and fake tans. The room's crawling with 'em. Why do you ask?"

"It's none of my business," he said. "I only asked because I wanted to get a sense of what you're like. Jessamyn Frost, Ben's boss, told me you interviewed her, and she mentioned you were a lesbian. I wondered why you chose this bar."

"Oh. Sam chose the bar." She took a drink. "But I'm not here to pick up girls, and you know that."

He smiled and pointed playfully at her. "Down to business, Inspector."

"Sam said you wanted to talk to me."

"He's right. I wanted to meet you. I realize you've worked closely with Mike Church, who is, of course, the lead investigator in Wiley's murder case, now that the Hughes case is considered closed."

"So?"

"The grand jury is convening in that case, and the case for arson against Ben is pretty strong, based on what he told the Raleigh police. I want you to help Ben. I want you to call Mike Church and arrange to testify before the grand jury."

Lombard smiled crookedly. "How can my testimony help?"

"He talked to you. Ben told me he explained everything to you. He was imprisoned and tortured and forced to set fire to that building. You know it."

"You know better than I do, counselor, that the subpoena power for a grand jury hearing rests with the district attorney. Badgering Mike won't do any good."

"It might. Their investigation begins and ends with what Mike found out. You're part of that. Please, Loy. You know it's the right thing. And Wiley would have wanted the right thing to be done. He's the victim. Doesn't his will count for something?"

Lombard studied his emphatic expression. "Will," she mumbled.

"You will?"

"I don't know. I mean, what you said about Wiley's 'will.' What will?"

"I meant that he would have wanted justice, and sending Ben up for arson and murder isn't justice. Loy, he could be charged with a capital crime. They kill convicted murderers in this state for a lot less than what he stands to be accused of." He nervously lifted his glass and sipped his scotch. "Wiley opposed the death penalty. So do I."

"Did Wiley leave a real will?" she asked casually.

"I don't know. I haven't heard anything. Why?"

"Hmm. Jasper Slade left a will."

Rhodes set his glass down. "Yeah," he said.

"You knew that, didn't you?"

He didn't look at her. His eyes were downcast and troubled. "I never saw it."

"Did Wiley? Did Mr. Do-the-Right-Thing get a hold of it somehow, right before Jay Hughes got butchered? Did innocent Ben dig that up along with all that other nasty ammunition he used against Slade and pass it on to Wiley?"

Rhodes pursed his lips and glanced at his watch.

"You want me to help you, Tyler? Help Ben? Then help me."

"I never saw it. I think Ben did get it somehow. I doubt he even remembers how."

"And he gave it to Wiley."

"I think so."

"Yet Wiley sat on it, because publishing that would be going too far, because the will was obtained by theft or extortion. You tell me."

"I don't know," Rhodes snapped. "I'm telling the truth."

Lombard rapped the tabletop gently with her knuckles. "Mmm, mmm, mmm. I need to know the truth. I need to know how Ben got it. But I guess it's good enough knowing that he did get it, and knowing, as I'm sure you do, that Wiley is the only one who could have sent it to Jay Hughes's family after Slade's death. It would have been the right thing to do, wouldn't it?"

Rhodes looked surprised. "I didn't know that."

Lombard gave a weak sigh. "I believe you," she said thinly. "It would have been the right thing to do, though, sending the will out to the beneficiaries?"

"Yes, it would. Wiley would do that."

Lombard raised her glass. "Here's to Wiley Faulks," she said.

Rhodes slowly lifted his glass and said, "Wiley."

15

LOMBARD SPENT THE WHOLE OF THE FOLLOWING MONDAY locked inside her office. She refused to take any calls. Retta had been startled when she knocked on the door at lunchtime and Lombard had shouted from inside, demanding to be left alone. McLean told Retta that he had seen Lombard in a similar state many times when they worked together in Charlotte, and it always coincided with the close of a vexing investigation.

Just after 3 o'clock, she opened her door and peered into the lobby. "Retta," she said, "I'm sorry I barked at you. Take the day off tomorrow. I'll mind the store."

"I don't want the day off," Retta said. "Stop telling me what to do."

"Fine, then. Sam!" Lombard yelled. "Where is he?"

"In my office," McLean hollered.

Lombard went into his office and shut the door. He was staring into his computer monitor. "What are you doing?" she asked, sitting down.

"Surfing the Net. Looking for a nice beach in Florida."

"Turn around. I made a report, and I want you to look it over."

He spun slowly around in his chair. "Who's it for?"

"Mike Church and the DA. Since Ross McKenna's a veggie and since he fired us anyway, after I stuck that gun to his head, I doubt he'll have much use for it."

"Go on," McLean said. "Talk. I'll read it later."

Lombard set the report on his desk, leaned back in her chair, and rubbed her hands together. "Murder is always about hatred or money, or both, right? Not exactly. I'm not sentimental, but I believe love is actually at the root of this case, though the murders were ignited by greed. I don't know what exactly was going through Jasper Slade's mind in his final days, but he was losing it. He was beset by the deepest conflict of his life, one that he had suppressed after A.C. Drinnon's death, until he met Jay Hughes. I have little doubt he treated Jay like a plaything at first. That's how you men are."

"That's not true," McLean said.

"Whatever, it's beside the point. Everything in this case leads to one conclusion on Slade's regard for Jay: He fell in love with him. It might have been a midlife thing, a yen for youth, I don't know. But he loved him. He admitted he had loved A.C., who had left him a bundle of money, and Slade intended to leave the same gift to Jay. What ruined him was the AFFC finding out."

"Why would he leave a pile of money like that to a hick like Jay Hughes?" McLean asked incredulously.

"What did Slade care what happened to the money? He'd be dead, and he had no other real family. Might as well leave it to his boy. Besides, by the time he made the will, he was burned on the AFFC."

Lombard snatched a mint out of a candy jar McLean kept on his desk and unwrapped it. "As I said before, the press rumors made Ross McKenna suspicious, so he had Grendel Roper follow Slade. Roper confirmed that Slade was fooling around with a pretty blond party boy, and McKenna confronted Slade. I believe that's what prompted Slade to make a will." She popped the mint into her mouth. "He shouldn't have done that."

"It was a mistake if McKenna found out," McLean agreed.

"Slade didn't think anybody would. He must have thought he was in danger either way, though. He knew A.C.'s death had been no suicide. Della killed him, or had him killed. Yet she got away with it, and Slade knew that. So when he found out McKenna was on to him, he thought he could be in trouble. So he made a will, not thinking the AFFC would find out about it.

"Slade was going through hell. Ben Hartley and Wiley Faulks were ragging him in their newsletters on one end, and the AFFC was pressuring him on the other. Then McKenna somehow discovered that will and ultimately bridged the gap between the hounds of the left and the hounds of the right when he had Grendel kidnap Ben Hartley."

McLean was listening keenly. "How did McKenna get his hands on the will?"

"First I have to explain the history of the money it meant for Jay to have. A.C. Drinnon's will provided that the $1.5 million be used for a conservative foundation, but Slade evidently kept it. He started the AFFC with funds raised by contributions. That's in the AFFC literature I've read, which doesn't say a thing about money bequeathed by A.C. Drinnon—just that he was the AFFC's inspiration." Lombard narrowed her eyes and pointed at McLean. "Della never raised a stink about that, to keep her husband's secret in his grave. But she knew, and she no doubt told McKenna." Lombard stood up and began pacing slowly.

"Now," she said, shaking an index finger at some invisible entity to which she seemed to be directing her narrative, "Slade's will was drafted by an Asheville lawyer whose associations were unclear to Slade in his desperation. He got the name from Jay Hughes, who therefore knew about the will. Slade had no idea that the lawyer had been Hughes's lover and had, in fact, been the lover of Ben Hartley as well."

"Tyler Rhodes!" McLean cried. "How could you know that?"

Lombard picked up her report and whipped out the last few pages, handing it to McLean. "It's Slade's will. Tracy Hughes sent it to me. Look at who prepared it, signature on the last page."

"Oh, my God. What bad luck."

"I bet that's eventually what Slade thought too, if he thought at all. He was clearly not thinking rationally in those last days. The pressure must have crippled his senses. A poor little hick like Jay dragging his lawyer friend in thinking it was no big deal. Slade couldn't use his own lawyers, nor could he use anybody who was part of the old-boy network. He had to rely on an outsider, a misfit. Tyler kept the will; I suppose Slade thought it was safe with him."

"So how did McKenna find out about the will *before* the murder?"

"That will is what motivated McKenna to conspire murder. I think Grendel Roper was constantly watching Slade's movements. So he would have seen him meet with Tyler Rhodes. He probably broke into the office and snooped around to see what they were up to and found the will." She shook her head and added dryly, "Imagine what went through Slade's mind when McKenna confronted him with that colossal fuck-up. No way of denying that, boy.

"Anyway, that's when McKenna's warped mind really started working. Pretty soon he and Grendel had arranged Ben Hartley's abduction and torture. Fearful, but having no clue what was in store for him, Slade slunk back to Asheville and despaired of what to do next. It wasn't long before he agreed to meet with Ben Hartley, thinking he might persuade him to stop the harassment on that end." Lombard sighed. "Slade had no idea he was by then playing into McKenna's hands, because by then Ben Hartley had become McKenna's unwilling agent in a plot to murder Jay Hughes and bully Slade into surrendering his entire estate to McKenna, under the umbrella of the AFFC."

She pointed at the will. "You'll notice the front page of that will has the word COPY stamped on it. Tracy had only a copy, one that was mailed to her."

"Who mailed it?" McLean asked.

"I think Wiley Faulks did. He opted not to publish it, probably out of some weird ethical concern of his. But Grendel Roper knew he had knowledge of it, and that knowledge, coupled with his part in McKenna's frame-up of Ben, would seal his fate."

McLean frowned. "Wait. Maybe I'm slow, but how did Wiley Faulks get it?"

"I think Tyler Rhodes discovered the will missing at some point after Grendel's probable burglary, got nervous, and gave a copy to Faulks," Lombard speculated. "He either had copies already or had it on his computer. Grendel Roper missed that."

She sat down. "McKenna decided to kill Jay Hughes and ruin Jasper Slade in one fell swoop. Two birds with one stone, so to speak. The ordeal would shake Slade to his foundations, and when he was taken to Stonebridge Farm, he would, under the influence of narcotics, sign over all his holdings and assets, including the money he had so stupidly made part of a ridiculous will. If questioned, McKenna could say it was for legal expenses, which no doubt would have capped a million in a trial like the one in store for Slade. But the case would never come to trial, and McKenna and Della Drinnon and Grendel Roper knew it."

"They knew he was going to die," McLean concluded.

"That's right," said Lombard. "His case wasn't going to cost them a dime more than a couple of private-investigating whores."

"But how could they just get him to sign over his life like that?" McLean asked. "Wouldn't they need a lawyer?"

"I think if we looked into Sig Mashburn's records, we would find that he knew all about the transfer of assets. I doubt he had anything to do with their plot, but he wanted to get paid. That's why they let him talk to Slade. They needed him as a witness to the transaction, and he complied so he could get the case. I can't prove that, but I would bet on it."

Lombard propped her feet along the edge of McLean's desk. "Anyway, Slade was dead little more than a week after Jay's death. That brings me to the autopsy report, page eight of my report."

McLean flipped through the report and withdrew the medical examiner's findings. Lombard went on. "There were nonlethal amounts of Demerol in Slade's body at the time of his death. If pressed, I think the pathologist would admit that it would be hard for somebody as doped up as Slade was to tie a knot strong enough to hold him up for a hanging. He was hanged, probably by Grendel, after being dosed with enough of that stuff to keep him from putting up a fight. I don't know why they didn't just OD him. I guess Grendel found hanging to be a more true-blue American style of execution, over that pussified lethal injection."

McLean threw down the report. "Why did McKenna still want us on the case?"

"I think he legitimately wanted us to pin the murder of Jay Hughes on Ben Hartley, like we discussed before. He didn't want the AFFC ruined. He had set Ben up as the perfect scapegoat, a jealous lover, spurned by Tyler Rhodes in favor of Jay Hughes. He was just crazy enough to try to engineer a scheme like that. He also played us against Grendel Roper, who scared him. Just like Dr. Frankenstein, he became a target of the beast he had created. They didn't see things eye to eye, he and Grendel. I think Grendel, who was in this to preserve honor in his weird way, saw that McKenna really only cared about the money. That offended Grendel. So he mutinied, and things soon spiraled out of control. But it was that internal war that led us to the truth."

McLean said, "And Wiley Faulks…"

"Died because he knew about the will, only they didn't get to him until after he'd sent it to the people he thought had a right to know about it. That was Wiley: Do the right thing." Lombard looked vaguely sad, but then shrugged. "He would have died anyway. He was part of McKenna's frame-up. And Tyler Rhodes was in real big trouble, and he knew it. That's why he was so scared, Sam. He would have been next, though he didn't know it was because he authored that will."

McLean shook his head. "I don't think Tyler knew what to believe at all."

"Maybe not." Lombard got up. "I'm going to deliver this report to Church and the DA. I'll be subpoenaed to testify at the grand jury in Ben Hartley's case. That will lead to a subpoena for Tyler Rhodes, I'm pretty sure. But he'll be all right. His only connection to this case is the will. Besides, even if he has darker connections to this case than we know, he's the sort of fellow who can walk through fire unscathed."

"What are you gonna do in the meantime?" McLean asked. "Catch up around here? Work on your garden at home?"

"Both, and more," she said.

"What's more?"

She smiled sheepishly. "I got a phone message from a lady friend. I might go out on the town Friday night. Time to relax."

McLean grinned at first, then his brow pinched a little, as though perturbed by some unwelcome thought. Lombard had left the room, and he mumbled, "Not Hunter, surely."

———

A few weeks later, in the early part of June, Sam and Selena McLean were on their way to Lombard's house in the country. It was a fine Saturday evening, still daylight at 8 p.m., though a light orange sun hung low on the horizon and scattered dimming light amid shadows of lush green forest.

"I've never been to Loy's," Selena remarked as they neared her house. "Who all is coming?"

"Retta and her gentleman friend," McLean said. "Mike Church and his wife. A woman."

"What woman?"

"I'm not sure," he said. "Loy didn't name her. I'm a little worried about why."

"What for?"

"I don't know. It's none of my business." In truth, McLean had been very worried, ever since Lombard had disclosed her intention to call back a "lady friend" who had left her a phone message. He knew Hunter Lyle had been calling Lombard and that Retta had taken her messages. He didn't want to believe Lombard could have called her back, though. Despite her unusual lifestyle, Lombard had always seemed practical and conservative where marriage and family were concerned. It wasn't like her to fool around with a woman she knew to be married.

Besides, he thought, Hunter Lyle had used Lombard. And he knew Lombard was proud and vindictive enough to shut out permanently anybody who dared to deliberately exploit her goodwill or her trust. It vexed him. It couldn't be Hunter Lyle, he insisted to himself. And if it was, what was happening to his friend?

They arrived at Lombard's house and discovered that Retta and her friend James—a man who was, in contrast to Retta, small, timid, and soft-spoken—were already present. Retta was helping Lombard in the kitchen while James sat in the living room watching TV. McLean introduced Selena to James, who smiled gently and kept his eyes on the television screen.

McLean went to the kitchen carrying a paper grocery bag stuffed with two bottles of wine. Lombard and Retta were in a heated discussion and barely noticed him. Retta was in mid sentence. "…and that's why it's best to crush the garlic. You get the juices."

"Don't tell me how to cook," Lombard snapped. "I minced twelve cloves like it was nothing. You mince it. That way it holds in the juices until you throw it on the hot oil, and the flavor just blends into the oil. Crushing bruises the hell out of it."

"It's not for hot oil," Retta grumbled. "It's for the salad oil, and crushed is best."

"Well, I was talking about the sauce. Hey, Sam honey," Lombard suddenly said, beaming at him. "Did you bring your kids?"

"No. We found a sitter," he said.

"Thank God. I can be myself."

"We brought some wine."

"Good. Set it on the sideboard. Make it look fancy."

"Say, where's the lady friend?"

Lombard looked down at her countertop, where she pulled out thin slices of eggplant from a marinade and began dipping them in a plate of seasoning. "She's coming," she said blithely.

"Who is she, anyway?"

"Oh, you'll see. You've met her."

McLean eyed Retta, who was chopping lettuce, celery, and red onions for a salad. Retta said only, "Where are those tomatoes, Loy?"

"Right here." Lombard emptied a colander of bright red tomatoes on the cutting board and said, "Don't forget the mozzarella. And don't chop the basil, for God's sake."

"Mind your eggplant. I know all about the basil and cheese."

"Sam," Lombard said, "You know how to fry veal? I've already breaded it and the skillet's ready. I'm busy breading this eggplant. My girl doesn't eat meat."

"Neither does Selena."

"Really? Well, there's plenty of eggplant to go around." She leaned through a window that overlooked the living room. "Who likes veal?" she hollered.

Mike Church, who had arrived after McLean, stood up with a woman he introduced as his wife. "Loy, I'd like you to meet Linda. Linda, Loy Lombard."

Lombard had no trouble confronting witnesses, lawyers, and killers, but she was helpless with proper social introductions, even in her own home. She looked kindly at Linda Church and said, "There's bread, cheese, and sausage on the table if you're gut hungry. Dinner will be a little while." She eyed McLean. "Get 'em a drink."

McLean had just begun turning a corkscrew when suddenly Mike Church said, "Turn that up! Sig Mashburn's on TV."

Lombard came into the room wiping her hands on her apron, and all eyes fell on the TV screen. There was Sig Mashburn, grinning ear to ear as a network news reporter interviewed him for a prime-time investigative-report show. The voice-over said, "Mr. Mashburn's lawsuit was brought on behalf of the family of the late Jay Hughes, the murdered lover of the late Jasper Slade, who is alleged to have made a will in which Hughes would have been the heir to a $1.5 million fortune. The entire nation was captivated for weeks by the bizarre saga of the final days of the former senator, a conservative leader accused of murdering his homosexual lover, then days later mysteriously dead of an apparent suicide. In the meantime, the family of Jay Hughes received in the mail a copy of what is purported to be Jasper Slade's last will and testament, recorded before his death. Slade was considered intestate until Hughes family spokesman Dean Hughes recently came forward."

A man who called himself Jay Hughes's uncle appeared on the screen, sitting alongside Mashburn and giving his account of the family's struggles against the American Family Freedom Campaign and its catatonic chairman, Ross McKenna.

"I am confident," Mashburn's grinning face exhorted, "that when all the facts are in, this poor, beleaguered family will finally be at peace with their departed loved one and with his legacy. It was, after all, the will of the late, great senator Jasper Slade."

McLean reared back in disgust, but everybody else was laughing. "Turn that thing off," he said. "I've seen enough. How about some music instead?"

Selena offered to help Lombard, and noticed a floral centerpiece on the dining table. "That's pretty. Is that from your garden?"

Lombard said, "Oh, no. That's compliments of Tyler Rhodes, in gratitude for my grand jury testimony, which saved his ass and Ben Hartley's as well."

McLean asked, "Has anything come of it?"

"There's no report yet," she said, "but Mike says it looks like they'll charge Ben with facilitation to commit arson. He can get probation for that."

The doorbell rang. McLean immediately started for the door and held his breath. When he opened the door and saw Lombard's guest, he smiled and said, "Well, isn't this a heck of a nice surprise! I wonder if you remember me? Sam McLean."

A thirtyish woman with curly straw-blond hair and a naturally tanned, freckled complexion stood on the porch, dressed in cream cotton pants and a Prussian blue sleeveless button-down shirt. Her clothes looked freshly pressed, and her riversport sandals looked new. "I brought chocolate cake," she said, awkwardly holding up a pastry box. "I didn't bake it. It's store-bought."

Lombard was standing in the kitchen doorway. "I've got fresh raspberries that will go beautifully with that." She smiled. "Most of you have met Christine Campbell, the park ranger that busted Sig Mashburn."

"Oh, I just filled out the paperwork," Christine Campbell said. "Anyway, it's Chris."

"Come in the kitchen and make yourself useful," said Lombard. When Chris Campbell was out of sight, Lombard whispered to McLean, "This is our third evening together and the first time I've gotten her in my house. I want everybody cleared out of here before midnight."

"You got it," McLean promised.

———

By 9 o'clock, everyone was crowded around a dining table that Lombard had lengthened by propping up the drop leaves. They were halfway through dinner when Selena, on her second glass of wine, more or less thought out loud, "We didn't say grace!"

McLean said, "Selena, baby, we're almost through. I think we'll be forgiven."

Lombard grinned. "How about a Bible verse instead?" she suggested merrily.

"Lord," Linda Church said, blushing, "I've never heard anybody make it sound like a dirty joke."

"Oh, I'm no blasphemer," Lombard said. "This is a real Bible verse, one that has a lot to do with the toast I'm about to make." She looked around the table. "So listen up and tell me which Bible story it refers to. You get extra points for the chapter number and verse."

"What prize do we get?" Selena peeped, hiccuping.

"Another glass of wine," Lombard said. "Okay. Here it is: King James Version, so all you Protestants can figure it out. 'And there came two angels to Sodom at even; and Lot sat in the gate of Sodom: and Lot seeing them rose up to meet them; and he bowed himself with his face toward the ground.'"

"That's the story of Sodom and Gomorrah," Campbell said.

"See? It was easy," Lombard said. "Sam and I talked about it, didn't we, Sam? Back at Stonebridge Farm right before Jasper Slade died. And old Della Drinnon dragged into the room while I was telling the story of how Lot knocked up his daughters…"

"He knocked up his daughters?" Selena squealed. "Oh, that's right," she giggled. "I remember that story now. I found it when I was thirteen, the same week I saw a naked Peruvian man in a *National Geographic*. It was too much for one week…"

"Selena, baby, let Loy talk," McLean gently suggested.

"Anyway," Lombard said, "that's beside the point. The story of Sodom is supposed to be about the ruin of a city that's run afoul of God by its sexual excess. Most people say it's a condemnation of homosexuality, but I've always thought it was really about sexual debauchery, using people's bodies, that kind of thing. I guess the reason I'm bringing it up is that there's an irony to how Della Drinnon saw that story, and Ross McKenna, and Grendel Roper, and even Jasper Slade, who probably read it the same way as they did. They didn't realize that any kind of overkill of desire is foul in the eyes of God. Whether it's sexual exploitation or corporate greed or rank laziness or the self-serving hunger for power, exploiting the weak, sick, and poor. For all its pretense of championing morality and decency, the AFFC was as base and corrupt as Sodom in its carnal excess. It was corrupted by power, by greed, and ultimately by murderous hatred."

Lombard poured wine into her glass and said, "Can anybody remember the words to Genesis 19, verse 13? I wrote it down somewhere, but I've memorized it. 'For we will destroy this place, because the cry of them is waxen great before the face of the Lord; and the Lord hath sent us to destroy it.'"

Mike Church grinned. "I think I see where you're going with this, Loy."

"A toast," Lombard said, raising her glass. She looked across the table at Sam McLean, her partner in crime of going on seven years, and said, "Here's to us, Angel."